When Bear Man took Tree for his bride, he went with her at night to the river. He knew what he wanted to say and do, but sat there, speechless.

Beside him, Tree had a quiet smile. She waited with a calm and slowness greater than Bear Man's hesitation.

Finally, when it seemed that his waiting could go no further, Bear Man stood and removed his breech clouts and soft moccasins. Then he waded into the water until he was buried to his waist.

Tree had felt the excitement of becoming a woman when she watched her husband undress. She shivered, but not from the night air; she trembled because her destiny had become clear.

Slowly, Bear Man faced her and pressed his dark lips to her palm. He gently lifted away the drape from her shoulders and then her skirt feathers. He pressed the large stone that he had found in the water against her womb. It was cold and damp, and then he started to sing.

In the morning, they walked back to their village.

Tree had already seen it in her vision when Bear Man said, "We shall name our first son

STONE

STONE

THE BIRTH

BY JAMES TUCKER

ZEBRA BOOKS

KENSINGTON PUBLISHING CORP.

ZEBRA BOOKS

are published by

KENSINGTON PUBLISHING CORP.
475 Park Avenue South
New York, N.Y. 10016

To Mabeljo Mills Tucker and Thomas J. Tucker, the Choctaw daughter and the Cherokee son who many seasons ago gave me life.

Acknowledgments and Apologies

I can't express too strongly my debt to the following: J. T. Alexander for his labors with the Cherokee language; and to Durbin Feeling, William Pulte, Agnes Cowen and their co-workers for the same. James Mooney and Frans M. Olbrechts for their research of Cherokee myths, sacred formulas and medicinal prescriptions; much of which I have made use. Also to Jack F. Kilpatrick and Anna G. Kilpatrick for their presentation of Cherokee folktales. And to J. Ed. Sharpe for his delightful introduction to Cherokee history.

To these and all scholars of the Cherokees, I apologize for inaccuracies they may discover in my representation of the Cherokees and history. My only defense is found in the words of Stone: "There are no realities greater than those which we create."

The Cherokee Indians in 1540 at the coming of the Europeans knew themselves as the *Ani Yunwiya*, the Principal People.

Their lands encompassed most of what is now Kentucky and Tennessee; and much of Alabama, Georgia, South and North Carolina, Virginia and West Virginia.

They had a highly developed government consisting of seven regional clans. They lived in cities and towns. They were fearless and were feared as the greatest of warriors.

BEAR MAN

1

Yona Asgaya, *the Bear Man*; *son of* Ajislvsga, *the Light Fire, the* ugvwiyuhi, *chief*; Hlgvi, *Tree, his wife.*

2

When Bear Man took Tree for his bride he went with her at night to the river. It was summer and the air was warm. The trees were thick and black against the sky. There were no birds singing, but insects were making their sounds, the sounds they always make on summer evenings, and with them the noises of toads and frogs.

Bear Man found a large flat stone and sat there with his bride. He kept grinning and not talking, just grinning and looking out at the water. He knew what he wanted to say and he knew what he wanted to do. His father was the *ugvwiyuhi*, the chief. Bear Man knew that a warrior and the son of a chief should have no difficulty with such matters, but he had never handled such things before and so he kept looking at the water flowing slowly

13

by the large stone upon which he and Tree rested.

Beside him Tree had a quiet smile and watched her husband. She knew that soon he would say what he wanted to say and do what he must do. She waited with a calm and slowness greater than the river's water, and greater than Bear Man's hesitation.

When it seemed to him that his waiting could go no further, Bear Man stood. Tree started to stand with him, but he put his hands gently on her shoulders. She sat again and looked at him without speaking.

"I've made a song," he told her. "It is a song about where we are, and what our lives shall be. I have spent many days coming to this place and watching the river to learn this song." He turned and stepped down to the bank. There he removed his breech clouts and soft moccasins. Then he waded into the water until he was buried to his waist. He turned to face Tree.

Tree watched her husband. When he had taken away his garments she had felt the excitement of becoming a woman start to grow within her. All her life she had seen men and boys bathing. She had helped her mother tend the wounds of warriors and had seen those warriors unclothed. She knew that if someday Bear Man had wounds she would turn the healing skills she had learned to him. As she sat on the slab and watched him it was the first time, though, she had seen him naked. Only days ago she had been brought from the central community of another clan, the *Aniwayah* or Wolf People, to the small community which was

14

part of Bear Man's clan, the *Anikawi* or Deer. Now she sat in the night and watched her husband waist deep in the river. She heard him as he began his song, facing her, looking deep into her.

> There are trees grazing in the valley,
> eating up the river that flows through
>   their midst.
> I am going to take you there
> and lay you down to listen
> to waters caressing the earth,
> and I will caress your bosom and tell
>   you
> I love you beneath the trees
> on warm grasses beside the river.
> I will hold your hand and touch
> the redness of my lips
> to the paleness of your palm.
> I will gather last year's leaves and say,

Bear Man held out his hands. In them were old, dried leaves that he had saved from autumn.

> These leaves we will forget.
> I will crumble them quietly and blow
>   them away.

He clasped the brittle leaves tightly, then again opened his hands. He blew at the broken bits of leaf and they flew away into the night, onto the river, and were gone.

Then I will gather stones out of the water
    and say,
These stones cannot be forgotten,

He bent and buried his head beneath the water.
When he emerged he held stones in his hands.

    and I will cast them back into the river
    where they can be found forever.

He hurled the stones far out into the stream. He
looked a moment at them splashing. Then he
began to walk from the water. He came to the
shore and then to Tree. He took her face in his
hands, and stared into her eyes.

And then I will gather your face into my
    eyes and say,
You and I cannot be forgotten. We are all
the stones in all the rivers.
And then I will touch your womb and
    say,
Come to the river. I will find our stones,
and I will flow through your midst and
    hide
our stones within your womb.
There they will soften.
They will become our sons;
they will become our daughters,
from all the stones
in all the rivers.

Bear Man took Tree's hand and pressed softly

his dark lips to her palm. Around the young husband and wife black trees rustled against a small wind. The insects and the frogs and toads made their sounds. The river moved silently to the music of Bear Man's song. Tree felt her husband's hands gently lifting away the drape from her shoulder and then her skirt feathers. She felt the large stone cold and hard beneath her back. She felt the wetness of Bear Man's skin. She felt him touch her womb and thought she heard again the last words of his song.

In the morning they walked back to their village.

"We shall name our first son Stone," said Bear Man.

"Yes," said Tree, and she followed beside her husband.

3

They became the ani unigimi, *the people who are gone. They were a part of the* Ani Yunwiya, *the Principal People. Then came the great* udehoisdi *of chief Light Fire, his disgrace. That is when the people of Light Fire left the Principal People and their seven great clans. They left because the udehoisdi had made them a people that no others would accept. They left to search for* udasdelvdi, *salvation. They became wanderers.*

But before they were wanderers they had been Warriors of the Principal People. And they had been Hunters. Bear Man was great among them. He was given his name because even as an infant he was larger than any other that had ever been born of woman. And Bear Man loved to hunt.

4

Nvda. Hnilgvi. Unidayvladv.
The sun. Trees. Shadows.
Bear Man watched his shadow, black across the ground. Shadows are neither cold nor hot, he thought, feeling the sun's heat burning at his back. He looked up from the shadow and let his eyes rove through trees, hills, other shadows. His eyes searched for deer, cool, lean creatures that had given his clan their name.

A small breeze eased the heat between his shoulders, along his spine. He took a slow step, another, and another. His steps were quiet, as quiet as his shadow. Quieter than the animals of the wood, quieter than deer. The breeze that had come and cooled him left as quickly, and again he could feel the sun reaching through the sky to touch the bare skin of his back.

He headed up a ridge that sloped swiftly

through the green and dark wood toward the sky, a blue soft cradle for distant white clouds. The way he followed led to the crest of a large hill. From the hill Bear Man could survey valleys, slopes, glades. From it he could spot any movement of a herd or a lone animal. And if he did he could then move quickly against it, after it, to send his arrow into it and through it. As the wind sends its messages through the trees, he thought.

At the top of the ridge the sun burned hotter than ever. Bear Man put his hand between his eyes and the sun and reached toward the unreachable fire. If this hill were a little higher, he thought, perhaps I could touch the sun. A bird flew past, calling its wild warning. Are you telling me that I'd burn myself? thought Bear Man. He laughed then and found a place for a moment's rest in the shade. He gathered a pebble from the ground and put it into his mouth. He sucked on it, drawing moisture from his mouth to his throat, temporarily easing his thirst. From where he sat he didn't have a good view for his survey, and he knew he would soon move. But the shade, and the pebble, and the waiting sun worked against him, made him want to rest longer.

He began to hum a chant that his mother had taught him years earlier, when he was a young boy and everything was both new and true.

The chant told the story of the creation of fish from the leaves of a great oak tree. The oak had gone to war with the autumn wind, fighting to keep its leaves. When the war was over the tree had lost and its leaves were falling. But the wind

19

had learned great respect for the oak and so carried its leaves to the river, and there they became the first fish, instead of dying as other leaves do. And from then on fish swam from that river to all rivers, lakes, and the sea.

Bear Man liked the song. He liked it because he was fond of trees, of water, and of the wind. They were sacred things. He suspected that there was little actuality in the song regarding the creation of fish. So many tales, he knew, were not told to teach the outer truth of things. What they taught instead was the more mysterious, sacred, inner truth of matters. The truth which cannot be seen with the eyes or touched with the hands.

He watched a *jisgwa*, a bird, feeding her young in their nest. It was the same bird that had called to him earlier. It was a robin. Not a rare or noble bird, he thought, but lovely unto itself. That is enough for any of us. He watched it fly away, hunting as he himself hunted for his family. The bird reminded him of his cousins, the Bird Clan. He felt pride in all his cousins of the seven clans. They formed together the mightiest people, the Principal People. But when he thought of his own clan, the Deer People, and of his own village, his heart beat a little faster. I love them most of all, he thought. It is fitting, too, that the deer, which provide us with so much, have also provided us with our name.

His thoughts wandered away from his hunt and came to rest with his father. Someday, he thought, Light Fire will become as all men become. Will I then be chief? Will I become a leader among the

People? My father will become a tale told again and again from the ends of time. I will become—only the morning knows its own mysteries. I'll wait until it unveils them. Today there is hunting to do. He stood and stretched. He raised his bow above his head and waved it softly through the air, challenging the sun, daring it to burn him to a cinder. He patted the quiver of arrows at his side, and then walked to the foremost part of the hill's crest and stood searching, scanning for game. Already the sun had moved enough to cast longer shadows. And already Bear Man could see that some of them were moving.

5

They were darkness dancing slowly through the trees. Then they were darkness moving into a clearing, flowing across the earth. And behind them came their masters, the deer, masters of shadow and motion. One was a great buck. The others were his wives and children.

Bear Man moved silently from the crest of the hill. The herd wasn't far away and wouldn't take long to reach. As he moved he kept watching them. He watched the buck bow its head to the grass, graze a moment, and then raise his head and antlers high into the air. Around him his harem and children also grazed, nibbling at green, green grasses, munching at greener leaves. Counting the stag there were seven of them. Seven is a fortunate number, thought Bear Man, the number of clans of the People.

He moved nearer the herd, taking an arrow from his quiver as he walked. He put arrow to bow-string and drew lightly, lighter than the spider draws its misty thread. All the while he moved nearer. He drew breath through his nostrils and they flared. The scent of the beasts was in the air, and had he been up wind from them they would have smelled him. He had planned his approach with that in mind. The breeze had returned, cooling his face, and he walked into it, thinking *hide me, hide me. Thank you. Thank you.* Of course the wind could turn on him. But he considered the wind his friend, and it seldom betrayed him. When it *had* done so, Bear Man considered that it must be for a right purpose, and so wasn't a betrayal. It was a message, an instruction. On those instances he thought carefully about what might be learned from what was happening when the wind had decided to stop or shift. By doing so he had learned not to abandon his awareness of other things happening around him. Once his concentration had been so completely upon his prey that he was aware of nothing else. And then the wind changed. What could it be? he had wondered. What is friend wind telling me? Then he caught the new scent. He tensed, turning and drawing his knife simultaneously. The result was a new bear-skin rug for his father's hut. *Thank you, wind. Thank you, wind*, he had said then, and had said it many times since. So he listened to the wind, tasted it, touched it, smelled it.

The buck separated himself from the harem. He pranced with his head held high. He knows his greatness, thought Bear Man, watching. Should I take him down from his high dreams? Or should I take only one of his wives? Each moment, each step, silent as the breathing of grass, Bear Man came nearer. When he was in range of the buck, he stopped. He raised the bow and drew the string smoothly to his lips, to his cheek, to his ear. He listened to the bow's almost silent bending. The flint tip of his arrow leveled at the buck's heart. Bear Man held still the aim, not wavering, but not loosing the arrow either. I won't take down this one, he thought. A doe will mean better, more tender meat. The buck would be harder to kill anyway. Even a doe might take more than one arrow. It was too likely the buck would be wounded and then run for hours before the arrow finished its work. Still Bear Man held the flint tip pointed at the big heart. He held it there until he knew that if he let it fly that it would find its mark, and that the stag could not escape. The arrow would be deeply, properly placed. And though the stag might run, eventually he would fall. Knowing that, and then giving the animal its life, would place the buck in Bear Man's debt. Now you owe me, he thought. And I will be repaid by your children, this season, and the next and next for many seasons. He eased on the string, gently lowering the bow. You are mine, he said silently. And then the wind, his friend, shifted slightly and brought him a new scent. He knew it at once. There was none other like it. He looked through the trees for some sign of its origin, and then he saw the brief flickering motion of death at the buck's side, and then the arrow protruding from its chest, above the heart.

The buck faltered, then stood again, pausing erect with its head once more held high. It looked quickly to its wives and sons, and then bolted away. The arrow dangled from its bleeding hide. Bear Man turned to the rest of the herd. One of the deer was stumbling, an arrow in her flank. Another was twisting on the ground. There were two arrows in her back. The fawns were following after the other doe, which followed the wounded buck. Then Bear Man saw the *ani soi*, other people, rushing into the clearing. He saw one of them take a knife to the throat of the fallen doe. Another put a second arrow into the doe that was stumbling. It fell, and the *soi* with the knife, red and wet as though *it* were bleeding, rushed to her and cut a large gash across her neck. The blood flowed instantly and unstoppable, flushing over the deer's neck and across her legs, then onto the earth where it sank slowly through leaves and grass and into the soil.

The *soi* was kind. He had cut the animal's neck so it would die quickly. And though it continued to kick, it was dead. And after a while the kicking stopped, and then the legs, like the rest of the creature, were still. Its eyes turned to dark, almost black glass. Its tongue, red with still warm blood, protruded from its mouth. Already flies were swarming over the carcass. It was dead, and had immediately assumed the pose of death, the place of death, and the smell of death.

Bear Man smelled the cold, musty odor of the blood. It was sweet and invincible, the eternal fragrance of mortality. He watched the men, busy at their kills. You have stolen from me, he thought to them, at them, wanting his thoughts and anger to pierce them, to haunt them and frighten them away. The *soi* continued at their tasks. There were smiles on their faces, songs in their voices. The youngest of them chattered quickly to the eldest, older than the trees thought Bear Man, and then he sped away in search of the buck. You have stolen my hunt, his thoughts went out like arrows, like spears. And you have killed my stag, and so have stolen my hunt for many seasons. The old one began to instruct the younger who had remained with him and together they started the work of preparing the animals. The young one got the first kill strung up from a tree branch. He took his knife in first one hand, and then the other, trying to decide how he could best get at the beast. When he decided he made a quick, smooth, unhesitant move and the creature's belly opened and spilled onto the ground.

Bear Man watched the thieves at their work and wondered if he would kill them.

There were three of them. Bear Man recognized them as the *Anvgadaninvda*, the Outcasts, *ani soi* from the south. They were those who had generations ago warred with the Principal People over the lands that the People now occupied.

Now and then they came into the People's lands, and now and then there were small battles between these *soi* and the People. But that hadn't happened for many summers. It had never happened since Bear Man had become a warrior. Will it happen now? he wondered. All *other people* fear us. Why are these so far into our lands? Surely they were doing more than hunting. Surely they are here to cause trouble, he thought. Perhaps these *soi* have forgotten to be afraid.

Bear Man turned his back on the two remaining *others* and followed after the one who had wounded his stag.

When the *soi* was in sight, Bear Man could see that the fellow was younger than himself. And of course he was smaller. Everyone is smaller than I am, though. Bear Man was huge, compared to most men.

The *soi* stopped to turn some leaves, looking for traces of blood. Bear Man halted and watched. The hunter found what he was looking for and continued after the buck. Bear Man followed. He couldn't decide what to do about the *soi*. He thought of killing him. That would be easy enough. One arrow would end the *other's* chase and would be appropriate retribution for the theft of Bear Man's hunt. But there would be other dangers, thought Bear Man. It was forbidden for a man whose wife was with child to look upon the dead. I should leave him alone, he thought. I should go home. Tree is waiting for me there. He thought of her, soft and large. He pictured her cooking and the glow of the fire illuminating the roundness of her belly. I should go home, he thought again, but he thought also of the food and clothing that had been stolen from him and his family, not just now but also for the unclaimable generations that now would never come forth.

The *soi* halted. He was looking at something. Bear Man couldn't see what. He came nearer, searching. Then he saw the buck. It was rubbing itself against a tree. It was churning against the arrow, trying to dislodge it. Bear Man could see that the arrow wasn't deep. It wasn't a serious wound. Surely, he thought, the beast can live. Then he saw the *soi* removing another arrow from his quiver, stringing it, aiming. Bear Man thought quickly. Which was the worse evil, to look upon the dead, even to kill, or to allow thieves to take food and clothing from his family? Surely the fates will make allowance, he thought, and his decision was made. He let out a low, well-sounded whistle and at the same instant disappeared into the trees.

The *soi* heard the whistle. He lowered his aim and turned, at the same moment seeking shelter. He knew he had been seen by a warrior or, more likely, warriors of the *Ani Yunwiya*. He knew that soon he might die.

He moved into a cover of brush. As he did so he spied the buck freeing itself of the arrow and bounding away. He searched the woods with his eyes, looking for his enemies. He thought of his friend and his father waiting for him. Or were they already dead? He thought then of the hunts he had never gone on and the battles he had never fought. He thought of the woman who was promised to him but that he had not yet taken as his wife, and of the children he had not yet fathered. And then he saw the brief shadow and felt the slight breeze. He turned and saw the dark giant standing over him. He saw the blade of the *galuyasdi*, axe, falling toward him. *Old Man!* he thought, his mind seeking swiftly but far too slowly for his father's face. And then he saw no more, and thought no more. He was gone to join the *didanvto*, spirits.

Bear Man cleaned the blood from his axe and then sheathed the weapon. He looked into the eyes of the other. They were frozen open. It was a good way to die, he thought, now he will be able to see his way into the world of spirits.

He turned and looked in the direction the buck had taken. Heal well, great one. Give me your children, for now you are twice in my debt. Then he headed back to the Outcasts who were waiting for the dead one to return. He had decided they should deliver to him his hunt.

While he walked he thought about the young *soi* he had killed. He thought about the warrior's apparent youth. He wondered if he had a wife and children. Those thoughts took him to his own wife who was waiting for him at their hut. He smiled thinking about her. They had been married for only one new moon when she told him she was carrying their son. Now she was large with the child. Soon Stone, his son, the grandson of a chief, would be with them. Then I will be fully a man, he thought. It wasn't enough that he was a great warrior and hunter. He must have a son. Otherwise he was not a complete man. If he died without a son then that would be the end of his tale and of the tale of all his fathers. It would not reach to both ends of time and so it would not be told forever. Bear Man wondered if the *soi* he had killed had a son. He hoped so. But if he didn't, I can't grieve too heavily about it. Many people die without sons and many tales are ended. There is no way of avoiding that. It is a part of life. It is a part of the earth, the wind, the leaves and water. Bear Man contented himself with these wisdoms. But part of him worried that he had brought bad luck to his unborn child by killing a man.

When he came near the clearing where the deer had been killed, he slowed his pace and made certain he walked without making sounds. *I am Bear Man*, he thought. *I move, though, with the same quiet as the roots of trees, and even the trees cannot hear my motions. And the trees hear almost all things, for they are the greatest listeners.*

Bear Man believed the trees in their tremendous, stationary calm had learned to listen to all sound, even to silence. And that when they spoke, whispering to the wind, that their words were the utterings of greatest wisdom. If only I could understand their language, he thought, then I would become the wisest of men, knowing all the great mysteries of the earth. And so he spent hours and days listening to the trees and the wind as they spoke together. And sometimes he thought he understood, but he was never certain. And so he listened more.

In the air he could again smell the perfume of death. And he could smell the smaller scent of the two *others*. He could smell their ease. He knew that it came from the joy of a good hunt. And he knew that they had no fears about the safety of the one who was now dead. A few steps further and Bear Man heard their voices. They were not talking loudly, but not quietly either. They have

30

no more fear at all, he thought. He heard them laughing. Their language was much the same as that of the Principal People, but different enough that Bear Man had trouble with some of their words, that and he couldn't hear everything they said. He could tell, though, that they were talking about an *udanvdi*, a whore. They were recounting her deeds. These are worthless people, he thought, that they rejoice in such things. Then he remembered that he might have to kill these men, and he chased the other thoughts from his mind. He didn't want to kill while thinking such small things about them. Death shouldn't be so small a thing. If he killed them while retrieving his hunt, that would be bad luck enough. It would be worse if he did so while having evil thoughts about them. Killing a man because he was a thief was justifiable, usually. Killing a man because you didn't like the way he conversed was foolishness and would bring the worst kind of luck. Not that Bear Man all together believed in luck, good or bad. He suspected that it was mostly something that witches and mothers taught to scare children into obedience. But he wasn't sure.

By the time they were in easy sight, he realized that he didn't want to kill them. If they will simply return my hunt and leave our lands, that will be enough. He was already regretting that he had killed one of them. Bad luck might be real, he told himself. He remembered being told that bad luck doesn't always come as it is foretold. Sometimes it waits for years, making you think that you've escaped it, and then it claims you. Thinking about it he started to sweat, and his heart beat faster.

The men were sitting on the ground. They were slapping the earth, playing a game with pebbles. It would be easy, he thought, to kill them. Their bows were out of reach. He could send arrows into them before they could defend themselves.

They started laughing again. This time they spoke of their wives and children. The ancient one talked loudly about his son and how proud he was of the young warrior. Bear Man quickly understood that the warrior he had killed was the son of the old man. He kept listening. He learned that the warrior was soon to be married. He forgot a moment about his own bad luck. He had ended these men's tales. He wasn't glad about having done so.

The old one went on to tell of his daughters. Oh, how he loved his daughters. He loved them as only one so wise and good as himself could, he told, but they weren't sons. And only sons can carry on the tale of a man. A daughter can only carry on another man's story. This is enough, thought Bear Man. Let them have the hunt. He turned to leave. That's when the wind betrayed him.

The breeze had been coming to him from them. Then without warning it changed. And before he was gone he knew that the two warriors had caught his scent. What to do now? he thought. He unsheathed his axe and held it firmly. From somewhere he heard the small cry of a robin. Then he whispered lightly to the trees around him. "I am going now to talk to these other people, the

Outcasts," he said. "I am going to offer them the chance to leave our lands and return to their homes. If they choose to fight me instead, I ask you to listen and record the story of what happens here, so that if I die the tale of it may be passed someday to my son. That is what I ask you to do." Then he walked out of the woods and into the clearing to face the two men.

9

Their laughter had stopped the moment they caught the scent. And then another moment passed and they were staring at the edge of the wood, at the face of death, at the dark figure of a man so large they knew he was a demon. There were shadows falling across the creature's face and arms, and the shadows looked like a deep, black paint against his already dark skin. His stone axe was ready at his side. He stood unmoving, waiting for them to move. His clothes and feathers told them he was a warrior of those who call themselves the Principal People, their enemies. They tried to hide their fear, keeping their faces and their eyes silent, blank. Were there other of the *Ani Yunwiya* around them? The two continued not to move. Not to speak.

After a long while, the giant spoke first.

"This is the land of the Principal People," he

told them.

They continued to make no movement or sound.

"You know that you should not be here."

The eyes of the young one narrowed. His lips tightened.

"Now," said the giant, "you must leave, and leave behind what you have killed." The deer had already been gutted and prepared for journey on a litter made of tree limbs.

The old warrior stood. "We have hunted them," he said. "We killed and cleaned them. We won't leave our labor behind us."

"It is best you do. Why have you come here? What trouble do you want to make for the People, and for yourselves?"

"We want to make no trouble at all," said the old one. His face was alive with wrinkles. "We have only come to hunt on our old lands. Lands that you who think you are the only people took from us."

"Go now."

"We are waiting for my son." He pointed in the direction his son had gone. As he did so his eyes searched the woods for signs of others. "We must wait for him. Then we will leave."

"You must leave now. You son will not return. He has gone to become a spirit."

The old one's face didn't move. His eyes didn't change. "What story are you telling me?" he asked.

"I have sent your son to the spirits," said the giant. "Now unless you go, I must do the same to you."

The old man's eyes rolled back into his head and he turned his face to the sky. He made his hands into fists and began to pound them against his head. "*He was my only son! What have you done to me!*" He started walking in a small circle. "*Now my tale has ended! My story is gone!*" He raised his arms to the sky. "*It has ended!*" he cried.

"Go home, old one. Father yet another son. Go—"

"*No!* I have an *old* wife! I can have no more sons. I am ended! My fathers are ended!" And then he quickly brought his hands down and faced the giant. "You are no *human being!*" he said. "You wear the garments of the People but it is plain that you are a *demon!* Look how large you are. White Hand and I must kill you so that you'll haunt these woods no more. Our enemies will call us their friends for doing this."

The young warrior studied the face of the giant. It seemed all his attention was on the ancient one. He moved his hand, which was blemished with a large white patch, to the knife at his side.

The giant spoke again. "Even old women have given such surprises. Go home. Weep for your son. Pray for another."

"*You must die!*" screamed the young one and he lunged to his feet and swung his knife through the air, then let it fly at the giant's face. The giant ducked the knife; reached to the earth. The young one charged him. The giant stood suddenly and threw dust into the young warrior's face. Then he kicked the young one's belly and sent him rolling into dust and grass, clawing to get the dust from his eyes.

The old one had stopped wailing and knelt to help his friend, heedless of their continuing danger. With his tongue he washed specks out of his companion's eyes. And then when his friend could see again they stood. The demon was gone.

The young one gathered his possessions, and then started to gather the litter. "Leave them," said the old one. He then collected his own belongings and they left, heading in the direction his son had taken. But it is not ended, the old one told himself, and he looked into the woods for some sign of the demon.

10

Bear Man watched their going. He followed them until he was certain they intended to leave and not return and attack him. Then he went back to the deer. They lay on the litter in the shade of a tall pine. Their bodies were hard. Hundreds of flies were swarming over them. Bear Man lifted the two long branches and began the walk home. Already the sun was low in the sky, and he knew it would be long after dark before he returned.

Pulling the deer was difficult. Much of the way back to the village was thick with growth. Still, Bear Man decided, it was easier to drag them than it would be to carry them. So he made his way slowly, and thought of Tree as he went.

He thought back to their first night together. He had taken her to the river and had sung his song to her. Then he took away her clothes and laid his body between her legs, and she encircled his back with her arms, and his legs with her own legs, and his hardness with her softness. And after they had spent all of their heat and he had planted his seed well within her, he pulled away and discovered her blood upon him. When he saw it he was glad because it was evidence that she was a pure woman. He put his hand to himself and felt the blood. Then with the blood on his fingers he brought them to his mouth and tasted it. Then he put his fingers to her mouth. "Our blood is one," he told her as she took his fingers between her lips. Then they went into the water together and cleaned one another. After that she again encircled him with her body. They began like that, he remembered. And they had continued like that each day since, except those days and nights when hunting and prayers took him away.

He knew she expected him tonight. He knew when he got there that they would butcher the deer together, and that they would lie together in their hut as they had done on the stone that first night, and that though she was large from their son that still she would welcome him.

Afterward he would tell her about his adventures with the others. They would cry together because he had ended two men's tale, and because he had endangered their child. And then they would sleep. That is what drew him most. Sleep. He was tired, weary. He wanted to cover himself with the warm darkness of sleep. He wanted to wash and cleanse himself in it. Sleep, he thought. Sleep. And then he felt the strange stinging in his arm. Casually he rubbed his hand across the soreness. When he brought his hand away it was red with blood. On the ground in front of him was a *soi* arrow.

11

Tree brought water from the creek. The creek was *Vlenitohv*, Life or The-Water-That-Gives-Life-To-The-Village. It ran through the village and into the woods until it found the river. The river was named *Nagoligvna*, which meant Unknown, because no one knew the depth of its deepest parts. It was the same river that Bear Man had taken her to on their wedding night. She was thinking about the river, and about that night.

She was thinking about those things because she had just felt a strange pain in her womb. The pain started her to thinking about the child. Is it hurting, too? Thoughts of the child led her to thoughts of Bear Man and the river Unknown. She wished Bear Man was home. *He'll be home tonight*. She wasn't afraid when he was away, but she always felt better when he was with her. That's what she was thinking when Bear Man's friend, Crawler, approached her. He was smiling the cunning smile she always saw him with. It made her distrust him, though she never spoke of that because he was her husband's friend.

"He'll be jumping down soon," said Crawler, admiring the roundness of her belly. He was a short, thin, quick moving man. He did a little dance as though he were a little human being jumping down and out of its mother.

"Soon enough, Crawler," she said. "And Good Cook's will be jumping down soon for you," she added.

"Not so soon as your's," said the man. Then he danced away, but not without again giving Tree the smile she distrusted.

Her thoughts returned again to the pain she had felt. It worried her. She looked to the western horizon. The sun was already down and soon it would be dark. If Bear Man were home I wouldn't be worried, she thought. Then she felt the pain again.

12

Bear Man dropped his burden and vanished into the cover of trees. It was nearly dark and he couldn't see far. He supposed that the Outcasts had decided to follow him. He wondered which one had shot the faulty arrow. Likely the young one, he thought. He would be more likely to be impatient and not wait until he could have a perfect aim. Such rashness, Bear Man told himself, was the formula for death. And then he saw a movement not far away. He couldn't tell if it was the young or the old warrior. He waited for it to stop. He watched the leaves gently rock to a motionless resting. *Behind them. He waits to die. Go straight, dear arrow!* He let go the string. An instant later he heard a cry. Then the leaves were again disturbed. The young warrior staggered out of his hiding. Bear Man's arrow was deep in his chest. The *soi* held it and tried to pull it out. He kept jerking at it and his hand kept slipping away. Then he fell to the ground and started moaning.

Bear Man didn't move. His eyes searched the dark. His ears listened. He could see no movement, and could hear no sound, except the now and then groans from the young warrior. Still he waited. He knew that if he moved while the old one was watching that he would be dead. His spirit would leave him here in the woods to join the world of spirits. He wouldn't move.

The time passed slowly and there were many thoughts threatening to come into Bear Man's mind but he wouldn't allow them. He had to concentrate all his attention, all his body and mind, on what was happening around him. If he allowed himself to think of things elsewhere he might be caught again as he had been while he was dragging the deer.

First came his thirst. *Don't think of it. There is*

no thirst. And then the pain in his arm. *There is no pain*. But the arm throbbed anyway and then he stopped fighting it because he realized it was his friend. Because next came the tiredness. His eyes wanted to close. His body wanted to rest. *Sleep*, it told him. The arm throbbed, *stay awake*. Listen to the pain, he told himself. Stay alive. Listen to the pain, and only think of the movement of shadows and the sounds of the forest floor, the leaves, the wind, and the smell of the old one. That is how he knew the old one was still there. There was no wind then but he could faintly smell him, along with the scents of the deer, and the young, dying *soi*.

His eyes were half closed when he picked up the new scent. It was strong and harsh. They were near, he could tell and there were several of them. Then he heard them, breathing loudly, then growling. He waited, listening to their growls and to the *soi's* moans.

He is taking a long time to die, thought Bear Man. He has come here to die, because his friend died. Bear Man thought of his own friends. Will they die because I died? he wondered. Crawler? Possibly. My father? Others? There was no way to know what future would be made.

Bear Man listened to the growls and the crying through the night. Sometimes he could hear the warrior praying. And then the cries and the prayers stopped. And then a short while before dawn the growls, too, ceased. Bear Man could see the dark shadows rolling and drifting away. Then there was only silence. And a little after that the smell of the old one was gone.

After dawn the old one's scent hadn't returned. Bear Man had not moved at all through the night. Cautiously, his muscles aching and his wounded arm numb, he came out of his hiding.

The carcasses of the deer had been stripped by the wolves. Their bones were scattered through the grass and brush. He turned from them and walked to the fallen warrior.

The *soi* was not dead, but was too weak even to moan. The pain had caused his fists to permanently clench and his face was twisted into a strange, wrinkled mask.

"You will die soon," Bear Man told him. The warrior couldn't respond. Bear Man took his knife from its scabbard and held it before the open eyes of the warrior. I should simply leave, he thought. I want to simply leave, put all of this behind me. His arm was swollen and the pain was getting worse. He looked at it. The bleeding had stopped. But it was so swollen he couldn't move it. He looked back at the warrior. His knife was still in front of the man's eyes. "Do you want to die now?" he asked him. He wasn't sure the man would be able to answer. I would want to die, he thought. The man's lips moved. No sound came. He opened and closed his eyes, slowly. His lips moved again. Bear Man lowered the blade and drew it quickly under the warrior's chin. It was the same thing the warrior had done for the wounded deer. Bear Man cleaned his blade, stood, and went in search of the old one.

When the other *soi* couldn't be found, Bear

Man started again for home. He had only crossed one ridge when he collapsed.

13

"You won't die," said the ancient one.

"*Who are you? Where am I?*"

"At first I wanted you to die. Now I've decided that isn't enough. You must live a while longer. Then I shall kill you."

"Are you a tree? Are you a spirit?"

"No."

"Who then?"

But then there was no one there and Bear Man wasn't certain there had been. Was it a dream? he wondered. It was nearly dark again. The pain had much eased and most of the swelling was gone. He carefully stood, looked around. A dream? he wondered.

It was late when she heard him enter the hut. She lay still as though she were asleep. She could tell he was standing in the doorway. *Don't linger there*, she thought, *the child will be difficult in coming out*. She suspected that he didn't believe such teachings, but she did. *Come in*, she thought. *Come lay beside me*. She could feel him watching her, watching the rise and fall of her breasts and belly. Then she heard him move inside, drawing closed the deerskin across the door, shutting out the light of the stars. He was very quiet. *He is always quiet*, she told herself.

She could only barely hear as he removed his band of feathers, and then his moccasins, and then his clouts. He was moving strangely. *What is it?* she wondered. She could feel the tension, the strain. Then she could feel him beside her, but he didn't move.

Touch me, she thought. Still he didn't move. She turned toward him, put her hands to his thighs, touched them lightly. She kept moving them, lightly, gently, almost not touching. The smell of him was good to her. She had missed his smell. She was glad to have him back. She had cried when the night before he hadn't returned. She had cried again when sunset came once more and still he wasn't there. Now she felt like a foolish child for having worried. *Touch me*, she thought again. And a moment later she felt his hands, gently on her breasts, making circles. Then circling her stomach. Then lower.

She moved her breasts nearer his face. He continued to touch her. She touched him. And then his lips were on her breasts. And though the child was still within her she could feel him drawing milk from her. It was something she had taught him to do, though she supposed that part of him remembered the ritual from when he was an infant in his mother's arms. *It's good to have you home*, she thought, opening herself to him, enjoying again his familiar scent, but noticing then something strange about it. *What?* she wondered. She was too tired to tell. Too tired and too excited at the same moment.

Later, as she drifted to sleep, she almost recognized the scent of his blood, but then the image was gone and she slept.

15

The old one had many names. He was *Sunale Didla*, Toward Morning, for that is when he had been born. He was *Dihltadegi*, The Jumper, because as a youth he was renowned at that sport. He was *Asdosgii*, The Brayer, because he often spoke loudly and angrily his opinions. And he was *Ganaqutisdi*, Hate, because his hatred for the *Jalagi*, who called themselves the *Ani Yunwiya*, had become legend among his people, and he had taken an oath that he would not die until they had been driven from the lands they had stolen. But most of his people simply called him *Utvsohnvi*, Old Man, because he was the oldest among them.

Old Man stood outside the village in the dark shadow of a tree. He had followed the giant warrior, and had often thought he could easily kill him. But that would no longer be enough, he told himself. So when the giant had entered a hut, Old Man was watching.

He wasn't so proud to think that he would live to see the expulsion of all the *Jalagi*, but he believed he could be the instrument that would lead to that end. He was getting older, though, and what he must do could wait no longer.

He watched the hut and listened to the village. He committed to memory the layout of the streets. From some other hut he heard a child crying. Then, a shadow among shadows, he moved away. When I return, he promised himself, many will cry.

16

It was forbidden for a man whose wife was carrying a child to be a gravedigger or in any way to help with a burial, lest the child be stillborn. While he slept Bear Man dreamed that he buried the two soi *he had killed.*

There were bird songs. There were the songs of waking, the waking of the village. There were the songs of Tree, breathing in harmony with the birds, breath flowing with the rhythm of the village.

Gray light. Songs. Pain. Bear Man woke to these things. The pain in his arm quieter, but still there, still trying to keep him awake, though the dangers were gone.

Gone? he wondered. *Danger never goes. It waits!*

Is it waiting? he wondered. He peered through the dim gray of the hut. He flexed his arm against the pain. He tilted his head and held still, capturing a moment of the songs of birds, village, and Tree. *The songs of home*, he thought happily, smiling.

He was slipping on his clouts when he heard Tree moving. He looked at her face, a soft petal emerging from deer and bearskin blankets, her hair long and dark, darker than night. Her eyes opening, blinking as though they had just discovered that her dreams were true.

"Welcome home from the night," he told her.

"Welcome home from your hunt," she said. She smiled, and then she saw his wound and her smile turned to a frown. She took his hand and drew him to her. Delicately she touched the wound.

"I met with three *ani soi* of the Outcasts while

on my hunt," he said. He said it with a soft voice, without any fear, not wanting her to be frightened. He touched her hair. His hand sank in the dark stream of it, then emerged on her shoulder.

"Are you hurting?" she asked. She took her hand away from his wound.

"No," he whispered near her ear, telling her only a small lie. *Don't be afraid,* he thought. "I'm getting well now." She turned from him, staring at the thin glow of light around the deerskin door. What is it? he wondered.

"There's something bothering you beyond my own pain?" he offered.

She shook her head, continued to stare at the light. Then, "Will our child be born without an arm now?" she asked. Is that all? he wondered. Is there something else?

"No," he answered. "I don't think so." Other women wouldn't speak their fears at all, he told himself. They would keep them to themselves. But Tree isn't other women. But is she telling me all her fears?

"Sometimes men who injure their eyes cause their unborn children to be blind," she said. She turned back from the doorway and looked at Bear Man, but not at his eyes.

"Who do you know," he asked, "that such a thing has happened to?"

"I've heard. It is taught."

"Taught by mad witches and old women," he said. "Don't worry. I'll speak to the medicine man, Broken Back. I'll ask him if there is any danger."

She turned back to the doorway. "What of these others you met?" she asked. Why is she asking that? he wondered. Women don't ask such things.

"They tried to steal my hunt. We played with each other a little. I hurt my arm. That was all. Don't worry about it." He didn't want to tell her about killing the *soi* or about his dream. He knew those things would only worry her more, and he was concerned enough for both of them, that's what he told himself. He kissed her then, holding his lips quietly against hers. When they parted she was still looking at the doorway.

"You paused a long while in the doorway last night," she said. She said it slowly, as though she were afraid she had finally said too much.

Is that what is bothering her? he thought. "Don't worry about anything," he said. "I'll speak to Broken Back. There will be no problems for us. Our child will be the grandson of a chief. He will not come to harm." Then he laughed a little, trying to make the moment lighter. "Come now," he said. "It's time for us to wash." He put his hand gently to her chin and drew her face toward him. "Let me hear you smile," he said.

She smiled, but the smile had no laughter, no song.

It was the custom of the Principal People that a man and a woman who were waiting for their child to come out to wash each other in the morning before they began their labors.

Tree donned her skirt of deerskin and a drape of woven bark. They went together to the creek. She had asked no more and Bear Man was glad for it. Partly because he didn't want to worry her, and partly because he felt ashamed of the bad luck he may have caused.

In two days the new moon would come. If the child hadn't arrived by then, then once more Bear Man and Tree and the priest would go to the river for Tree's monthly washing. Bear Man thought about that as he washed Tree's face. The monthly washing was important to their child's safe delivery, so the priest assured them. And it was even more important to its prosperous life. *And laws, and traditions?* he wondered. *Looking upon the dead? Standing in a doorway? And injury to a parent? Eat this but do not eat that?* Were all these things real, or superstitions? he asked himself. He thought about the dream he'd had. It was only a vague memory, but it was clear enough that he remembered putting the dead men into the earth. I must consult Broken Back, he thought. If there is anything to all of this, then he will know the sure way to fight the ill fortune I have brought.

He cupped some fresh water in his palms and rinsed Tree's face. Then he took her hands and slowly washed them. And then her feet.

The sun was already warming the day. It sparkled on the shallow water. Bear Man laughed while washing his wife. Tree saw two fish swimming near her feet and pointed at them. Bear Man reached for one but it swam quickly away. They laughed together. Already their worries seemed distant to him. Then Tree began to wash Bear Man.

"We'll have a strong and happy son," she said.

"We are strong, happy people," he said. "Of course we will."

"Our son will grow to become a great leader of the Principal People," she said.

Bear Man stared at her. He felt a strange movement within. He wasn't sure what he should say or do. He listened to himself, tried to understand the motion he felt. *A tugging.* Then it was gone.

"Is something wrong?"

"No," he said. He wondered though. The feeling had been unmistakable.

"Your wound is already healing, like you said," she told him, pouring water over it.

When they were again at the hut, Tree prepared some medicine. He watched her mixing it in a gourd dipper, her hands fine and precise, the way his mother's had been, he thought. An image of the long gone woman came briefly to his mind. *Whispering eyes, whispering voice, whispering smile.* Tree offered him the gourd. He put it to his lips and drank it quickly, sucking against the sour taste. Then she was putting her medicine made from the paste of oak leaves onto his wound. "Thank you leaves," she said. She took the cup from him. "Thank you flowers," Bear Man echoed her words.

He watched her turn away, putting medicines in their place. Her stomach seemed larger each day, he thought. "Do you think it will come out before the new moon?" he asked.

"Second Daughter, the midwife, says not." She started to walk away. He stopped her with his hand on her stomach. He held it there lightly. She started to move. "Wait, please," he said. *Where are you?* he wondered. *Dance for me.* There was nothing. He laid his hand more firmly against her. *Dance,* he thought, and waited, waited. And then came the motion. The child moving within her. And he knew. He knew what had happened within himself at the creek, at *Life.* It had been as though he had felt the movings of his son within himself. "I think it will come out soon, though," he told her.

"Perhaps," she said. "I hope so."

When she was busy making clothing, Bear Man stood to leave. "I'm going to Broken Back now," he said. She said nothing.

He moved to the door, waited.

"Hurry out the doorway," she said quietly, not looking at him.

Without speaking again he pushed aside the deerskin and stepped back into the day. It was already too hot, he thought. And then again he felt the motion inside. And almost he thought he heard a whimper come from his hut. He started to go back. No, he thought, she would rather be alone.

20

Tree put aside the skirt she was making. She wondered why she hadn't spoken to Bear Man about the pains she had felt. Was it because of his wound? Because of fear for the child? It doesn't matter, she told herself. The knowledge is tied within me, she thought. But I can't keep it there. When Bear Man returns, I will untie this knot within myself. I will release the fears, let go the pains. *The fears will echo through the world, the pains will journey through the wilderness*, she heard herself think. *Songs*, she thought, *Songs like Bear Man*.

The pain came again. At first she had thought it might be her labor. But it isn't, she told herself. She knew labor was different, though she had never experienced it.

She had felt the pain once at the river, while Bear Man was washing her, and then again as he left the hut. Is the child in distress? she wondered. Has its arm been injured? Does it know it will have difficulty jumping down? Is it turned upside down? The midwife says no, but couldn't she be wrong? The thoughts plagued her, rolled around inside her mind until they became a pain behind her eyes.

Come back soon, Bear Man, she thought. *I've things now that I'll say. I'll tell you about pains. I'll tell you about fears.*

21

A clean orderly town, he thought. That was the village. His village, Chief Light Fire's town, generations old. Children of the Deer Clan. *Strong huts! Tall gardens! Tasty crops! The best hunting!* His thoughts were a song to it. He passed his father's hut. *The tallest, broadest, finest house! Only the council lodge and the menstruation lodge were larger. All the houses are right-sized, clean, suited to their tenants! A clean orderly town!* When a family had more children, a larger home was built for them. Usually it was made from both new materials and materials that were usable from the old hut.

In the cradle of hills! He walked through the

village, his thoughts singing, casting out fears. The village rested in the nest of two hills, a sheltered valley. *Through it runs Life! And Life leads to the Unknown! That is the way of all living things. The Unknown. And then the land of spirits! And what then? Do even spirits know?*

There were more than five hundred people in Light Fire's town. Each year the village grew a little larger. The warrior-hunters warred when they could, hunted always. There had been few wars in the south. Many of the men journey north to join their cousins against the northern *ani soi*.

The women made clothing—white clothes, brown clothes, skirts, shirts, moccasins. They founded feasts!—Corns, meats, greens, fruits! They erected huts, told tales, gave birth to children, taught those same children they bore—*the ways of the People!* And the children played, boys at games that grow them into men! Girls at games that *tamed* them into women! Ceremonies! Harvest! Feast! Fire! *Life! The Unknown!*

At the far end of the village was the hut of *Gashoi Ulsgwalida*, Broken Back. The medicine man had gotten his name years earlier when as a boy he had fallen from a tree. He fell on his back. The *crack* of the bone is still talked about. The then medicine man, Red Eyes, took Broken Back to his hut. Months later the boy emerged, healed. Red Eyes who was childless, renamed the boy. Named him and claimed that the boy was his because he had saved him. Before the injury he had been known as Hard-To-Come-Out, because he had taken so long coming out of his mother. Red Eyes named him Broken-Back-Who-Used-To-Be-Hard-To-Come-Out, and called him that. Everyone else in the village only called him Broken Back. No one liked to say the long name, except Red Eyes, and Broken Back himself. He took great pride in the entire name. Red Eyes made him his apprentice, and when the old man went to the land of spirits Broken Back became medicine man to Light Fire's town.

Bear Man came to the medicine man's hut. It was finer than most. He was treated with great respect and admiration. Everyone knew he was a powerful man, more powerful than witches or priests. Many times he had been asked to come to other towns to live. He had refused, never saying why. No, he would say. That was all.

Bear Man thought about Tree's warnings of doorways. The song of the village was still lingering in his mind. He resisted the worries that wanted to flood him. Broken Back's doorway waited in front of him. He stepped back from it. "Broken Back!" he called. "This is Bear Man. You know my wife has a son in her so I can't stand in your doorway!" Then he waited for the old man to answer. No sound came from the hut. Perhaps he isn't there, thought Bear Man. He called again. Still there was no sound from the hut. He decided to wait until the medicine man returned. He sat on the ground and stared down the street at the simple row of buildings, starting to listen again to their song. Then he heard instead a movement behind him. He turned. The medicine man stood in the doorway of his hut. When he spoke his lips didn't move. It was a trick he had learned from Red Eyes. It never ceased to amaze others.

"Broken-Back-Who-Used-To-Be-Hard-To-Come-Out is very busy. Come and talk tomorrow." His lips hadn't moved. He turned to go back into his hut. Bear Man stood quickly.

"I have urgent need of the great healer," he said. He stood and waited for the medicine man's reply. Broken Back came again out of the doorway and stared at Bear Man.

"Come in quickly," he said, and then he vanished inside.

They sat facing each other. Bear Man started to speak. Broken Back stopped him by placing two fingers against Bear Man's lips. Then the medicine man closed his eyes. He didn't move or talk. After a while his lips moved a little but no sound came out.

Bear Man waited. Everywhere in the hut were the sacred objects of the medicine man's craft. The collected remains of animals. The leaves of many plants. Roots. Barks. Drawings on skins, drawings of animals that the medicine man had cut open and studied. Bear Man had never seen anything like that. But it was obvious that's what the drawings were. There were stones. Cups of soil. Masks. Bear Man avoided the masks. Looking at a mask might make the child ugly, he thought. He didn't believe it, but it was the sort of thing that Tree worried about, so he didn't do it. Besides, he wasn't certain she wasn't right. *There are truths unseen in many things*, he thought, *and though the masks may not cause a child's face to be ugly, who could know what it might do to his spirit?* Yes, he wondered, who could know? *The trees, the wind*, he told himself.

The medicine man's lips were still moving; still there was no sound from them. Then he raised his hands and turned his palms toward Bear Man. He held them there and Bear Man put his own palms against Broken Back's. The medicine man opened his eyes and seemed startled to find Bear Man in his hut. His lips stopped moving. "Tell me why you're here," the unmoving lips said.

Bear Man told him. Everything. The Outcasts. The deaths. The wound. The doorway. The dream. He told him that he had kept some of these things from Tree. He told him what things. His voice went on and on with the story of it, until finally he realized that he had told it all but was still hearing it. He wasn't talking, and Broken Back's lips were still, but he could hear a voice, Broken Back's, reciting all the things he had said.

When he had finished the discourse, the medicine man took away his hands, folding them in his lap. Bear Man did the same. "This is a terrible thing," said the medicine man. "I could tell you it isn't, but what good would that do?" He stood and began gathering medicines. "I must see your wife," he said.

"What can be done?" asked Bear Man, still sitting.

"I must see your wife," he repeated, and then he walked out of the hut. Bear Man waited a moment and then followed.

"What can be done?" he asked the medicine man as they walked. The medicine man's lips moved, but again no sound came from them.

22

Crawler watched Bear Man and Broken Back leaving the medicine man's hut. He started to go after them but then thought differently and turned to walk to the creek instead.

Crawler had gotten his name because of his reputed quickness and quietness at crawling. The skill served him well as a hunter and as a warrior. The skill came from his size. He was small and slender, light and agile. And so his size was a blessing. It was also a curse.

I am a curiosity, thought Crawler, looking into the water at his reflection. Why can't I be as other men? he wondered. He slipped off his moccasins and let his feet sink into the water, cold, rushing, clear, draining the heat of the day out of his body.

If only all things were so simple as cooling your feet, he thought. He had just come from his hut. *There lies the center of my sorrow*, he told himself. *There, and in this caricature of a body*.

His wife, Good Cook, had never refused him

her body. No wife would. But she had also never welcomed him. And who is she, he asked, to close her eyes to me? She is fat, she is ugly, she is stupid. And now she carries my child. A creature that will be a rodent like myself or a monster like its mother. Which is worse?

He thought back to when he had married her. Had he felt differently then? He could no longer remember. He did remember the silent laughter of other women. *He is a lizard*, he imagined them saying. *He is toad. He could never be a husband.* But Good Cook hadn't said those things. Instead she had said that she would marry him. And then sometime after that she had changed. She had stopped whispering and stopped moving when he was inside her. She had stopped touching him unless he told her. And then when his back was turned to her he thought he could feel her laughter. But when he turned to look at her she was always silent, never smiling, no laughter even in her eyes, so there was nothing he could do to answer her ridicule.

23

As they walked the medicine man crumbled leaves into a wooden cup. Then they stopped at the creek near Bear Man's hut. He put some powder from a bag into the cup. Then he sprinkled water into it until the cup was full. He stirred the water and the mixture with his finger. "The powder is from grain-root," he said. Then they went to Bear Man's house.

When they were inside, the three of them sat in a circle. Broken Back talked to Tree, sometimes moving his lips, sometimes not. Always moving his eyes. First looking at her face, her nose, her mouth, her eyes. Then looking elsewhere. Her feet. Her hands. Her large stomach. Then sometimes closing his eyes.

His eyes were closed. His lips were moving. "How does the little human being inside you act?" he asked. The woman looked at her husband but said nothing. Broken Back opened his eyes. He told her some of the things Bear Man had told him. He didn't tell her about the deaths, about the dream. Don't tell her that at all, he had told Bear Man while they were at the creek.

"These are the things Bear Man has told me," he said. "Now you must tell me things." He put his hand to her stomach. He held it there, pushing hard but not hurting her. "The little human being is dancing," he said. Then he took his hand away and gathered up the cup he had prepared. "Drink this," he told her. She drank it. "How does it taste?" he asked. She made a strained face at the cup. "*Mmh!* I think so, too," he said. She laughed, and then he smiled at her.

"Don't be afraid of things," he told her. "There may be some bad luck from these things. But there may not be. Being afraid of them can be the worst bad luck of all." His lips stopped mov-

61

ing but his voice continued, deeper, sounding far away. "Your unborn doesn't understand things that have happened outside you, but he does understand the fear within you. It will make him afraid, and that can cause him trouble." He looked at her long and steadily. "Do you understand?" he asked, moving his lips again. She nodded. He stared at her again a long while. Then, "Tell me now. Tell me some things. I know there are other things you haven't told." And then Broken Back and Bear Man saw her holding back tears, and she continued to hold them as she told them of the pains.

"Tell these things, too, to your midwife," he told her. "She must know about this. I think it is probably nothing. Don't you know that many women have such pains?" She nodded. "Good! Then don't be afraid of them." Then he reached forward and put his hand under Bear Man's clouts, holding the warrior firmly but not severely. "Have you been putting this inside her?" he asked. Bear Man nodded, startled. "Do not do so again until the child has jumped down and the time of purification is over." He got up to leave. Bear Man stood and came to the medicine man's side. He whispered in his ear.

"I, too, have pains, not strong pains. I feel something within me," he said. The medicine man grinned. "You've nothing more than grasshoppers in you," he said. "Soon enough they will hop away." He turned again to Tree.

"That is all I have to say to you now." He

smiled at them. "Broken-Back-Who-Used-To-Be-Hard-To-Come-Out will talk to you again after he has prayed." The lips were still. "There are other medicines for him to prepare." He turned and walked out the door; then stepped back again. "And laugh some," he told them. And then he laughed loudly through broadly smiling, but unmoving lips. And then he was gone.

Bear Man took hold of Tree's hand, warm and soft in his own. She put her head to his shoulder, her face touching his. What has happened? he wondered. He thought to the trees. He thought to the wind. What have I done? he asked them, but they didn't answer.

24

Old Man stood before the two new mounds. Beneath them were the two men who had been killed, his son and White Hand. He had finished the rituals of their burial. Now there was nothing to do but to return home. There he would tell his people how he and those who had died had dared to hunt on the old lands. And he would tell them of the demon. Then he would ask other warriors to join him, to end the cruelty of their enemies.

It was a long way home and there was much to think about, much to plan. Many of his people would oppose going to war, perhaps more of them than those who longed for it. There will be a way to deal with all things, he thought, for I will not be stopped.

25

They filled the air with happy prayers. They filled their voices with laughter. Inside them, the fear was hiding, waiting.

The medicine man returned with more medicines. Second Daughter, the midwife, came with good things to say. *All is well*, she proclaimed. Your pains, and Bear Man's feelings inside, she said, are only the voices of your fears, fears deep within you. If you listen to them they will gain hold on you. Let them cry out, but don't listen to them.

26

"Father, let me tell you what has happened," and Bear Man told Light Fire everything. The *soi*. The dreams. The pains.

Light Fire listened without speaking. Then when

Bear Man was finished, Light Fire spoke. "What will become of our son?" he asked.

"They say all is well," Bear Man told him.

"What will become of our fathers and the tale of our fathers if all is not well?"

"All must be well."

"What will happen if this ancient *soi* you speak of returns with warriors and makes war against the People?"

"Then they will die, father."

Light Fire looked at him without blinking. He wasn't an old man. He had been only a little older than Bear Man was now when Bear Man had been born. But he was old enough to remember wars. Old enough to know that he didn't like them, didn't cherish them as many young warriors do.

"With the *soi*," he said, "you did what you had to do. Now we must wait and see what they have to do. Perhaps nothing. If they are wise they will forget this."

"If they were wise, father, would they have hunted in our lands?"

"Then we must be wise."

27

He watched the smoke curl out of his pipe. It felt like it came from his heart instead, clouding not the room but his body, and his dreams. Light Fire was alone in his hut, thinking about his children, Bear Man and Tree. He had no others. He worried for them, and for himself. *Is all well? Are there only grasshoppers jumping inside their bellies?*

The end of a man's tale is a sad thought, he told himself. He thought about the *soi* and his father. His eyes were wet. Too much smoke in the hut, he told himself. He wiped the wetness from his face. Stay away you people, he thought to the *soi* in their distant town. Stay away. We don't need your war. You don't need it.

His thoughts sought a safer place to be, a place without these troubles. In his mind came the image of a long past face. The image was sharp and clear, but he wondered if it was the same face he had known. He wondered if the years had changed his memory of it.

"Woman?" he asked aloud, and the sound of his own voice in the quiet of the hut disturbed him. *Woman? Where are you?* Her name had been The-Woman-Who-Loves-Everyone. Truly she had, he thought. "*Ulihelisdi*," he said aloud. It was a shorter name that he had given her. *Ulihelisdi*, Joy. "Where are you?" he asked. His voice was so alone in the silence that he hated it. *There are troubles in my heart*, he told her. He wondered if she could hear. Some believed that the spirits could hear all things, and could converse with all creatures. Could it be? he wondered. And then he told her of Bear Man's troubles, and after that of his own. He told her about his own dream. The vision that came to his sleep each new moon for three seasons. And in it he had seen his town burning and his people leaving, leaving the town and leaving the Deer Clan and the Principal People. *I've told no one but you about this*, he said in his mind, hoping to reach her. *What can such dreams mean?* He waited, praying for an answer, but none came.

28

The new moon lit the night. The medicine man and the priest had told them that in the morning Tree must be washed. Then they had left them alone, standing in front of their hut, staring up at the great white light in the evening sky. They could see heavy clouds coming from the north.

"Rain?" asked Tree.

"I think so," said Bear Man, and they went inside.

Later, beneath their blankets, they touched each other's hands and faces, and smiled at each other through the darkness.

Half way through the night they woke.

"Rain," said Bear Man, giving name to the countless tears he heard falling to the earth.

Tree touched his face. He sat unmoving, listening to the rain. Listening to it beat and fall and wash at the world. She kissed him. The rain became a song inside him, but he couldn't understand its words, couldn't put measure to its motion. With her hand she drew a circle again and again across his chest, and then across his stomach. Still he didn't move. He listened to the song. The rain is jumping down, he thought. It is the song of newborn creeks, newborn rivers, newborn lakes.

When she lowered the reach of the circle he said, "We mustn't." But she continued.

"Tree," he said softly.

"We can't put it in me," she said, "but I can love you in many ways," And she continued her touch.

"I have never loved or touched another," he told her, whispering.

"I know," she said. "And I, too."

Outside, the rain sang down from the sky, sang with the trees and the soil, and sang with the motion of Tree and Bear Man's love, and sang to small streams running to the creek, which was Life. And the creek grew larger and moved swiftly to the river, which was Unknown.

29

There was the morning, clean from a night of rain. There was Tree and Bear Man, waiting for her cleansing. There was the priest. And there was the river.

Light Fire, Broken Back, and others were waiting. The priest, He-Has-No-Hair had had no hair when he was born, and so he was named. In keeping with his name he kept his head shaved. Most men of the Principal People let their's grow long, or shaved only on the sides allowing to grow in a patch on the top.

The priest and Tree walked to the bank. Bear Man followed. The three of them stepped into the water. Bear Man held the white beads of life and the white threads that lead to and from the land of spirits. He also held the cloth, folded. The priest held out a hand. Bear Man gave him the beads and thread. The priest began the prayer.

"Ha!" he cried. "The white thread has come down! The soul of Stone has been examined! Stone who is Bear Man, who is Light Fire, who is Under-The-Tree," and he went on to name the names of Stone's fathers, which were also his own names. "The soul of the small human being has been examined where it is growing. Soon you will come down and be born to this woman. He will be born to her! He has been examined!

"From above you have caused the white threads to come down. The soul has been examined." He again named Stone's names. "In the upper world he was let down. The soul has come to rest on the white thread. The soul has been lifted up as far as the first upper world, the place to where it has been raised.

"In the second upper world the white threads have been let down and the white cloth has come to rest upon them. The soul has come to rest upon the white threads. The soul has become examined! The soul has been lifted up as far as the second upper world." He went on and on to the seventh world. And then he petitioned for a long life for the little human being. Bear Man held forth the cloth. The priest put the beads to the thread. He then put them into the cloth. Bear Man folded the cloth.

"You have sipped the brew of bark and cones," he told Tree. "I have prayed." And then he began to wash her. First her face, touching it lightly with water. And then her hands, and then her feet.

When the washing was through they stepped to the shore.

"What are the results? What are the prospects?" Tree asked. Bear Man, his father, and Broken Back waited also to hear the priest's answer.

The priest stared at the folded cloth as though it held the answer captive. Then he looked at Tree. "You will have a strong baby human being," he said. "That must be true. Don't have any fears about that." Bear Man felt his arms calming, his breathing ease. "But there may be other problems. There may be problems at the delivery. That is because once Bear Man lingered in a doorway. We will have to wait to find that out. Nevertheless, the little one will come out."

"What about his arm?" asked Tree.

"We won't know that until he jumps down."

Bear Man looked at Tree. She had turned away from the group, was staring into the creek. He walked to her, started to touch her. She stepped away.

"There is a strong human being inside you," the priest continued though Tree had stepped away. "He wants to come out. That is certain. He has many strong names. They want to live. That is certain. But things have happened that should not have, so there may be difficulties. Certainly you have avoided most of those things that each of you should avoid. You have not worn anything around your neck. Nor has your husband. You have not eaten squirrel, nor raccoon, nor trout, nor rabbit. You have not eaten deer that your husband has hunted. You have not used salt. Is there anything you have done that you should not have, except what you have already told? No?" The priest stared at Bear Man. He knew that Bear Man had killed the *soi*. That knowledge had been kept from Tree and from the village. Looking at dead men is a serious thing, the priest thought. But he was certain the child would jump down. "There is much good here," he told her. We will have to wait for the little human to come out before we know how much bad may have happened. Not much perhaps." He then took the cloth and beads back from Bear Man as payment for his services, and then left.

As they walked back to their hut Bear Man told Tree a story. It was not an old story which she would have heard many times, but was one that he made as they walked. It was about a turtle that ate its shell. By the time they reached the hut Tree was laughing and Bear Man was laughing with her. But when he started to touch her she became silent and held still.

They were outside their hut. Nearby some children were playing *anetsa*, chasing a small ball of deer-hair and deer-hide between two trees, hitting the ball with their hickory sticks. The game was rough and some of the smaller boys were covered with scrapes and bruises. Still they played. It was a game only for boys, for boys learning to be men. It gave them fun, and taught them skills of speed and endurance.

Bear Man laughed again. "I have not played the game in so long a time," he said.

Tree said nothing.

30

Long after sleep should have come to him, Bear Man sat and watched the breathing of Tree. *So you have breathed this life for fifteen summers*, he thought to her. Soon your child will breath it. But I have harmed you, and I may have harmed your son, my son. And I may have brought new danger to our village.

Am I a fool? he had asked her. She had kept silent a moment, and then told him to remember what his father had said. And she assured him she would never have married a fool, that she would not have a fool as the father of her child. *You are the wise one*, he had told her. She had said nothing more, though, and he hadn't tried to touch her again.

He stood and went outside, walked to the creek. It flowed glistening through the night. He knelt and dipped water into his hands. Then brought it to his lips. Its coldness rushed through him. He cupped some more, sipped again. Then sat back on grasses and watched the water pass him by.

Where does the water come from? Where does it go? he wondered. Where do I come from? Where do I go? There were no certain answers. If only there were answers, he thought.

Perhaps I should go now, journey to the south. There I could face the Outcasts, deliver myself into their hands, rather than tempt them to come here seeking revenge for those I have killed. Then some of my shame would be taken. I must do something, he thought, but he didn't know what. He tried to imagine leaving, never seeing his son, never again holding Tree, hearing her voice, resting his body within her. The image wouldn't come. It isn't a possible thing, he said to himself.

Later, again beside Tree, he closed his eyes and hoped that answers would come from somewhere, but neither answers nor sleep came to him.

Adageyhdi. Love is.

Udageyuha. He loves. I love.

Ugeyuha. With love we own. I own him. He owns me.

Bear Man I love, thought Tree. But when I hear his voice, when I watch him move, and when he touches me, there is pain.

She heard him come back into their hut. He can't sleep because of my sorrow, she thought. If I smiled for him, if I touched him, then he would know again that he is a good man. Then he would sleep. I should smile, she thought. I should touch him. But there is pain! She tensed, but there is also Bear Man, and love, she thought.

She felt him moving beside her, getting warm beneath the covers of animal furs. I shall smile for him. I shall touch him.

The decision eased her thoughts. The pain eased. I shall, she thought . . . but then before she moved again her thoughts had turned to dreaming, and it was only in her dreams that she reached for him.

Bear Man woke her in the morning. *I'm going to the woods*, she heard him say. And then he was gone and she didn't see him again until the afternoon when the labor pains had begun.

Silence. Silence. The trees and wind sang no song. They uttered no whispers. Are there no answers? Bear Man asked them. *Silence.*

He hadn't slept through the night. He lay beneath the bough of an old oak, closed eyes. *Come to me slumber,* he asked. Sleep wouldn't come. Answers wouldn't come. *I am alone then,* he thought, *and must find my own rest, and my own answers.*

When he returned to the hut he found Tree gasping, clutching her belly, folding her legs up against herself.

33

He is trying to jump down!
When Tree began the labor, they took her to the menstruation lodge. A bed was made for her near the fire. The fire was low because it was afternoon and still warm out. They wanted her to be warm, though, and they needed warm water to wash the child and a warm flame to keep the child from a chill.

Bear Man had already made arrangements with four women to attend Tree in the delivery. One of the women was Tree's mother. Another was her sister. Another was Sweet Fruit, Tree's friend, and there was Second Daughter, the midwife. Second Daughter would catch the little human being when it jumped down.

Second Daughter had come with Tree's mother and sister from their village. Tree knew Second Daughter from her childhood. The woman knew the necessary formulas and what to do if the priest's warning came to pass.

After the delivery Tree would remain at the lodge for twenty-four days. The period of purification. Bear Man would be allowed to visit her, but not to stay with her.

"When I come home again," she told him, "I'll hold you inside me." Then she tensed with pain. These pains were different, she told herself, from her earlier pains. *The child wants to jump down!* The water had already flowed out of her. The child will soon follow, they told her.

"Don't worry about me," Bear Man told her. "All that matters is you and our child." And then she tensed and tensed again, and he tensed with her and said no more. He held her hands more tightly. With a white cloth he wiped perspiration from her brow. The fire made the lodge too warm, he thought, but Second Daughter had insisted it be that way.

Second Daughter went outside. She walked around the lodge and spoke the proper words, telling evil spirits and witches to stay away. When she was certain no witches were near she posted young girls at each corner of the lodge to watch for intruders. Then she went back inside and began instruction to Tree and Bear Man and the other attendants.

"You must keep your clothes on," she told Tree. Tree knew that. "You must keep them on so that your little human being will know that his mother is modest and virtuous." She then turned to Tree's mother and sister. "Help her to stand," she said. The women stood on either side of her and lifted her to her feet. "Stand behind your wife," she said to Bear Man. He moved behind her, held her. "Allow her to lean against you." Then to the women, "Hold her feet and knees. Spread her legs." They did so. Second Daughter knelt before Tree and lifted her skirt. She put her hand into Tree's body. "It is going to jump out," she said. "This is not false pain."

"Now?" asked Tree.

"No, but soon enough. When the pains come, push down."

The pains were coming more rapidly. Second Daughter turned to the woman Sweet Fruit. "Keep the warm water ready," she told her, "and the blanket." She turned back to Tree. "Wash her face," she said to Tree's mother. Then she took a bowl from near the fire. It contained a mixture with which she washed Tree. "You must be clean here when the child comes out," she said.

The pains were stronger, closer together, but the child wasn't jumping out. He still hadn't shown his head. Tree began to cry quietly. Behind her, Bear Man held firmly and whispered comforts into her ear.

Tree turned to him. "Say no more," she asked. "When I hear such sweet things it makes it more difficult to accept the pain."

I only want to help! he wanted to tell her, but said nothing. Instead of helping, I hurt her. Can I do nothing but bring sorrow?

"What she says is true," said the midwife. "It is better only to hold her and to help her push. It is better to say nothing." Bear Man nodded and spoke no more.

"The child is scared to come out," said Second Daughter.

"He *will* jump down!" insisted Tree.

"He is scared, though. The mixture I washed you with has scared him. It was then that Light Fire and Broken Back came into the lodge.

"The priest is at the river," said Light Fire, "praying for both of you."

"He should be praying for the child as well," said the mother.

"He prays for the child as well," he told her.

"Perhaps it is not a man," said Tree's sister. "Perhaps it is a woman and she is afraid to come out, knowing you want her to be a man."

"That may be," said the midwife.

"That is nonsense," said Light Fire. "It is a man." He turned to Bear Man, expecting his son to support what he had said. Bear Man offered nothing.

"If it is a woman," said the midwife, "then such talk is scaring it more." She turned again to Sweet Fruit. "Bring me some of her drink," she said. They gave her a drink of brew from a gourd.

"This will make the jumping down, and the pain, easier," she said. Then she knelt again and lifted the skirt. She came close to Tree and whispered to the child. "Don't be scared," she said. "Come out quickly. We are waiting for you."

The pains continued. The child didn't appear.

Tree, with Bear Man helping her, continued to push. The midwife whispered again. "There is an ugly old witch coming. She'll take you out and steal you if you don't hurry."

She stood and turned to the others. "The child won't be frightened by my threats," she told the others.

It was getting dark outside when Tree began to scream. The midwife had done all she could. After trying to tempt the child with toys, playmates, and its mother's milk, she had reached into Tree's womb to try to catch the child there. It hadn't worked, but she had learned for certain that the child was turned the proper way. She sighed in silent relief. She had been afraid it was turned around.

It was far into the night when the child's head appeared. At that the medicine man blew a liquid through a reed onto the child's head to help it come out. Then they waited. And Tree continued to scream.

"Will it ever jump down?" asked Tree's mother.

"It will," said the midwife.

At midnight the child jumped. Second Daughter caught it, and then held it for the others to see.

Tree's screams faded to quiet sobs. The child was a man, and it was silent. Tree tried to speak. *Is it alive!* she tried to say. She had no strength for her voice.

Second Daughter held the infant gently, and with her fingers she firmly tapped the bottom of its feet. A moment later the infant started crying, not loudly, but loud enough to tell everyone present that he was here, though he had taken a while making the journey.

"He is bigger than Bear Man was," said Light Fire. "Perhaps we should name him Stone-That-Is-Bigger-Than-Bear-Man."

"That is a good name," said Broken Back. He liked long names because he had one. So he said, "Perhaps we should name him Stone-That-Is-Bigger-Than-Bear-Man-And-Is-Hard-To-Come-Out." He laughed. "That would be a wonderful name!" he said. He especially liked it because it was partly his name, too. Bear Man said nothing during this. He kept holding Tree, waiting for the midwife's instructions, washing perspiration from Tree's face.

The midwife signaled to Sweet Fruit. Sweet Fruit brought water and the blanket and the knife. She placed the water and blanket before Second Daughter. Then Sweet Fruit cut the navel string and tied it. Then she took away the afterbirth.

Second Daughter washed the child with warm water and then wrapped it in the blanket. It was still crying, though less loudly after being washed. Then she took it to Tree's bed near the fire. She turned to the other women. "Wash her now," she

turned his attention again to the lodge, only this time to the silence. What is it? he asked himself, but knew that the answer could not come until the end of the night, if then. And so he contented himself with listening, but no more voices came from the lodge, at least not loudly enough for him to hear. It is making much the same sounds as death, that place, he thought.

Beside him his wife rolled over and murmured, half speaking from some unknown dream. Why can't you be so silent as the lodge? he said, not speaking. She murmured again.

35

"It isn't right for you to touch her," said the midwife.

"Is it right for her to die?" asked the medicine man. Then he looked to the husband and the chief. Bear Man hesitated but the chief nodded, and so the medicine man knelt before the woman and began his work. As he did so he thought back to the many animals he had killed and cut open simply to learn how the earth had made them. And so as he reached into the woman he knew what was wrong and what must be done, though it was something he had never done before, and so far as he was aware neither had any other.

It was when he asked for a knife that Bear Man

spoke and said he must stop. "Then she will die," said the old man, and he got up and found a knife. No one stopped him when he started to cut. And when he was finished they all stood in wonderment as they watched him take a small sliver of wood from one of his pouches and with it draw thread through her wounded body, none of them aware that he was only doing what he had done with the animals. After learning to take them apart he had learned how to put them together again.

At last he put away the remaining thread and then washed her body. Everyone could see that where he had cut her there was now only a line like a scar and that it was laced with thread. And everyone could see that she was no longer bleeding.

"Will she live now," asked Light Fire.

"I don't know," said Broken Back. "But she hasn't yet died. Perhaps she will live." And then he told them to let her rest by the fire. He then gathered his materials and walked out of the lodge. In his mind was the memory of his old teacher, of the many months he had spent healing from the break in his back, and of the one thing the old one had insisted upon above all others, that in nature there may be found medicines for all things. And so Broken-Back-Who-Used-To-Be-Hard-To-Come-Out had spent his life in search of those things. Soon he would know what he had found.

He was near his hut when someone from behind put a hand on his shoulder. He stopped and turned. It was Bear Man.

"She will live," said the warrior.

"I hope so," said Broken Back, weariness in his voice.

"I know that she will live," Bear Man insisted. He bowed his head. "But no thanks to me. My misdeeds brought such bad luck that she nearly died. I—"

"There is no luck," said the medicine man, his lips poised and unmoving. "Luck is only what we call the working of nature. Learn the motion of nature, and you will learn the motion of luck."

"But—"

"The things you did were nothing. Perhaps her own fears made things worse. I don't know. But nothing you did hurt her or the child."

Bear Man considered what he was hearing. It was so like many thoughts he had often had, but he had never heard anyone speak such things.

"Still you have healed her. She will live long and have many children!"

The warrior's fervor was almost enough to convince the medicine man, himself. *She may live*, he thought. *But if she does will she have more children?* He thought of his knife, cutting within. *At least she has this child*, he thought, *if she lives*.

"I hope so," he said again. "Now I am a tired old man. I must rest." He saw a little of the light die in Bear Man's eyes. "Don't tell others the things I have said about *luck*," he added. "They *need* to believe in it." Then he turned and walked away.

36

There is no luck! You have done nothing to harm her! Tell no one these things! All is the motion of nature! Learn that motion!—These are the things he told me, thought Bear Man. And he is a great healer. He has learned the motions of nature. But if what he says is true, then why not tell them? Why do they *need* to believe that which isn't true?

It was nearly dawn when Tree opened her eyes. Bear Man was beside her, holding their child. She was too weak to move and so Bear Man lifted away the blanket and laid the infant to her breast.

"This is Stone," he told her.

She looked at her husband and tried to smile. "Now I have two of you to love," she whispered, and as the child suckled she again fell to sleep.

37

Far to the south Old Man gathered young warriors around him. "The time will soon come," he told them, "to kill those who so long ago drove us from our sacred lands, and who so recently killed my son and ended the tale of his life, and of my life, and that of my fathers." And he could see the fire in their eyes, blazing, burning, hot and angry, almost reaching out to lick the night, and he knew that these were his, and that though others had tried to stop him they could never do so.

38

This was the way of the People:
The afterbirth, that which has remained, was wrapped in an old cloth and taken by the father. He then crossed one or more hills. Each ridge he crossed signified the number of years he wished there to be before his next child arrived. Then he made a deep hole in which he buried the bundle.
He had to be careful that no one followed. Witches were known to remove the bundle from burial and then to bury it again, too deeply, placing stones upon it. When that was done the parents could have no more children. If it was removed and thrown away, then they would have a child at an undetermined time, either before or after they wished.

Some children were raised to become witches, most especially twins. A single child, though, could be raised to be a witch. This was begun by denying the child of mother's milk for the first twenty-four days. During that time they were fed with the liquid potion of corn hominy. This was given them only during the night. And the child was kept secluded from all visitors during that time. After that other potions were given to the child.

When a child was raised to be a witch, it was said that they could fly and that they could move through the earth, and that whatever they thought would happen, *even as infants. And when it was twins raised as witches, it was said that they could speak to each other's minds, even from a great distance, and that their minds, when joined in thought, could shape the thinking and actions of others.*

39

A cold morning in summer, a cold song.

Silver-gray sun on the new horizon, silver-gray bundle in his arms.

Bear Man ascended the final steps to the third hill. The wind spoke the coming of cold rain, sang the delight of warm blankets. Bear Man stood on the ridge and heard its voice, heard it first whisper and then shout and then whisper again. *Rain! Shivers! Run! Run! Hide in dark warmth!* He grimaced at it, wanted to spit at it, wanted to order it to stop. Instead he stepped down from the ridge, started the descent.

He found the clearing without looking for it. He

had forgotten what he was looking for, forgotten everything, even the weight in his arms. Then the clearing spread before him. It opened to him as a door opening out of darkness. It spread wide, deep, holding back trees, keeping away branches.

Silver-gray grass called him. Here. Here it will rest.

He carved the earth, carved deep and clean, and then laid the bundle into the darkness. "*I'll want another child in three years*," he sang in whisper. Then he began to lay earth upon the bundle.

When he was finished he scouted for witches that may have followed. And then he hid, waiting and watching to see if anyone tried to disturb the grave. None came. The summer-cold morning became summer-warm noon.

Bear Man's thoughts took him to Tree, to Broken Back and his strange message, to the *soi*. Finally he was tired of thinking, tired of waiting, simply tired. He hadn't slept for two nights. It is time to go home, he thought. Time to open myself to sleep, if I can.

40

They watched him go, the eyes.
They walked to the grave, the feet.
They dug into the earth, the hands.
"You are hidden here, and cannot escape," said

the witch's voice, and then the witch's hands put seven stones on the bundle within its new grave. Then the hands reached to the throat and lightly touched an old scar. She remembered and her sister witch remembered with her.

The memory came like a dry wind through their minds, the long ago playing, the accident at play, the injury of the older twin's throat at the playful but careless hands of a boy, Bear Child who was the son of Light Fire, chief of their village. *Now this is avenged,* thought the mind of Number One. *Yes,* came the inner voice from far away. In the village Number Two raised her hand to her throat, free of blemish.

And now, they thought, there is nothing more to avenge. Number one gazed at the stony grave. Now, she thought to her sister, we must give where we have taken away.

Number Two held her days old child to her breast and watched it suckle. Yes, she thought. Now we shall prepare them to receive you. First we will prepare the woman, Tree, and then we shall help her to prepare her new son, Stone. And you and he shall become leaders of the Principal People.

Yes, came the echo of an inner voice. It was the beginning of a formula they had planned for many seasons. It was a forbidden thing, the formula, for it required damning the placenta, and preparing a marriage that could not be allowed by their laws. But anything is possible, they knew, to those who willed it so.

And whoever stands in the way of the formula,

they convenanted, *shall die. And in our daughter we shall stand above them all.*

Number Two's infant moved away from its mother's empty breast and began to feast on the other.

41

Tree held the infant to her breast and watched it suckle.

"Are you strong enough to hold him?" Bear Man asked. He had just come in and was sitting down beside her.

"Strong enough," she said.

"Are you hurting?"

"Yes. When I move." She caressed the infant's head.

"You shouldn't be holding him."

"I don't lift him. Sweet Fruit helps me."

"You look so tired," he told her, feeling more tired himself, anxious to go to his hut and sleep.

"I'll be fine," she said. "I sleep a lot."

"Good." Then he added, "I hope when you're better that you'll make him save some of that for me."

She smiled. "Of course," she said.

Bear Man leaned over her, kissed her gently. Then, "May I hold him?" he asked. Tree nodded. He carefully took the little human from her and held it against his chest. Its lips searched for milk. "You'll find nothing there," he whispered to it.

"Are you pleased?" she asked.

"Yes," he said. "I'm very pleased. And aren't you? Look at his arms!" He laughed and she laughed a little with him.

"I'm so very pleased, too," she said. "He is worth all the pain."

The baby started to cry and Bear Man put him back to his mother's breast. Later, when the two of them were sleeping he went to his hut.

In dark of the enclosed room he closed his eyes and asked for sleep. He could hear songs from outside. Sleep, he asked. Thoughts of the night, of the *soi,* of Broken Back again filled his mind. Sleep. He saw the faces of the *soi* warriors. He heard the unmoving lips of Broken Back. He felt the weight of Tree leaning against him. He saw the blood from her body. Sleep, he asked, but sleep was hard coming, and when it did there was little rest in it.

He was sitting beneath a tree. *This was the dream.*

Everything was silent. Everything was still. There were leaves in the air, but they held still, not moving, not falling. They were caught in turned, twisted mid-flight to earth. There were birds, wings spread, wings ready to carry them away, but they, too, held still, not moving, not wavering. There were no songs. Even silence had lost its song.

Bear Man wanted to move. He looked at his

legs and tried to move them. They wouldn't move. He looked at his hands and tried to move them. They held still. He thought that if only he could move, then the songs would return, the leaves would fall, the birds would fly. He couldn't move.

Then in the silence he heard a voice.

Bear Man, it said. He looked for its owner, saw nothing.

Here, Bear Man. He looked to his right. There stood the great stag. There was dried blood by its wound. The stag walked toward him. Nothing else moved. *Hello, Bear Man,* he heard it say.

"Hello, my friend," he told it. "I can't move. Nothing here moves but you."

Don't worry about moving, said the stag, *only listening. That is the great art.*

"Why are you speaking to me? Have you good news?"

I have come to settle our debt.

"I have spared your life twice. How can you settle against that. You owe me your sons and daughters for many seasons."

I have come to settle all. It waved its head of antlers through the windless, motionless, songless air.

"How can you settle now?" asked Bear Man, afraid the animal wanted to cheat him out of his debt. He tried to stand up again, but still was bound.

Listen, Bear Man. It was a different voice. *Be still, and listen. Don't move even within.* It was the voice of the tree where Bear Man sat. Bear Man could tell it was the tree but didn't understand how it spoke when it had no mouth, no lips. But then he recalled Broken Back who spoke without using lips. Perhaps he had learned that from trees. He was a mysterious man.

"Why haven't you spoken to me before?" he asked the tree. "I've so often listened to hear you speak. Why haven't I heard you?"

Because you are always in motion. You must learn to stand still. Then you can hear all things.

Bear Man looked at the deer. It was eating leaves that held still in the air, half way between tree branch and earth. "But the stag moves, and yet he hears."

The stag is a master of motion. He has learned to move with sound, so that even when he moves he hears, and he speaks. First you must learn to be still, and to listen. Then you may learn to master motion and speech. Listen now. Don't speak. Don't try to move.

The buck moved closer to Bear Man. *What the tree tells is true. Now I have given you the key to hearing all things. You may or may not learn to use it, but you know it. That is my first payment of the debt for the first time you spared my life.*

The creature turned and ran through trees until he was nearly out of Bear Man's sight. Then he turned and spoke again. His voice was as close and calm as it had ever been. *My final payment is this*, it said, *Beware of Bird-Song!* And then it turned again and vanished.

Bear Man held still, and listened, and after a long, long while heard a song he had never heard before. Gradually, like someone walking slowly toward him, it became clearer, louder, richer. And at last he understood its voice. It was the song of his heart, beating, beating, telling him who he was and that he must stay alive. *This was the dream*.

When he woke it was morning, and he heard first the songs of birds.

42

Light Fire's town was small. Five hundred hearts beating. The town lay in the south and east part of the People's lands. There were no other towns of the People south or east of them. There was only the land, and beyond that the lands and towns of *ani soi*. Because of that Light Fire's town was important. It was a barricade between the People and *others*.

After waking Bear Man decided that he would go hunting to the south and scout for signs that *soi* were near. They probably aren't, he told himself. But I'll go looking for them anyway.

So he went to Tree and told her his plans. She smiled and told him to travel safely. Take Crawler with you, she said. That's a good thought, he told her. I'll ask him, he said.

"*Adanasinusdi*, Crawler," said Bear Man, standing at his friend's hut. Crawler came out. He was half his friend's height.

"Hello, Bear Man! How wonderful! Your son jumped out I hear! How wonderful!" He reached up and slapped Bear Man's shoulders, then danced around him.

"Yes! Yes!" said Bear Man. "He came out this morning, after making us wait all yesterday and night!"

"Ha! Ha! You must have stood in too many doorways then!"

"Yes! I did! But he is here now."

"And you are here now, talking to Crawler. What can little Crawler do for his big friend?"

"I'm leaving soon to go south and scout for *soi*, and hunt for game."

"*Soi?*"

"I saw some just a few days ago." He nodded at his nearly healed wound.

"They saw you too, brave one. I trust their injuries were greater."

"You trust the right person then," said Bear Man.

"Then I'll come with you. Wait while I get my belongings."

"I'll get my own. Then I'll meet you beside the creek, friend. We'll leave from there."

"From there will be fine. Shortly then?"

They each gathered their bows, their axes, knives, quivers, food. Bear Man was the first to the creek. He stood by the shore and watched shadows from the sun playing on the water. He knelt and drank. It is clear, cold, *Life*, he thought. Then in the water he saw Crawler's reflection.

"You are a quiet one," he told him.

"I practice," said the little man. Then he knelt and with his hand cupped water into his mouth. "I would have been quicker," he said. "But Good Cook begged me to put it in her before I left!" He laughed hard and Bear Man laughed with him.

"Then Good Cook is much like all other wives," said Bear Man.

"How could I know? I've never been with other's wives. Have you?" He laughed again, this time patting his groin.

"No. No. I was just saying something to join our laughter!"

"In any event, she is at least what our wives want us to think they are. How can we really know what women are, what they think? They are far too strange to understand!"

"Not only are you the silent one, you are the wise one."

"I practice."

Then they started off. While they walked through the village Crawler began to sing a song. Bear Man joined him.

Women are the strange ones.
They make the best witches.
Women are the sad ones.
They make smiles when they are not happy.
Women are the happy ones.
They are happy when men don't know how
    to be.

They sang new lines to the old song and kept

singing it until they were out of the village and beyond the fields. In the distance Bear Man could hear the voice of bird-song.

43

Tree held the child against her breast as it slept. The pain in her kept her from moving about, but it didn't keep her from embracing her son.

Here you are, she thought to him. *Stone, my son.* In his sleep his lips sometimes tried to suckle, so she gently put her pap to his mouth. *Drink all you like, young Stone. Grow as tall and strong as your father.*

A woman with an infant in her arms came and sat beside Tree. The woman had borne her child only a few days earlier. The woman's name was Number Two. She was the second of twins. She had named her child Tear Maker because the mother had cried loudly in giving birth.

"He's a handsome one," she told Tree.

Tree smiled. "And your Tear Maker is lovely," she said. "I know it was terrible for you last night, during the delivery."

"However hard that may have been for us, it was much worse for you two," said Number Two.

"We'll be quiet now, though."

"Don't you worry about it. Sometimes that little man will cry, but don't you worry about it. My Tear Maker makes her own tears sometimes, and she isn't quiet when she does."

Another woman came into the lodge. It was Number Two's sister. She joined the two mothers.

"Lovely babies," she said. She turned to Tree. "Are you going to raise him as a witch."

"No," said Tree. She hoped that didn't offend the women, because she knew they were witches.

"Not all children should be witches," said Number One. "Tear Maker won't be a witch. My sister wants a man witch. When she has a son, he will be taught."

"That's right," said Number Two.

Number One reached out and touched Stone. It frightened Tree. She tensed inside and wanted to pull him away, but it was dangerous to offend witches, so she let the woman touch him. "He's going to be a strong, healthy one," she said. Then she looked at her sister, nodded her head toward her sister's place in the lodge.

"I'll talk with you later," said Number Two and she followed her sister away.

They are strange women, thought Tree. But then all witches are strange. Especially strange is the older one, she thought, the one with the scar on her neck.

Stone woke and began to cry so she held him a little tighter and helped him again find her pap.

44

Before they slept, they talked. They had come across five small mountains and it was late. There were already many stars about. Both of them were tired, especially Bear Man. But they wanted to talk. They wanted to recount their boyhood. They wanted to talk about their hopes, their dreams, their fears and laughter. They were full of all the things that all men are always filled with and can only empty to another man. They told stories. They made stories. Crawler told of a witch woman who once made a town vanish. Bear Man insisted it wasn't possible. Crawler shrugged and said no one could find the place. Because it was never there, Bear Man laughed. When the tale ended they sat and listened to the choir of the night, the sounds and songs of the woods. Frogs were singing. Crickets joined them. Wind and trees harmonized. And there were birds. Bear Man listened especially to the birds.

"What are they singing?" he asked Crawler.

"Which of them?"

"All of them, any of them."

"They are singing themselves. It is the only song they know."

Bear Man thought back to his dream. Hadn't the deer and the tree known his song. "Not all of them, perhaps," he offered.

"All of them, I think. It is what makes people different from them. We learn songs other than only our own."

"But do we learn our own?"

Crawler smiled. "Only sometimes," he said. "And then we are seldom able to keep it, I think."

"Do you know your song, Crawler?" Bear Man was staring at him through the starlight.

Crawler hesitated. Then, "No. I don't know my song. I have never learned my song. And what is more, I'm not certain that I want to." He paused. "Their songs are lovely enough. But how about you? Have you learned your song? Heh?"

"I heard it once, in a dream. That is all."

"What did it sound like?" He leaned forward. "Can you tell me about it?"

"It was the beating of my heart. I heard it sing to me in a dream."

"That is a wonderful thing!" He laughed a little. "You're a lucky man, Bear Man. Perhaps I'd like to hear my own song after all. Was it frightening?"

"No," he said. "It was peace."

"Like them," Crawler said, and he nodded into the night.

"Why is their music so much purer, do you think? Why do they sing so clearly?"

"Like I said. Because they sing their own song. We sing so poorly because we only imitate them and imitate ourselves."

After that they spoke no more of songs but instead listened to the night voices. Bear Man paid special attention to the birds, trying to understand them, trying to hold still and stay quiet. But no understanding came.

Then Crawler started talking again. He talked about his family, his fathers. And then he asked Bear Man about Light Fire. "Why has your father, our chief, never remarried?" he asked. It was a question many in the village had asked themselves. No one knew.

"I know no more than anyone about that," said Bear Man. "I'll tell you this. When my mother died, he went away for a long time. He went somewhere into the mountains. I don't know where. But he was alone, I think. I was very sad about her death, but I think he must have been even sadder. He stayed away a very long time, and sometimes I thought he would never return. After he did return, he never spoke of her. She was called The-Woman-Who-Loves-Everyone. That was because she had such great love for others. She was known for that. I think he must have loved her as much as her love for all. But now she is in the land of spirits, and I think maybe he is simply waiting to be with her. I don't know. Perhaps he will marry again. It might be good for him if he did."

"It would be good for the village," said Crawler.

"Yes it would be, but it is nevertheless not my business or yours."

"If Tree were to die, do you think you would take a new wife?"

"How can I know such things?"

"I know if Good Cook died that I would certainly want a new wife. If I had children I would need her to raise them. If I had no children, then I would need her to carry them." He paused, then laughed weakly. "Besides that, there is little more than amusement in putting it in the belly of a whore."

"What is that?" asked Bear Man. "Have you been to a whore?"

"I shouldn't have spoken," said Crawler, but he went on. "Only once, though. I was angry at Good Cook. She's good at making me angry. That's what she's good at. Much better at that than at cooking. Anyway, I went to that whore whose hut is on the north end of the village."

"Was it good in her?" asked Bear Man.

"It was good enough. I learned some things I wish Good Cook knew!"

"Then why don't you teach them to her?"

"And how would I explain where *I* learned them?" They both laughed at that. And their laughter went out into the night, chasing at the songs of animals, trees, wind, the songs of purity.

When Crawler was long asleep Bear Man still stared into the sky. I have had little sleep, he told himself. I should be able to sleep well and long. But it wouldn't come. He let himself think about the evening. He thought about his talk with Crawler. He thought about the things they had said about his father and his mother. Why hasn't he taken another wife? he wondered. There was

no answer. And then he thought about their con-
versation over the whore, and their laughter. And
suddenly he felt ashamed. Not because they had
spoken of a whore, but because of the thoughts he
had had for the *ani soi* when he had heard them
talking in a similar way. Were they so wicked
then? he wondered. Am I so good?

He got up from his bed and went walking
through the night woods, thinking it would later
help him find slumber. The songs of the night
were quieter. The bird-songs were gone. There was
no wind. The frogs were quiet. Mostly there was
only the raging tune of the crickets.

He came to a pool of water, dark and glistening
in the night. He knelt to drink, and as he did so he
heard in the distance the faint sound of bird-song.
Next he heard the motion of brush behind him.
He turned quickly, his axe already in his hand.
Something caught at his feet and he fell forward
onto the grass. And then there was laughing and
someone rolling away.

"Crawler has brought down the Great One!"
the small man cried and laughed and rolled. And
then Bear Man was laughing and rolling with him.
And when they returned to their camp Bear Man
slept. And had no dreams.

In the morning they each took down a deer.
Gutted the animals and then started for home. At
the pool where they had played as boys during the
night the grass was still crushed, and the three men
standing there could see that the place had been
visited the night before.

When night came Bear Man shared his kill with others. They sat around a fire, watching it cook in the smoke. Many were singing. Others were telling tales. Then there was dancing.

It was late when Bear Man went to the lodge to visit Tree before he slept. When he got there she was already sleeping and he wouldn't wake her. He wanted to. He wanted to laugh some with her, to tell her about his hunt, about rolling with Crawler, to tell her about the feast. Instead he watched her in the dim firelight. He watched her face, golden and soft, softer he thought than strands of sunset. *How gentle you are*, he sang to her in his mind.

When he left the lodge the sounds of feasting were over and a quiet had settled in the village. He walked slowly to his hut, past his father's hut, past the council lodge, past Crawler's hut. From inside Crawler's hut he could hear the song of bodies. When he came to his own hut there was a figure sitting in the doorway. It was a boy, the son of Dark Snow. The boy's name was *Ugalogv*, Leaf.

"I've waited for you," he said.

"Waited?"

"You are the town's greatest hunter. I want you to take me with you. I want to learn to be as great a hunter as you."

Bear Man looked down at the boy, smiled. "One day," he said.

"Tomorrow?"

"No. But soon enough. Go home now. Go to bed."

The boy smiled broadly, jumped and danced, and was gone.

Was I once a boy? Bear Man wondered. And from the far woods outside the village he once more heard a solitary and clear bird-song.

46

Old Man stood with two of his warriors and looked down upon the dying fires of the town. "This is where we shall come," he told them. "This is where we must begin. These must die first."

"They are strong," said one of the warriors. "They have more warriors than we can gather."

"That is why we must wait until the moment is right. And that is why we must be clever."

"When will the moment be right then?" asked the third warrior.

"Soon," said Old Man. "Soon," he repeated, and there was an aching in his chest when he spoke and he knew that unless it was soon that he would never be a part of it.

On the twentieth day after the birth of Stone, Bear Man took Leaf hunting in the mountains. After they had walked all morning and had seen no game, they stopped and sat beside a small stream.

"Why are there no deer?" asked the boy.

"There are deer," said Bear Man. "Only they are elsewhere."

"Where are they then?"

"On the hills. In the valleys."

"We have walked many hills and valleys and have seen none. Why is that?"

"Do you always ask so many questions?"

The boy lowered his head and was quiet.

Bear Man smiled, summer warmth on his lips. "I've answered your questions, Leaf. Now I've asked you one."

"I thought you wanted me to be silent."

"Hardly. I wanted to know if you always ask so many questions. That's why I asked that."

"I always ask many, many questions. Sometimes my father, and others, even other boys, sometimes they say I talk too much, ask too much. I thought that's what you were saying."

"Why do you ask so many questions?"

"Because I want *to know the answers!* And because the questions rise up inside me, pound at me from within, force themselves out of me. *I don't know why!* I just know that I ask, and ask. Is asking such a terrible thing?"

Bear Man held still, listened to the torrent from the boy. Remembered his own boyhood, remembered the first discovery of nature's songs, remembered his first hunting, his first kill, remembered the loneliness and cold of *passing through* to become a warrior. Remembered above all not knowing, and wanting to know everything. Still I don't know, he thought. I never will. But some things I have learned.

"You'll never have all the answers, young hunter," he told the boy, "but keep hunting for them. Questions are your arrows. And sometimes they pain others. That is why others tire of hearing them. But they are the only way to hunt for knowledge."

The boy thought about it. Closed his eyes as though he were letting the words settle down into him, purge themselves within his memory. Then he opened his eyes and stared at Bear Man. "Why haven't we seen any deer?" he asked.

Bear Man laughed. "Because we've been loud and open and talking, and they have seen us before we have seen them. If you want to hunt deer, you must first learn to be silent, and listen. The same is true if you want the answers to your questions."

They stayed in the woods for four days. On the twenty-fourth day after Stone's birth, the end of Tree's purification, they came out of the woods. They carried with them their kills.

"He is a good hunter," Bear Man told Leaf's father. "He knows how to be silent and still, to listen. If you'll allow it, I will hunt with him again."

"Will you? Will you?" the boy begged his father. "Of course, of course!" the father assured. Bear Man was the town's greatest hunter. That he had paid such a compliment to Leaf made the man's face glow.

"And next time," said Bear Man, "we shall hunt not for deer, but for bear. And for even greater game that that."

"But what is greater?" asked the boy.

"Answers," said Bear Man. "Answers to our questions."

48

"I've been walking for days now," she told him.

"I know, but it's a long walk to our hut. I should carry you."

"But I can walk, Bear Man."

"No more easily than I can carry you."

And so he carried her, brought her home. Then brought home Stone, their son.

When they were in the hut, Tree began to cry.

"Are you hurting?" he asked. *No*, she said, *there is little pain*. Then she took his face in her hands and held it to her own face, and her tears washed him until his own tears were washing her

face as well. "It's good to be home," she told
him. "Don't ever leave me."

"I won't," he said. "*Ever.*"

49

Are we enough? Old Man wondered. He knew
too that was what his warriors wondered. Twenty
warriors. It was all he had managed to call to his
side. Twenty who were willing to die while killing
the *Jalagi*, those who called themselves the Principal People. I've waited too, too long, he told
himself. Now I am too old. They won't listen to
my words, the others. They won't follow me.
Twenty. It is but a few. But even a few can do
much.

He watched from a hill. He saw the giant with
his woman and child. He saw them go into
their hut. They at least, he thought. They shall
die.

They were preparing for sleep when Tr⌐
and went to the doorway.

"Let's go to the river," she said.

"It's late. You haven't the strength."

"Let's go there to sleep tonight. I've been inside walls for days and nights too long." She looked out across the night hills. "I want to be out there," she said.

"You're not strong enough," he told her.

"You can use a litter. I'll hold Stone while you pull us both."

"Is there no changing the mind of my woman?" he asked, not expecting her to reply, asking more the stars than the woman.

And so he prepared a litter and helped her onto it. And put the child in her arms.

"This way," she told him, "our son will learn where he came from." Bear Man smiled. "Yes," he told her, and he started off, hauling them behind him.

The town was quiet. People were already sleeping. From some huts, though, they could hear singing voices. From others, singing laughter. From some the singing of making little human beings. "We can sing such a song tonight," said Tree.

"It's too soon," he told her. "Broken Back said we should wait longer now, since he had to open and close your body."

"It will be all right. I'm in very little pain. Be

t will be all right."

said nothing. He only continued to
itter, listening to it grate against the
ones, and grass.

They went along the creek until they came to the
river. And then they headed north. As they traveled they listened to the frogs and insects and
breeze. All just as they had done so many nights
before, when they had first gone that way
together. Bear Man listened closely to the songs.
There were no bird-songs that night. It is strange,
he thought, that there should be none. He wished
for a moment that he could hold perfectly silent
and still, so that he could again hear the song
within him, and understand the voices of the trees.

"Will their words forever be beyond me?" he
asked.

"Not always," she said, understanding.

"Perhaps not," he told her, and kept listening.
When they came to the great flat stone, they
stopped.

"This is where your father first put it in me,"
she told Stone. "This is where you began. This is
where you come from." Bear Man took the child
and laid him on the stone. Then helped Tree to it.
Then Bear Man took off his garments and walked
into the water.

"The water here is warm almost," he said. He
turned back to his wife and saw that she had un-
dressed herself and the child. He walked back to
them and helped them into the water. He watched
her as they walked. She looked strong again. The
swelling was gone from the child being inside her.

112

The wound was healing well. And her breasts were large with milk. He had refused to take milk from her while she was at the lodge, but he remembered what it had been like before that and wanted to again.

When they were waist deep in the water, he gave the child into her arms. Then he knelt and gathered stones from the river. "These," he whispered to his son, "are your brothers and sisters." He touched them one at a time to the child's lips, and after touching each one threw it far out into the river's deep. "No matter where they fall," he told, "they may be found. I will find them. I will bring them to your mother, and to you."

With that they walked back to the stone slab, Bear Man carrying Stone. They made a bed with blankets they'd brought, and settled down into the warm softness. The night air was still. The river had been warm. All the cold and loneliness of the past days were gone. Then Tree was touching Bear Man's back, and then his legs, slowly drawing them near her. His hands found her waist, and then her breasts. And then his face was against hers and his lips against her lips. The night song of insects was a serenade. His kiss traveled from her face to her neck, her shoulders, her breasts. And then, gently, gently suckling he lifted out of her the white fluid life.

Tree began to pull herself toward him, parting her legs, covering him with her thighs.

Bear Man again kissed her lips, and then he easily pulled away from her. "It's too soon," he said. He touched her stomach, allowed his fingers to trace down across her scar. "I've almost lost you once," he told her. "I'll not lose you. Never."

She reached to his neck and drew his head once more to hers. She tasted her milk on his lips. "No," she whispered. "We will never lose each other." Then she kissed him once more. "But it isn't too soon. You are the greatest of warriors, but you are also the most gentle of men. Be gentle with me now." And then she folded herself around him and pulled him to her until he was inside her. And slowly their motion became music with the night creatures, as it had long ago on their first night together. And the songs of night were everywhere, and could be heard by all who listened.

Old man and his companions listened to the village. Soon, he thought, and he signaled the others to move nearer.

51

As one approaches death, dreams are frequent. The dying person sees some of his departed friends and relatives as they beckon him to join them in the spirit land.

52

Bear Man dreamed. In his dream he saw his mother, beckoning to him, calling to him, but he was afraid to go. *Come*, she cried. *Come*, and she held open her arms. And then Bear Man woke, and didn't know if in the dream he would have gone to her or not.

Bear Man opened his eyes. He looked at the stars. He hadn't slept long. Then he turned his attention to the sound of Tree's sleeping breath, to Stone's sighing. How much I have, he thought, watching them, listening to them. And then he heard the silence. It was everywhere. Silence. All the songs had ceased. No wind. No insects. None of the familiar melodies. Silence. And then through the great cavern of no sound at all came one, faint, bleeding, solitary song. It was distant and uncertain, like the last words of someone walking away forever. But Bear Man knew its sound. It was like the sound of a great and far away bird-song. But it was not. He could understand the song clearly, and knew that what sounded like bird-song was the crying of pain and fear, and that it came from the village. The *soi*, he thought. They have come at last.

He woke Tree and quickly moved their blankets into hiding in the trees. "Wait here," he told her. "You'll be safe from them."

"Don't go," she said.

"I'll come back for you." And then he touched his lips to her cheek. "Be still. If you hear someone approach, don't move." Then he ran back to the stone slab. The far cry of the village called to him. He looked at his clothes beside the stone, reached for his knife, and naked turned to go to his people. Sprinting, leaping, bounding along the shore of the river and then the creek. The nearer he got the louder the song of despair became. And before he could see the village he could see the light of flames. And then he was in the streets. Children, women, warriors were running everywhere. Then he saw *soi*, running with torches, setting fire to huts, shooting arrows into crowds.

A boy was running toward him, bow in hand, stringing an arrow as he ran. Then the boy stopped, was aiming at a *soi* warrior. His arrow flew, and the *soi* fell twisting to the earth. Bear Man looked again at the boy. He was down on the the ground, lying across his bow. Not moving. There was an arrow buried in his face.

Bear Man screamed. And then he ran at a *soi* warrior that was putting a torch to a hut. He came to the lifeless body of the boy. It had been Leaf. *You are with the spirits now*, he thought, and he kept running.

Tree held her son to her breasts. The child had woken only a moment after his father had run away to the village. And when he started crying, Tree held him. Sang to him in whispers. Tried to cloud out of her own mind the voice she heard from the village. The voice of her people suffering.

When the child again slept, Tree wanted to sleep. The village tears were quieter then. Almost gone. Perhaps it's over, she thought. But what will remain? Sleep, her body whispered to her. She forced herself to stay awake, to wait for Bear Man's return. But what if he doesn't return? she wondered. But the thought of that was too dark and so she wouldn't allow herself to think it again.

She was almost asleep when she heard the steps. Bear Man! She started to move from her hiding. Bear Man! She carefully covered Stone and left him lying on the ground. Bear Man! She moved eagerly, her heart pounding, tears rolling down her face, streaming. Bear Man! She saw a shadow standing beside the stone. Bear Man! She rushed into the clearing, out of the shelter of trees and darkness. Bear Man! The figure standing at the river bank turned to face her. Tree stumbled, then stood motionless, staring into the face of the *soi* warrior.

Bear Man moved at the warrior with the torch. It was Crawler's hut. Flames were already covering it. The warrior was running for another hut. Bear Man could hear screams coming from inside the hut. Then he saw a woman running out the door. There were flames across her body. He turned his focus back to the attacking warrior. The man was no further away from him than a good jump. And so Bear Man jumped, dove, and aimed himself at his enemy.

He hit and they rolled together. The *other* still held his torch, tried to push it into Bear Man's face. Bear Man dodged, swung wide with his knife and struck the flesh of the warrior's back. Then his knife came up and slashed across the warrior's face. And then under his face. And then the warrior was still and silent. And Bear Man stood, no longer naked, clothed in the dark war-paint of blood.

He looked at the scene around him. There was a lot of confusion, it seemed, but not much happening. He looked for the *soi* warriors. There were dead ones everywhere, but he saw no live ones. Are they gone, he wondered, or have we killed them all?

The screaming was coming less often and less loudly. There were many people rushing bags of water to already destroyed huts. There were many others tending the wounded and the dead. Near him he saw a man kneeling over the body of a woman. The man was Crawler. The woman was Good Cook, his wife. The man was crying, and when Bear Man approached them he could see that the woman was dead. Her body was blistered with burns and there was a spear in her side. The spear, it looked, had no doubt pierced the unborn one inside her as well.

"Oh, you were a good woman," Crawler was crying. "I should have told you that." And then he cried some more. Bear Man knelt beside him and put his hand on his friend's shoulder.

"She is well," he told him. "She is with the spirits."

The small warrior turned to the giant. "She may be," he said. "But I am alone. My wife and my child have left me." Bear Man knew there was more than that that his friend was thinking but not saying. But it didn't matter now. What mattered now was searching the woods, setting up defenses, making certain there could be no more destruction.

"Leave her for now," he said. "Come, we've work to do."

The little man stood and the two of them walked to Bear Man's hut to get his weapons. The hut was untouched, unharmed by fire. But many homes had been unharmed. In all perhaps only twenty or so have burned, Bear Man thought. "Wait here," he told his friend, and he stepped into the building.

It was dark inside, but familiar, and he easily found first his axe and then his bow and quiver. And then some moccasins and clouts. He was about to leave when the cold, stone edge of a knife touched him under the chin.

"Don't move, giant demon," came the voice. It was an old, vacant, angry voice. "Don't move and you'll have another moment before I send you to your fathers."

Bear Man knew it was the old one whose son he had killed. He knew it was because of that incident that all this tonight had happened. He knew it was because of that incident that Tree had nearly died giving birth to Stone. He knew that what he had done had been the cause of great suffering. And he knew that now the time had come for him to yield, to make amends, to reconcile his folly. "Do what you must do, old one," he said. "I have no fear of you."

"That is well for you," said the old one. And then Bear Man felt the coolness mixed with warmth across his throat. He thought briefly of Tree and Stone. And then he saw his mother. Her arms were open to him and he was running to her, a child again. And then there was the dark, and for the briefest moment bird-song.

55

"I'm waiting, Bear Man," said Crawler, growing impatient, trying to hold back his tears and anger. And then he threw back the door and stared into his friend's hut, and a blade met his arm, slashing him, and he saw the old one running as he fell to the ground. And then he was up and after him, running along the creek where the warrior had run, coming to the river, looking through the dark. His arm bleeding, his eyes bleeding tears. And he ran. And then he stopped, and in the distance saw the old one with his knife against the throat of a woman. He took an arrow from his quiver, strung it. Pulled quickly against the bow. His arm trembled from the pain of his wound, and he fought to keep his aim steady.

56

Tree faced him, unmoving. He was old. Older than any man she had ever seen. And there was blood all over him. And when she looked at him she could see in him that he knew her, knew who she was. And then he was drawing his knife and walking toward her. Then taking her hand and drawing her to him until they were standing together on the stone slab. "Upon this altar you shall pay," he said in a voice as old as his face. And then his knife was against her throat. And then she could feel it moving lightly, teasingly, cutting but not yet destroying. And then it was gone, and so was the warrior. It took her a moment to realize that he was dead at her feet, an arrow deep in his neck. And then she turned and saw the warrior of the Principal People walking toward her. Bear Man! she thought again. But it wasn't the large figure of her husband. It was a small man. And when he was near, even in the dark, she could see the strange grin that so often he gave her.

TREE

1

Alone.

Alone she sang the songs that he could never sing again.

Alone she sang songs that he had never sung, because they were her songs. They were the songs she learned after he was gone. They were the songs of her new world.

This is the place.
This is the land where darkness shines.
And in the earth insects softly eat the mind.
This is the place where he has gone,
That man.

She walked in the woods at night when women were never supposed to be out alone. She walked there and listened as he had listened. She saw the stars. She saw their brightness and thought of him.

He was the man with eyes.
His eyes saw me and told me I was alive.
Now he has gone, and I have gone.

She walked days, and often avoided the work she had. She carried her son with her on her back.

She sang to her son of his father. "Stone," she said to him. "This is about Bear Man, who was your father." Then she would sing.

> He had strong arms that held all things.
> He had a strong voice that sang great
> songs.
> He conversed with trees, with deer, and
> with spirits.
> He conversed with his own heart.
> He died because he loved too many
> things.

And some days she took him to the river. "This river is named Unknown," she told him, though he was yet too young to understand her words. And then she would show him the great stone slab with the *other's* blood upon it. "This is where you began," she told him again and again. "This blood is the blood of the man who made us alone."

And then when walking nights and days, and when working, and daily living were done, she would lay herself down in the hut. And she would listen again to the songs of the sleeping village and the night forest. And she would reach her arms out for the man who was no longer there, and her mind would reach out for the words she would no longer hear, and the sights of him that she would no longer see. And it would be long after midnight before her tears had stopped and sleep would come.

This was the fourth season after her husband had been killed.

2

"There is no wisdom in being alone," said Light Fire. His daughter-in-law bowed her head and didn't speak.

"The village has healed itself of its wounds," he continued. "Now you must heal yourself." Still she didn't speak. He wanted to help her. He wanted to see again the happy woman his son had married. He wanted it for her and he wanted it for his grandson. He knew that and admitted it to himself. If it weren't for the boy he would no doubt leave her to her sorrow and allow her to waste away without any effort to intercede, to stop her slow dying.

"You *are* dying," he told her. "You still live with a dead man, and it is killing you." Silence was her reply. "Do you want to be with him so badly that you will allow yourself to waste away? What then of Stone? What will he do without a mother?" Tree wouldn't answer. Light Fire grunted and rose. There was nothing more he could offer. And besides, he told himself, I understand her pain. He remembered his own loss, so long ago and yet seeming like yesterday. Have I ever stopped mourning her? he asked himself. The answer was obvious. But I don't do so so desperately. Or do I? He wasn't sure. Just because he ate well, laughed, told stories and did all the things that all people do, that didn't mean that within him there wasn't a desperate struggle to recall and have again that which could never be recalled. I do miss her, he thought. And then he left Tree alone and walked into the bright day of the village street.

My town, he told himself. He inspected it carefully. Saw that children were laughing. Men and women were working, but not too hard. A good life still, he thought. He worried about that. When the attack had come four seasons earlier he thought that his dream of the town's destruction had finally proven itself. But the town hadn't been destroyed. And the people still lived here. And the dreams continued. And sometimes in the dreams he saw strange, white, hairy faces. Men who didn't look like men. And that worried him for he could find no understanding for it.

There must be answers, he thought. But where are they? And he realized that he missed his son, not for what answers Bear Man may have had, but because loving the young warrior had been one of life's answers in and of itself. And *that* he knew was Tree's difficulty. Loving her husband had been her life. Now even her son wasn't enough for her, and she spent her days doing nothing more than living in a long past season.

3

"They think that I shall die," she told her son while washing him in the creek. The child laughed at her. She smiled. "You know better than that now, don't you. You know I wouldn't die and leave you. They just don't understand that there are some things greater than being with them and laughing and playing with them." She took him from the water and dried him.

Then with him strapped to her back she started off again through the woods. The light in places made the leaves glow, as though they had a light of their own. Everywhere, as always, there were the songs.

"I've begun to learn their songs," she told him. "I'll be teaching them to you." She turned onto a path she hadn't traveled before.

When she had first begun her walks into the woods all paths looked alike. Now every path was different, distinct, itself. Every day she met new places, new trees, new clearings, and new thickets. She met them and came to know them and be at home in them. For in them she discovered herself, or at least a reflection of herself. And the reflection was clear and true, she thought. And what more can I ask of these walks than that?

She ate from fruit and roots and berries that grew in her woods. She sat beneath trees and listened, hoping to hear them talk. And when they never spoke, she never minded, for in the silence she heard an echo of herself, and of her lost love.

And she sang and spoke it all to her son.

Tree drew a circle on the ground, through grass and dirt.

"Let's see what there is here," she told Stone. The infant crawled through the grass, moving away from her. "Don't go far," she said, and smiled. Then she turned back to her circle. It is like the village, she thought. She saw in it a community of life. Insects, grass, weeds, flowers. She dug with her fingers, a bit here, a bit there, turning up roots of grass, and then weeds, revealing grubs, worms, and gray beetles. They live here together, she thought, all their lives. So do the people of Light Fire's village live. Moving together, working together, maintaining the order of their world.

There was no wind and the wood was filled with a majestic, pervasive silence. Tree bent to the earth and put an ear close to the ground within the circle she had drawn. She listened to see if she could hear a voice, a sound, a song.

From what seemed faraway she heard a motion, a gentle sweeping across the world. It was Stone, crawling, not far away at all. But he crawled quietly and the sound of it seemed distant. Tree let the sound of her child stray from her concentration. She wanted to hear from within the circle. She wanted to hear the beetles with their thread feet crawling. She wanted to hear the worms burrowing. From somewhere came the songs of birds. Then the louder song of Stone crying. She looked up. He was sitting in tall grass, sucking his thumb and crying.

She went to him, on her own hands and knees, crawling as he crawled so she could learn again what it was to be a child. "Is there something wrong?" she asked. He only cried, but not so loudly. She inspected him for cuts or bites. He seemed fine. Hungry then, she thought, and she opened her blouse and brought him to her breasts. And the crying stopped, and while he suckled she listened to the sound of that. "This is what your father loved to do," she told him, as she had told him many times before. "When you are old enough to understand," she said, "I will tell you all things, about yourself and about your father and about your mother. Then you will know who you are and where you come from."

The wind began to stir, and as he fed from her body, she watched the sky and watched white clouds move slowly to tell whatever tales the eye could see within them. There she saw deer and trees and once for a moment she saw herself, and then for a long moment she saw Bear Man. And so she sang Stone a song about that.

In the sky they hide,
all the things of the earth.
They hide there in the clouds.
The deer are there, the trees are there.
You and I are there, my child.
And the rains are all things weeping.
They weep because your father is there,
but can't be found here on the earth.

When the child was sleeping, Tree returned to

the circle she had drawn. She saw that already the beetles and worms and grubs had gone back into hiding. And the roots had already shed the moisture of their life. That too, she thought, is like the village. We live there so long and so well until something comes along to disturb what has been. And then some of us die. She then took tears from her face and moistened the roots, and planted them again. Then she carefully removed stones from their place within the circle to see what might be living or dead beneath them. Under some were insects. Others hid roots. Others merely cold, dark soil. Under one, hiding where human eyes had never looked, was another stone, a red stone, in the shape of a heart and no larger than the end of her thumb. She picked it up carefully and cleaned it with her fingers and then with her tongue. *This is Bear Man's heart*, she said to herself, and she held it to her breast. *This stone is the father of my child.* She thought back to her first night with Bear Man and to his song. *All the stones in all the rivers.* But don't all stones come from rivers? she wondered. She didn't know, but she knew that this stone she had found must be the emblem of Bear Man's heart, and that his spirit had brought her to it.

That night when she came home she found a gift of deerskin left inside her door. Who has done this? she wondered, but could think of no one who would give such a thing and not happily say they were doing so.

Unelanvhi, God, the Center Being, the One Spirit, the One Self. This was the being that some followed. They believed him the center and the source of all things. By talking with this one, the One Self, they believed they could talk with all things, with the spirits of all things and all people.

Witches who were twins learned to speak to each other's minds by speaking through the One Self, and they learned to control the minds of others by the power of the One Self. The One Self, the One Spirit, the Center Being was the source of their magic.

We are servants of the Center Being, said Number One.

We are his servants, said Number Two. They were speaking with their minds.

He has chosen us to bring his will to the Principal People, came the thoughts of Number One.

He has chosen us, echoed Number Two.

He has given us the formula we must use.

And so they began the second part of their plan.

When we rule the People there will be none who will not follow the true way to life.

Among the Principal People it was forbidden that human beings should marry within their families. It was even forbidden that they should marry within their clans, but that is the false way, said some. The ancient way is the true way. Only when a brother weds a sister, or a mother weds a son are the seeds of life kept pure. Those who taught this and sought to practice it were put to death.

Morning.
Cool air.
Sweet breezes like the last kiss of summer.
*The first embrace of autumn circling the mind
and heart of the world.*

The witch stood in the doorway.

The woman, Tree, watched her. Watched the
smile like a clean white knife unsheathe itself.
Watched the child in the witch's arms, a witch's
little human being. Or a witch's little human
thing.

"We've come to say hello," said the witch, the
witch named Number Two, and she let herself inside and found a seat near Tree where Tree had
been busy preparing a meal for herself and Stone,
her son.

"Hello, hello," said the witch, once for herself
and once for her daughter, Tear Maker. Then she
made a circle in the air with her hand, a small spell
against evil spirits that might want in.

"Why has a witch come to see me?" Tree
asked, not afraid, but concerned. She had talked
to the witch often while they were both in the
menstruation lodge, awaiting the end of their
period of purification after having given birth. She
liked the woman. And Number Two was the only
witch she'd ever come to know.

"You've been alone a long time now," Number
Two said. She opened the front of her drape and

started nursing her daughter. "People are saying you are a strange one."

"Is that why you've come to see me? To tell me what people are saying about me? I already know what they say."

"*Because* you already know. *That* is why I've come. Because you already know and you don't care."

"How do you know I don't care."

"Because you know that what they say is true, and that you have chosen to be as you are."

"And what does a witch have to do with this?"

"Witches, even twins like my sister and I, are masters of being alone. I have come to teach you. I've come to teach you to be what you are seeking."

"I'm far too old to become a witch, even if I wanted to be, which I don't." Stone was crawling nearby, about to get into mischief with the food, so Tree picked him up, and like the witch started nursing her chiid.

"I'm not talking about teaching you witchery. I'm talking about teaching you something else. Something that often only witches learn. But others can learn it too. You've already started yourself along the way."

"What then?"

"I'm talking about teaching you to become yourself."

Tree stared at the other woman, older than herself, pretty, her breasts larger than Tree's. And she recalled the days they had spent together in the lodge. The witch had always been kind. Had never been frightening as witches are reputed to be. And then she wondered, to be myself? Is that what I'm doing, searching for that? And what has that to do with Bear Man? Had he learned to be himself? But I already am myself, she thought. Everyone is. But when she thought it she was looking the witch in the eyes and she knew it wasn't true at all. No one is themself. We are like the circle I drew in the woods, a community. We are together. We are all parts of a whole. None of us is complete without the rest. She was still staring the witch in the eyes when she spoke.

"When do you start to teach me?" she asked.

"I already have," said the witch. And in her voice there was a sound that for a moment made Tree think that she had heard two voices.

6

The little man's eyes followed them out the village, and then he moved, following them with his feet, moving with the quiet and quickness for which he was known. My name is Crawler, he thought, both proud of it and hating it. And when the two women turned at the mouth of the creek to walk along the river, he was near enough that had he wanted to he could have easily hit either of them with a rock. But he had no such desire. His desire was a different sort. So he followed. Watched. Listened.

"This is where we first mated," he heard Tree say to the witch. "And this is where the old *soi* was killed." The *soi* that I killed, Crawler thought. His mind went back to that night. To following the old one as he left Bear Man's hut. Following him along the creek and to the river. Finding him with a knife to Tree's throat, ready to kill her. Killing him instead. Saving her. Saving her life and the life of her son. And that same night his own wife having died, carrying within her the unborn child who would never open his eyes onto the world. And then he had walked with Tree and held her son because she was trembling. And when they got to her hut they discovered Bear Man, limp and lifeless, covered with blood, his eyes staring into the darkness of the hut. And she had started screaming. He had tried to comfort her, to hold her, but she had grabbed the child from his arms and ran. Ran and had never stopped running. And I love her now, thought Crawler. And I've waited four seasons to claim her. To tell her that I saved her life and the life of her son. To tell her that I have a rightful claim to her.

And then he saw that the women had put their children on the ground, and that they were removing their clothes to bathe. And as he watched them his desire for Tree grew. I brought you a deerskin yesterday, he thought to her. I'll bring you more gifts. All so that when I claim you, you'll know that I am a good provider and that you'll want to be with me. And he watched them move into the stream of the river. Watched them wade out. Watched the current curl and glide around their waists. Then watched the water touching their breasts, then covering them.

I love you, he thought to her. And he knew that she had to say yes when he claimed her.

7

Tree let herself sink in the cool darkness. She let the waters swallow her, engulf her, embrace her and hold her as she so often held Stone. Somewhere above she could see the dim glow of daylight. She let herself sink further, deeper.

"Go down," the witch had said. "Go down and don't be afraid. The river's deeps are unknown and so it has its name. But we are not far out. The bottom seems far, but is there. Go and find it. It is a quiet, dark, place. When you get there, stay as long as you can. You'll know why once you're there."

And so she made herself sink, pushing herself down through the currents, sweeping both along the current and toward the floor of the river. And finally her feet touched stones and mud, and she curled herself on the bottom and waited for the understanding that Number Two had assured her would come. Already her lungs were aching and

138

she desperately wanted to return. But she made herself wait. She looked up and saw the far, far away light. Her body kept wanting to float up and she kept having to hold herself to the bottom. She found a large stone and grasped it, and that kept her safely there. Safely? she wondered. For a moment she thought the witch had sent her here to die. That the witch's words had been a ruse to bring her to her death. And then a voice within her asked, and what harm in dying? All men and all women die. Haven't I once cheated death by the miracles of Broken Back, the medicine man. Her head was whirling. She felt like she was drifting with the current, moving away. But she could tell she still had hold of the rock. And wouldn't life be better in the spirit land? That's where he is, waiting for me. Shouldn't I now go to him. Is this then the witch's gift. To find myself by finding him? And then her lungs were hurting more, were crying, pleading, screaming to her to move to the surface, to stay alive. *Live!* they called out. *Live!* And then the song of her heart was pounding and roaring in her mind. *I'm alive! I'm alive! I'm alive!* And her eyes were telling her their story. *We want to see again! We want the sun! We want the light of stars and moon! We want the colors of rainbows!* And her ears cried to hear all the sounds and songs of all the world. *Don't take them from us!* And suddenly she felt herself soaring up, kicking, crawling, fighting to regain the surface before she lost her strength. And the air came flooding into her and filling her and she panted and gasped and lunged for the shore. Then crawled, naked and shivering, to the blood-stained stone slab and lay on her back, letting the sun bake away the wetness and cold. And then hands were touching her, caressing her, the hands of the witch, and the witch was humming softly. And when she had quit shivering the witch bent to her ear and whispered. "You've done well this lesson," she said. "You took yourself close to dying. Now you know that you are alive. Now you know that you want to live. That is the first thing we must learn about ourselves." She kept caressing, soothing with her fingers.

Tree considered the woman's touch. It was the first time she had been touched since her last moments with Bear Man. The feeling was both good and strange. Number Two's touch was nothing like she recalled Bear Man's to be, and yet there was something familiar about it. What? she wondered. The woman's hands lightly ran up and down her legs, and then one hand again and again circled her stomach. And then the woman stopped touching her, and still naked herself, she laid down beside Tree and held her gently as a mother holds its child. And as Tree's head cradled against the other woman's breast, she recalled what was familiar about Number Two's touch. It was the same kind of touch and embrace she had long ago received from her mother. There was nothing sexual in it, only the pure loving of someone wanting to give comfort and asking for nothing in return. And so, because she hadn't been asked to do so, because there was absolutely no compulsion, she held Number Two more tightly, and began to caress her as she had been caressed. And much later, when the sun was low in the afternoon sky and the two of them had been crying quietly but didn't know when they had started to do so, Tree opened her eyes and stared into the other woman's face.

"I know I'm alive," she said. "I know I want to live. I know why I want to live." She paused. Touched the woman's breasts. "What I don't know," she said, "is how to live. How to live without Bear Man."

The woman took both her hands and held them. "Haven't you begun now to learn that?" she asked. Tree thought about it. Have I? How? And then the hours of touching and holding swept through her in a single moment and she understood. "Yes," she said. "By loving, by giving and receiving love. But never by requiring it." And the witch smiled at her kindly, a small, glad smile.

When they were walking back to the village Tree turned to Number Two and stopped walking.

"What's wrong?" asked the witch.

Tree stared at her, searching her face. Trying to find the answer to the question she was about to ask without having to ask it. Looking for some clue within the woman's smile, within her eyes, within her voice.

"Why?" Tree asked. "Why are you doing this? Why have you come to me?"

"We have come to you," she said, and again Tree sensed that quality of two voices in her words, "because when debts are paid it is good for people to again be friends. Bear Man, your hus-

141

band, owed us a debt. I can't tell you what it was, but it was paid. Now you are our friend."

"Who is we?"

"My sister and I. We always travel together. Well, not always, but always when we want to. She is with us now." And the woman put her face close to Tree's and put her hand over Tree's eyes. "Listen," she said. And for a brief moment Tree was certain she heard someone singing, a woman, but it wasn't the sound of a song that she heard, it was the feeling of one.

8

They left their children with Number One for the day. And they ran. They ran through the village valley, and out of it. Ran through woods that neither of them had ever seen. Ran fast and furiously, up and down hills. They crossed the small hills, crossed the small valleys. Ran north. Ran east. Ran south. Ran west. They ran like deer, and sometimes they thought they might fly, like birds. And running became a chant and song to them, and sometimes while they ran they sang, together, songs with words, songs without words. Songs of running, not to be somewhere, not to hurry, not to escape, merely to run. To thrust themselves across the earth, to feel themselves in motion, in near flight, to feel themselves heaving with their breath, to feel the sweat pouring down their faces, backs, necks, and legs.

It was noon when they stopped. They had been running since the dawn. Stopping only for brief moments at streams to roll in the water, swallow some of it down, and then get up again and go. But at noon Number Two said it was enough. And so they stopped, holding to their sides to ease the aching there.

"We've run too far," said Tree, heaving harsh, deep, gasping breaths.

"Never too far," said Number Two. She laughed and smiled at her companion.

"But now unless we turn around and *run* back we'll be tomorrow getting home. And I don't think I can run another step. I'm not even sure I can walk."

"Then let's sit down." And they found a shady place beneath a tree. They were in the hollow of two small hills. They had passed more deer, squirrel, birds, trees, flowers, *everything* than Tree had ever seen before.

When their breathing was quieter and they could talk without gasping, Number Two turned to Tree. "This is *where* you live," she told her. "If you want to learn how to live, you must know some things. One of those things is where you live."

"And what else?"

"What else do you think?"

"I don't know." She thought about it, though. What had she already started to learn? That she was alive. That love was a gift, and was part of being alive. "I don't know," she said again.

"You will."

"I will if you tell me."

"No. You will if I don't tell you. If I could simply tell you, then I would. Learning can't be told, it can only be experienced."

"Then what is the experience? What are we waiting for?"

"I'm not waiting for anything. What are you waiting for?" The witch smiled at her.

"Are these riddles?"

"Yes. And no. They are questions. But they're questions for you to answer, not me. But you have the answers. You just haven't looked at them. I'll tell you that much." She kept smiling, pleased, Tree thought, at the perplexity she was causing.

"I still say we've come too far," Tree said. "We'll never make it back by nightfall. We probably won't be back until morning."

"Do we have to be back before then?" asked Number Two.

"Have *you* forgotten we each have a nursing child?" She squeezed at her breasts. "I'm already ready to feed them. And I'm sure they are plenty hungry. Whatever Number One has cooked up for them, I'm positive they won't consider it as good as this!"

"Oh, mother, mother, mother you are. You have a child. And so now everything about you belongs to the child? Is that it?"

Tree stared at her, considering the questions.

"Aren't you hungry, too?" the witch asked. "Don't you have hungers now and then to be away from the little human and to be by yourself?"

Tree continued to think. Do I have such hungers? And for that matter, have I ever been by myself? "I'm not alone now," she told Number Two.

"No, you're not. Not yet."

"Are you going to leave me out here?"

"Should I?" She smiled. "Weren't you alone at the bottom of the river? Weren't you alone when you gave birth to Stone?"

"There were many people there. You were there."

"There was no one sharing your pain. You were alone with that."

"Those then are two times I've been alone. They weren't happy times."

"But you learned from them, didn't you."

"Yes. But, is that what it's always like to be alone?"

"That you'll have to discover yourself. Until then, tell me what you learned running today."

"I learned how tired I can get."

"Is that all?"

Tree paused. The wind caught her hair and sent it gently, coolly away from her head. Around them leaves were already turning their autumn colors. Browning, graying, yellowing, burning red and orange. "I learned," said Tree, "to move. To be in motion. To travel." The witch smiled. Does she want more of it than that? wondered Tree. What else have I learned. I ran, and ran, and ran. I did nothing but run, and when I thought I couldn't run another moment, I still ran. And then she knew more. "I can do," she said, "*more* than I knew I could do." Still the witch grinned, waiting. What more is there? That is all that's happened. What more does she want of me? What does she want me to find in myself? She looked at her. The witch stared back, waiting, unmoving, as though she had been sitting there forever and would go on sitting there until the end of time. Tree said nothing. Nothing more would come to her. Why am I here? she wondered. Why am I doing this? Why am I here?

"Yes," said the witch, as though she had heard Tree's thoughts. Had she? Tree wondered. "Why are you here?"

I don't know! Tree cried within, and then blurted out, "Because you brought me here! That's all! Because you came here and I followed you, running like a mad woman through the hills! Following another mad woman! Following you! That's all! Just *following* you!" She stopped. Out of breath, blood flushing through her face, sweat dripping from her chin, her lips twitching with tension. The witch didn't move, only smiled. Tree sat still, a great immovable object on the earth. Running was the farthest and last thing she could ever do again, she was thinking. Her legs seemed frozen. Her arms seemed like heavy weights.

"Is that what you have learned?" asked the witch, her smile never dimming, but never becoming mocking, Tree realized. It was a smile of love, and just as suddenly as her anger had fired her, now her entire body felt flushed with peace. And, "Yes," she said. "I learned to follow you. I

146

already had learned that, though. But now I have learned that I have learned it." And she laughed, and they laughed together.

And after a while they were quiet and there was a cool breeze in the afternoon air. Tree started rubbing her feet to ease the pain in them from the running. Then she looked up at Number Two who was doing the same thing.

"Yes?" said the other woman.

"I learned something else. Running is like living. You can get tired. You can move along, change the place where you are. You can do things that you hadn't thought possible. And sometimes you follow others."

"*You*," said Number Two.

"That's right," agreed Tree. "*I* can do these things. And sometimes running, like life, can hurt. Like my feet hurt now. Like I've been hurting to be without Bear Man. Like I hurt when Stone was born." She went back to rubbing her feet, massaging roughly.

There was a long, low, unnatural silence between them. Tree looked up again. Number Two was staring at her.

"Something else?" Tree asked. "Something more?"

"Yes, but you'll learn it later. Running has much to teach us."

The sun was low in the sky when they started back. They walked.

"We'll never get there," said Tree.

Number Two said nothing.

"My breasts hurt. Should I squeeze the milk out?"

"No. You should save it for your son."

"By the time we get there, there'll be more."

"Perhaps." Then, "Do as you like."

Tree considered Number Two. Was the woman worried about her own breasts? No. Didn't she also have a child to feed? Yes. Was she squeezing the milk out of her breasts? No. What should I do? She thought of the running. *Follow*. But sometimes it hurts, she thought.

It still wasn't sunset when they turned into a valley that soon turned into another, that soon joined yet another, and that one was the village valley.

"But we ran so long and so far!" said Tree.

"But you were following blindly," said Number Two.

"But—"

"Yes?"

Tree stopped. Thought. Considered what they must have done. That Number Two must have led her in a circle without her realizing it, and that they had never been far from the village. She looked at her teacher. Then smiled the same smile her teacher had been giving her all day. "There are many things to learn while running," she said.

"Yes," agreed the witch, and they continued into the town.

Before they parted Tree asked Number Two, "What will I learn tomorrow?"

Number Two answered, "Whatever you decide to teach yourself."

9

The hut was waiting for them as it always waited, quiet, open, an empty shell waiting for its masters to come and fill it. And waiting at the door were the gifts. Fruit and corn. From whom? she wondered. The gifts had come each day now for several days. She had asked Number Two about it. The witch said she knew nothing, but added that it was a matter they would discuss, sometime. She didn't say when. She seldom said when about anything. In fact, thought Tree, she says little, except to question me, or rather to give me questions to question myself.

She picked up the fruit and corn and went inside. She was so tired she could hardly stand and the bed of blankets was a welcome place to be. And it felt good to have Stone suddenly suckling her breasts. Empty them please, she thought.

She suspected the gifts were from a warrior, some young man who decided she was the woman he wanted. She tried to imagine herself again with a man. No visions of it would come. The idea of it held no interest for her. She had no idea who had been leaving the things. It didn't really matter, either. No man can claim me, she thought. And I'm not ready to give myself to one. Of course her parents and her father-in-law were upset about that. They were telling her she should have remarried long ago. They would speak and she would only wonder why. They couldn't understand that she already had a husband. And that just because he had gone to the land of spirits that didn't mean she wasn't his wife. She had told them that and of course they had agreed, but then they insisted that there was no harm in her marrying another man in the world of the living. They said the boy needed a father. She told them Stone had a father and needed no other. And then she refused to speak of it further. But from time to time they did, hoping that she would relent.

I won't, she promised herself.

10

Broken Back thought of the two women. He had twice now seen them together, and he wondered what the witch's business was with Tree. He recalled the instance many seasons ago when Bear Man had only been a boy. And when he had carelessly let fly an arrow that had caught the young girl named Number One across the neck. She still carried a scar from it. She had almost died, he remembered. He had had nothing to do with saving her, though. Her parents had taken care of her and refused to let him or the priest near her. Broken Back thought it strange that now this woman's should befriend Bear Man's widow, if that is what had happened.

And then he thought about the young warrior, Crawler. He knew the man's intentions toward

Tree. He had seen him leaving gifts at her hut. He had seen him sometimes follow her while she went on her walks. That isn't a good thing, he told himself. But there was nothing at present for him to do about it so he put it from his mind.

He turned his attention to the sore on his leg. It had appeared seven days ago, and it was still growing. And though he could still walk, walking had become painful and he had to concentrate to keep from limping. He had seen such sores before, but only on animals. He had heard of them on people, but he had never seen it. Now it had happened to him. His reaction was both curiosity and fear. Curious because of its novelty and because it presented a challenge to his healing craft. Fear because so many of the animals he had seen so infected had died.

11

The sun was straight up in the sky, and it burned down on an autumn land with all the heat and anger and brightness of a fiery torch thrust in a face.

It was Tree's thirtieth day under Number Two's guidance.

The two women were again naked under the water. Both of them were moving to the bottom of the river. They were further out than Tree had ever gone. For a moment she could see her friend swimming nearby. Then she was alone, moving down, ever down. They had been doing it every day for twenty days. Every day she went deeper. Every day she learned to stay longer. Every day she learned a little more why she was doing it.

The bottom of the river seemed to her like the bottom of the world. And perhaps it is, she thought. But she had been taught of the sea, though she had never been to it, and she knew that if there was a true bottom to the world that it was within its depths.

She sat on the river's bed, feeling at home. She had already learned to rest there without having to hold to anything. Sometimes the current would roll or turn her. She didn't mind. She was at peace for the moments she spent there. That was what mattered. She had learned a comforting peace from the river's deep. And she had learned new songs. Songs that cannot be sung, but can be learned. Songs that are only heard in deep, rushing, cold, dark and familiar waters. The song sang to her of motion, of circles, of life. The river is life, she had learned. It reminded her of something Bear Man had once told her. The river is life, and that its name is Unknown is appropriate because much of what *is* and what *will be* in life is unknown. Almost all, she thought, except what little we can learn of ourselves. She had learned that, too. That no matter how much she knew, she only knew little. There was always much more to learn. There always would be. And she had learned that a great part of the joy in *being alive* was in always being able to learn.

And as she sat upon the river bottom she closed her eyes and looked within herself, searching for what new thing she could learn of herself while there.

There are certain things, she thought, that Number Two is waiting for me to learn. That's why we keep coming here. I haven't learned those things and she's bringing me here until I do. But what?

Every day it is easier to stay, she realized. Easier to reach the bottom, and easier to stay there, resting, relaxing, being at ease and peace with the river, with the unknown.

The water held her gently, like the gentlest of lovers. She was home and she knew it. And then she realized, if I'm home here, then I'll be home anywhere I choose, and the thought both excited her and calmed her. Excitement for the discovery, and calm because she now knew another truth about herself. And she relaxed then more, sinking back, lying upon the stones and mud. And I can stay here, she thought. I don't have to leave. I can stay here forever. And as she thought it she knew that it meant dying, but there was no fear in the thought because she knew that wherever death took her that she could make a home there as well.

And when there were only the barest moments left for her to safely return to the surface, she did so, not flailing and gasping, but relaxed and at peace. And when she stepped to the shore, Number Two was waiting, with a knowing look on her face.

"You were gone longer than ever," said the witch. "Why did you return?"

Tree knelt beside her. The water was already drying beneath the heat of the sun. "To tell you what I've learned," she said. The witch waited. "And to tell another one day. I decided I want that."

"To tell your son?" said the witch.

"Yes."

"And what will you tell him?"

"That I am alive. That he is alive. All the things I've learned with you. And that not only am I alive, but today I learned that it is all right to die."

Number Two gave her again for what seemed to Tree the thousandth time the quiet, loving, understanding smile that agreed with all that Tree was learning.

"You've learned something else then, too," the witch told her.

"I know. I've learned that not only will I sometimes follow, as I have followed you. But I will sometimes lead, as I will lead Stone."

"That is good," said the witch, and it was the first time she had spoken the words that her smile had so often said for her, but she spoke them because what Tree had just learned was the most important part of her task. She had not failed in what she had set out to do. Tree would lead her son, she would teach him as she had been taught. And that, the witch knew, was necessary. In her mind there was a far away voice. Not a voice she heard, but one she felt. *Yes*, it said, *now we have*

154

paid our debt. And Number Two answered, *and not only has a debt been paid, but we have gained a sister*.

Then she spoke to Tree. "You have learned all that you have to learn, dear Tree," said the witch. "But there is one more thing I hope you'll teach yourself."

"And what is that."

"That is how to embrace a man. It isn't an easy thing to do, for men are seldom embraced properly, since they do all they can to hide from such love."

"But I love no man except Bear Man, and he cannot be held."

"There are still things for you to learn, sweet Tree."

12

Light Fire watched the smoke rings rise from his pipe. It comforted him to know that smoke at least could be depended upon. If you blew it the right way, it always made lovely gray rings. And that they vanished almost as soon as they appeared was nothing to be concerned about, it, too, was something that could be counted upon. Vanishing, he thought, going away, those are things that can be trusted. They will happen to us all.

He thought of these things because he again considered the strange dreams that haunted him. And in those dreams he saw his town vanishing in flame, and then his people vanishing into the wilderness, seeking out the setting sun. All these things must be, he supposed, but he was no nearer understanding why. Except that a new vision had been added to the dream. Now he sometimes saw Bear Man standing before the strange white, hairy faced people. And he was afraid that Bear Man would die again. And so he was afraid of the peculiar *others*. And once an old, old warrior had stood beside the gathering of people and had pointed at Light Fire and laughed, saying again and again, *I've won! I've won!*

He recognized the old *soi* as being the one who had killed Bear Man and who had tried to kill Tree. He supposed that all these new things added to the dream were only his heart's sorrows and fears.

He thought then of his daughter-in-law and his grandson. He was sorry and afraid for them, he knew. Yet there seemed little more he could do. The woman had taken up with a witch. Now, surely, there was nothing to do for her.

It was late at night when his pipe burned low and his dreams and thoughts settled away with the smoke rings. And as he climbed into his bed and closed his eyes, he hoped the dream wouldn't come again that night. But there was a new moon, and it always came with the new moon. And that night it did again. But this time he saw that it wasn't Bear Man who stood before the strange

156

soi. It was Stone, a new young warrior. And they were about to kill him.

13

They walked between the rows of huts, brown and gray in autumn afternoon. Number Two listening to the voices of village and nature singing. Tree watching her woman friend, watching her peaceful and quiet face, her silent lips moving slowly, keeping the rhythm of the songs she heard.

The huts, the women, the children, the men, the village. The woods surrounding them all; Tree knew without doubt that there was purpose and reason in it. That the village, all villages and all people gather for some purpose and intent beyond the complexity of their customs and beliefs. That within it all there resides a will and declaration that she didn't yet understand. Nevertheless she knew it was there. And in the songs that she heard, and knew Number Two heard, she guessed there might be understanding, and she knew that this had to be the purpose of her lesson today.

Number Two said we would learn about embracing men, she thought. What has that to do with *this*, and her eyes swept through the village.

When they were out of the village Number Two started running. Tree, as always, followed. They took a familiar path and followed it for half the afternoon, stopping only now and then for water.

Eventually Tree knew they were at the place where if they were to make a return trip before nightfall, that they would soon have to head back. There they stopped. Number Two said nothing. She let herself fall to the ground and rolled there, laughing like a child happily at play.

"Come play with me," she called to Tree. Tree dove to the ground, caught her friend in midroll and they twisted and turned together through the grass. Then they stopped and rolled away from each other, so far away that they couldn't touch each other's hands even by stretching. "You're all alone over there," said Number Two. Tree smiled and then laughed. "I'm all alone everywhere I am," she said. "It isn't so terrible to be alone."

Number Two stopped smiling at her then. She stopped moving. She stopped talking and laughter and gladness, and she held so still, with her eyes wide open and glaring, that for a moment Tree was afraid the woman had instantly left the world of men and gone to the land of spirits.

"Number Two?" she asked quietly.

Number Two said nothing, moved nothing.

"Is something wrong?"

Nothing.

Tree stood and walked to her friend. Then knelt beside her. The witch still didn't move. "What is it?" Tree asked. She had seen the witch do many strange things. She had never seen this.

Then she heard a voice, she thought, but couldn't understand it. Then she realized she wasn't hearing the voice, she was feeling it. It was inside her, and it was the voice of Number Two, and the voice of Number One as well. And the voice was trying to instruct her. Trying to call her somewhere. She closed her eyes, wanting to hear. Wanting to understand.

Don't move. Be more still than ever you have been. Don't move. Learn who and what you are. Don't move. Listen to your name. It has something to teach you. Don't move.

And so Tree held still, didn't open her eyes, didn't speak, didn't move. Only listened. *Listen*, the voice told her. *Listen and learn. Keep listening until you know everything about who and what you are. Keep listening until all the questions are answered. Don't move, don't see, don't speak, don't sleep, don't do these things. Only listen.*

And then the voice was gone. And Tree held still, kneeling in the grass. She could hear motions of the earth around her. She could feel and hear the motion of the wind. She could feel the motion of the blood in her legs, wanting her knees to ache. She wouldn't move to relieve their discomfort. She could feel the heat of the sun against her hair and shoulders. She could almost hear it, she thought. But that must be my imagining, she told herself, and then tried to tell herself no more, wanting only to listen.

The silence was long. The wind had faded. The sun was becoming cool against her and she knew that evening must be near. And then she realized that Number Two was no longer with her. She didn't know how she knew it, but she was certain it was true. She didn't know, either, when the woman had left. Certainly she had heard nothing of her leaving. But that meant nothing, as the witch could move without making sound. Perhaps she can even move through the earth or the air as some say that witches can do, she thought.

Her arms felt to her like enormous heavy limbs, and her legs had long ago lost any feeling at all. It was as though, she thought, they were buried in the earth, as though they had become roots and had reached down into the ground to secure her to the spot.

She didn't move.

When again the wind came and it was full of chill, she knew it must be dark. She wondered then if she should get up and go home. After all, she thought, what purpose can there be in this? I've been here all this time. I've held still. I've listened. I've listened and listened and heard all the songs again and again of the woods, songs I already well knew. What more can I learn? I've listened to the pain and then the numbness in my body. What can I learn new from that? I already know about pain. I've held still. I've held still. I haven't moved. I haven't moved. And I've listened. What is there for me to learn?

She didn't move. I'll stay here, she told herself, until I have learned. Once I've learned, I will know. Then I can leave.

It was a long time later when she smelled them. The wolves. She didn't move. She could hear them next, breathing near her, walking lightly around her. Inspecting her. Then one was rubbing against her, scratching its back. Still she didn't move. One of them licked her face. She felt little of it, but could hear the creature's breath, could hear its tongue coursing across her face. Could hear then her own heart beating a little faster. *Slow, heartsong*, she sang within. *Slow. Slow.* And her heart beat slower. And she didn't move. And after a while the wolves were gone. And she was immovable. I am here forever, she told herself, forever or until I learn. What can it be? What can it be? What can it be?

She gave up asking when she felt the sun against her face. I'll never know, she thought. I shall stay here forever. I belong here. I am indeed a tree and cannot be moved. I have been named well. This is the place where I shall stay. And she realized then that soon her body would fall into the earth, bit by decaying bit and she would indeed remain forever here, because she could not learn what Number Two had left her here to learn. And perhaps, she thought, a tree *will* grow from me. *No*, she told herself. I am already a tree. I have already planted my roots. I am a tree. I am a tree. I am a tree. And she kept saying the words, listening to them inside her mind for that was the only place they were spoken. And when she had said them a thousand times, she understood that it was true. *I am a tree.* And she realized that she had at last learned the first part of what she was waiting for. And so she smiled within, though she never moved at all without. And she waited to see what more she might learn, but realized that a tree cannot seek truth, a tree must wait for it to come her way. And so she learned the second part of what she had waited for.

It was toward night again when she said to herself. *I am a tree, and I am alone. And alone a tree cannot survive, and alone cannot be itself.* A tree needs the sun. A tree needs the insects. A tree needs water. A tree needs the earth. And there is something else. Something else. Something else.

It was the middle of the night when Tree stood and started her walk back to the village. It was morning before she got there.

She went to the house of Number Two where she knew her son would be. Number Two said nothing to her when she came for Stone. Tree said nothing to Number Two. She took her son and walked away through the autumn morning cool air.

Inside her hut she lowered her drape and after what seemed to her a thousand summers she once more put her son to her breasts and felt the sweet aching of the milk rushing from her into his small, hungry, anxious mouth. She smiled at him.

"A tree needs fruit," she told him quietly. "A tree needs fruit."

And when he was finished and sleeping she laid beside him and started to also call herself to sleep. But before she met that dark waiting prince, she reminded herself once more of the other thing that a tree needs in order to be itself. *A tree needs another tree. A tree needs the woods. A tree needs not to be alone.*

14

The arrow went through the air and became a vanishing dream. A dream of speed, clarity, and instant death. Crawler watched it sail, watched it vanish, smiled. It had been his arrow. Sending it away was his way of saying to himself and to the world that the time had come for him to claim his bride. He was the arrow, and its high flight over dozens of trees was the symbol of his waiting, and journey to this moment.

He was outside the village. The sun was still low in the morning sky. He had watched her through the night. He had watched her in frozen exhibition through most of two days and two nights. He had watched the wolves come to her and had fought with himself as to what to do, wanting to kill them, not wanting to disturb her withdrawal.

He had watched her and the witch for days. Gradually he'd come to understand a bit of what was happening. Again and again he had watched her dive into the river, and had waited and waited for her to emerge. Always just when he thought she would never surface, she had. Always. Then he watched her come to the woods two days ago. He watched her enter the trance. And he waited.

Several times he slept. When he awoke, she was still there. He was nearly asleep when she finally stood and left. And so he followed her back to the village. Always he thought of himself as her silent, unseen protector. Now, though, he told himself, I will be seen. I will go to her and tell her that by right she is mine, and if she will, by love.

But I must have her, he thought.

15

"You must embrace a man," said Tree to the witch, "as a tree embraces the wind, and as the earth embraces the roots of the tree."

"And how is that?"

"By being there to hold and be held, but by never claiming."

"Is that all?"

"No. A man must embrace a woman in the same way."

16

The warrior stood in her hut and offered her gifts of food, skins, jewelry, and love. He said love, she told herself. And then he claimed her as his wife.

"It is only right," he said. "I avenged the death of your husband. I saved your life and the life of your son. It is my right."

It's all true, she told herself. He has done all

these things. I am in his debt. He loves me?

She looked at the small, thin man. The familiar smile was still there, the smile that made her afraid to be with him. Can I live with that smile? she wondered.

"You love me?" she asked.

"I said so. Of course I do. Does that matter so much? But of course I do. Otherwise I wouldn't have waited for more than four seasons for you to finish your mourning. But the time has come to go on with living. The time has come for both of us."

Of course, she thought, he lost his wife the same night I lost my husband. Of course. He's never done anything to show himself other than an honorable warrior. But his smile. And his size. He stands beneath my shoulder. And he *claims* me.

"Must you claim me?" she asked.

Crawler's face tightened. He kicked the gifts laying before him. "What is this?" he asked, his voice cutting quickly into the peace of the hut. "What is this?" He kicked again at the gifts. "I've done only honor to you. My claim is my right. How can you question it? I've watched you all these days, watched your face. I've seen you change. I at last saw you new again. I understood then that you were ready to once more have a husband. That is why I've come now. And you challenge my right!" He spat on the gifts. "I am no fool! I know that many laugh because of my size and many think my face is funny! But you cannot challenge me and you cannot laugh at me! I claim you. It is my right! There is nothing more to be said of it."

Tree rose and stood before him. There were tears rolling from her eyes, not from pain but because part of her felt for this man. None of her wanted to scorn him.

"If you have been watching my face," she said, "you should have looked more closely. You would have seen that I have been becoming myself. Certainly you are right that it is time for me to have again a husband. But I cannot be claimed! Not by any man."

Crawler's hand reached for her face, and almost struck her, then stopped. Suddenly it seemed so wrong for him to be there, he thought. He looked up at her, this woman who dwarfed him as though he were merely a child. This woman who told him he had no right, and he believed her. It was something both in her voice, in what she said, and also in her face that told him she was right. He could not claim her. No man could. But especially him, and he hated her for it.

He turned. Kicked again the gifts. Spat on them again. Then spat on her and on her son. "I should never have saved you," he said. "You aren't worthy of such honor." And then he left.

Tree stood in the silence with the spittle dripping down her face. After she had cleaned herself, she cleaned her son and then she put all the gifts that Crawler had given outside the hut.

They stayed there for several days. Then one morning she woke to find them gone. She didn't know if Crawler had taken them or if it had been another. She hoped that he had retrieved them for himself. They were fine things, not to be lost.

That same afternoon she was at the creek, Life, washing her clothes, when another warrior stopped beside her and knelt to drink.

"The water from this creek is always good," he told her.

She looked at him. She had never seen him before, though he wore the garments of a warrior of the Deer Clan. And he was tall, and strong. Not so tall as Bear Man, she told herself, but taller than most. And his face was happy, one moment making him look like a boy, and the next convincing her that he was wise with age.

17

"I am Tree," she told him as she continued to wash. "You're right, the water *is* always good."

"It's been a long time since I've had some of it," said the warrior. He cupped some more in his hands and brought it to his lips. Then, "I've been away from my home far too long, serving our brothers in the north in their battles." He stood then and started to walk away.

"Your name?" Tree asked.

He stopped and turned again toward her, his face almost laughing with warm delight. "I am Archer," he said. "I was born with the name Clear Sky. Since I have become Archer."

"And are you home to stay, Archer?"

"First I must go to another clan to find a wife. Then I'll be home to stay. The water here is too good to leave again."

"Yes," she agreed. "The water is far too good for that."

Then she watched him walk away, and inside she felt something she had not felt for a long, long while. At first she didn't know what it was. But by the time she got back to the hut and the feeling was still there she had recognized it well. And she was hoping that the young warrior with the ageless face would not leave too soon to find himself a wife.

He came to her hut that night, just after sunset, before darkness had fully settled.

"A walk?" he asked.

"My son," she explained.

"Bring him," he said, gladness in both his voice and face. She brought the child, and they walked through the village, talking only a little, and most of that to Stone, who seemed glad to be out.

"He's a bright one," said the warrior. "He'll be a fine man one day."

"His father was the best," Tree offered.

"I know," said Archer. "I knew his father well."

Tree stared at him. Knew Bear Man? But of course. They would have grown up together.

"Bear Man was a friend," he told her.

"You knew him well?"

"Everyone in the village knows everyone," he said. "And he was the son of chiefs. I had to have known him. But we were friends, but not close friends. His close friend was the odd one, Crawler. I never understood why."

"Nor have I," she said. "Except that the little man seemed to worship him."

They came to the end of the village streets and Archer started to turn back. "No," said Tree. She nodded into the darkening woods. "There," she said. And she started off while Archer watched.

"Do you walk in the woods at night often?" he asked when he caught up with her.

"Often enough," she said.

"You're a strange woman," he said.

"Life is strange, too," she told him. "The land is strange. Only a strange person can find their way through it all."

"You are a poet?"

She smiled.

"Tell me some of your poetry. Sing me some of your songs."

"Perhaps someday."

They were far from the village and had headed back when Archer stopped her, putting his hand across her shoulder. She froze. His grip firmed. She started to tell him to release her when she too heard the sound and smelled the heavy, musky scent.

Then Archer's hand was off her and he was stringing his bow, then putting an arrow to the string.

"Where is it?" she whispered.

"Don't move," he told her. "Be still and listen." Yes, she thought. I am a tree, she told herself, and held her fruit tightly.

The shadow moved through the trees casually, thinking it had nothing in all the world to fear. And when it smelled the humans, it got angry instead of afraid, and it turned toward them.

Archer's arms were flexed tight against the draw of the bow. Even in the dark Tree could see his muscles, sleek hard lines coursing through his arms. And then she saw the shadow emerge from the trees. She heard the bow empty itself and saw Archer draw and empty four more arrows in rapid succession. And still the shadow came toward them, growling, screaming, pawing the air as it lifted on its hind feet. Archer let loose one last arrow, grabbed her and started to run. But then there was no use. The bear was motionless at their feet. The last arrow had been too much. There wasn't even any last hissing of breath. It was over.

They spent the rest of the evening preparing the carcass to bring it home. It was dawn before they returned.

"A nice walk," Archer said as he left her at her hut.

"Yes," she agreed, and she watched him walk away.

That day she told Number Two about the warrior, and about what had happened earlier with Crawler.

The witch smiled at her kindly and told her then to be careful. *People are dangerous animals*, she said. *Be careful*.

18

Crawler watched them walk into the village. It had been a long night, following them through the woods. The warrior was a good hunter and it took all of Crawler's skills to remain undetected. And when he saw the bear attack them, he surprised himself to be saying a prayer for the animal. And when the bear was dead, he knew what he must one day do, for it was obvious that the woman had given her heart to another, making worse her denial of his rightful claim.

19

The medicine man limped through the street. His leg hurt more than ever. There was no longer anything he could do to keep it from pain and weakness. The limp though came more from the leg's loss of muscular control than from pain. Pain was something the old man had long ago learned to hide from. This he couldn't hide from. The black sore had spread from his knee to his foot, was getting deeper, and, he realized, was something he couldn't heal. So he covered himself with pants of deerskin, and gathered what things he thought he might need or want, and he left. It wasn't unusual to see him walking from the village into the woods, so no one noticed his going. It wasn't unusual for him to be gone for days, so no one would notice his absence. That is all good, he thought to himself as he passed the last hut.

The woods waited for him. They were a good place for him to be, he told himself. They are a good place for all of us, said his lips but no sound came out. It was something he liked to do, speaking without sound, and making sounds without speaking, without the movement of his lips anyway.

He crossed three mountain ridges, something that would have been easy for him only moons ago, but now was almost impossible, though the mountains were only large hills.

After the third ridge, he hoped he was far enough, because he knew he could go no further.

He found a warm place out of the autumn wind. And then he took off the deerskin pants. The dark sore glared at him. He almost felt it hated him and that was why it had come. He certainly knew that he hated it.

He had stopped near a small pool of water, a clear spring bubbling up from the earth. I'll need the water, he told himself. He drank from it, its taste was good, sweet, cold.

Then he took his knife from its scabbard. It was his best knife. It was the same one he had used to cut into the woman, Tree.

He thought back to all the times he had done with animals the same thing he had done with her. Many of the animals had died from the surgery. But many had lived. It pleased him that the woman had lived. It pleased him for her sake. But even more it pleased him because he knew that it was a singular achievement of his craft. He had done what no one had ever done, and likely, he thought, would ever again do. Cutting into the woman's womb. And there treating the wounds within her that had made her rupture. And then tying together all the wounds, the ones he had made himself, so that the bleeding would stop and so that everything would grow again as it had been. Everything but one thing, he recalled. The woman would almost certainly never bear children again.

And then he thought of his other experiments with animals, and the many things he had learned from them. He thought about the thing he was about to do. He had done it time and again with creatures other than men. He had never had reason to try it with a human being, until now. It had often worked well with the creatures. Will it work now? he wondered. There was only one way to find out.

He held the knife firmly. Touched it lightly to his leg just above the knee, just above the infection, just below a tight strap that was cutting off the flow of his blood. And then he bore down on the blade, cutting at it the way a hunter cuts at an animal he has killed. And he forced away the pain. And forced away his weariness. And made himself keep cutting, and keep cutting, and keep cutting.

20

Archer watched her run. It was like watching a creature who had been born for nothing else but running. She ran with the same ease and comfort and grace as the deer. And while watching her run he always thought how unlike her name she is. And then other times, while watching her sit still and listen, listening to him, or to her child, or to whatever sound of nature was around them, then he knew she had been named truely.

I want to marry this woman, he thought one day when they were walking by the river. They had come to a large flat stone. He had started to sit upon it but she had kept walking, so he followed her. She is a strange woman, he told himself, but she is kind and she is wise. I want to marry her. And when she did stop, sitting on a grass covered mound, he told her so.

"To marry me?"

"I want to love you," he said.

"*Ugeyuha?* To possess me?"

"I love you."

"*Udageyuha?*"

"Yes."

"There are too many kinds of love."

"I love you."

They stared at each other, neither knowing what to say or do next. And then after a while they walked some more. They didn't talk. They didn't discuss anything. When at last they came back to the village Archer stopped her and asked her for an answer.

"Ask me again tomorrow," she said. "*Adageydi ulsgeda*," she told him, "Love is important." Then she added, "I must think about this. I must learn what I feel."

The next day when he asked her, she kissed him, and allowed him to hold her gently. "Will you become my wife?" he asked once more.

She rested a moment in the warmth and taste of him.

"Tomorrow I will tell you," she said.

21

They stood on a cliff that hung above the river. From the cliff to the water was at least five times the height of a man. From there they watched the flow of currents, and listened to windsong in the trees. Tree held Stone in her arms. Archer held his bow and aimed across the river.

"No arrow can travel that far," she said.

"If I can send it across the river, will you marry me?"

She smiled. "No, she said. "I won't marry you for that. But if you can send it across the river, I'll kiss you again. And for your kiss, and for your love, I will marry you."

He raised the bow, pulled it until Tree thought

175

it might break. Then released the arrow. It sailed high. It sailed far. And when it fell, it struck the distant shore. Buried its tip deep in the earth.

And she kissed him then, and held him. "Now we will grow together," she told him. And she put her son safely in the grass away from the edge of the cliff. And then she drew the man to her. Touched him. Felt his touch. Let herself open to him. "I'm now your wife," she told him.

"And I, your husband," he said, neither of them caring that they had not waited for the ceremony of their people. Their love was enough. Ceremonies could come later. Now everything was in their touching, holding, being. And Tree closed her eyes, and for the smallest moment she thought herself again with Bear Man, with her first love within her. And then she knew she was with Archer, and that she loved him as she had loved the young giant who had given her his son. And she knew that she never wanted to be away from him. And that whenever he traveled, hunting, to war, anywhere, that she would be with him.

"We are three trees, you, I, and Stone," she said, "growing in the shade of each other's strength."

When they had touched again and again, and held each other again and again, and when again and again Tree had brought him into her body, then they stood and walked once more to the edge of the cliff.

Standing there was like standing at the edge of time and eternity, at the brink of all beginning and ending, at the pinnacle of greatest height and deepest sorrow. For standing there, watching the water move below, Tree realized that just as sorrow and aloneness come to an ending, so too does joy. This will end, she told herself, but I shall stand beside and within it as long as I may. And then she watched Archer string another arrow, and aim it as he had the other to the distant shore.

"It is bad luck," she told him, "to attempt the same miracle twice."

He turned to her, smiled. "We've just given each other the same miracle more than twice." he said. And then he turned back to the object of his arrow, bent the bow, and let the arrow fly. Again it sailed, free and seemingly forever on its way. But when it began to fall, they both could see it would find its rest in the waters. And they watched it descend. And when it hit the water, slipping away as though it had never been, Tree turned to Archer to offer her regrets. And she saw the deep look of pain in his face, his lips tight, his eyes searching the sky.

"It's only once," she said. "Don't hate it so much." And then she saw that it wasn't the arrow falling short that caused him pain. It was another arrow, one caught firmly between his shoulders. He staggered, reached back, trying to pull at the deadly enemy. And then he toppled, fell not to the ground but over the cliff, and Tree saw him falling all the way. And though it was only a moment, it seemed forever while she saw his body plunge and fall, and then send up great clear thin walls of water. And then he was gone.

177

She turned to run for Stone. And standing over the child was the man who had killed Archer. The man who had in an instant severed all the new found joy and hope. Crawler grinned, his sad, frightful grin.

"Now you are mine," he said. "And never another's." And he moved toward her.

She tried to run. He moved faster, blocking her way. She started to scream. He was on her, forcing her down.

"Scream!" he cried. "Scream! No one will hear you. Scream the way you screamed when your fatherless child was born!" And then she could feel him lifting away her skirt, and then the hardness of him pressing against her. And all the joy and tenderness that touching and closeness had meant only moments ago now meant nothing more than pain and fear and hate.

When she felt him moving within her, she knew what she wanted to do, what she must do. She searched around the ground about her for a weapon, for anything. And still he moved, heaving and twisting. And at the same moment that she could tell he had spilled himself, had mixed himself within her, she found the rock. And while he was pushing himself more deeply than ever, she brought the rock down, and down, and down upon his head and shoulders. She was still hitting him when she realized that he had stopped moving, was lifeless upon and within her. And she pushed him away, stood and stared at him. The tiny, little, awful animal calling himself a man, she thought. And she started to roll him off the cliff but decided that he did not deserve to share the waters with Archer.

Stone was crying and she went to him and took him in her arms, and then she went to the edge of the cliff and stared down into the depths. And she cried with her son.

She was still sitting there, still crying, not seeing when the small man began to move, began to crawl, moving toward her. It wasn't the sly, perfect and artistic crawling he had done as a warrior and hunter. It was a hobbled, broken motion. And he moved nearer, guided only by the sound of her sobbing. He was close behind her and raising his hand to push against the small of her back, to send her to her lover, when she stood, and without looking back at him, walked away. He forced himself to watch her go, seeing that she was not headed to the village, but away from it. And later when it was dark, and he finally had the strength for it, he stood, and started after her.

22

The night was her friend, and she moved through it as one familiar with all the contours and secrets of shadow. Behind her, far behind by now, she thought, was the village, was the river carrying away her second husband, was the cliff with the dead man who had once saved her and

179

had now all but destroyed her.

She sang to Stone whenever he woke and started to cry. She sang to him, held him to her breasts, laughed with him. He was all she had now. Everything seemed to have left her. All the lessons with Number Two seemed like far away dreams, dreams that had never been true and never would be. Dreams that belonged to someone else.

Late into the night, Stone began to sleep well, riding easily on her back. But Tree wouldn't sleep. I must go on, she told herself. I must go on. I must never go back. She didn't know where she was going. She hadn't even given attention to what direction she headed. Just away, she told herself. Away. And so the sun rose against her back, and she kept walking, singing songs with the morning birds. But not singing their gladness. Singing instead her own sorrow.

It was late in the morning when she came to the pool. She knelt there to drink. The water was dark and cold. And while she drank she heard first the steps, and then the heavy sigh. And then she looked up and saw the man across the pool, standing awkwardly, gazing at her.

23

The old man stood on one leg and held himself up with a staff. He laughed to see the woman.

"What brings you to my retreat?" he asked her, still laughing.

The woman didn't laugh. Didn't smile. Only stared up from the pool.

"What's wrong?" he asked her then, aware that her silence was due to fear and confusion.

"Where is your leg?" she asked.

"Oh, that!" he said. "I buried it. It was no longer a good leg, so I cut it off and buried it." She stared at him in disbelief.

"I have some food here," he told her. "Come and eat and I'll tell you about my leg and you can tell me why you're here and what you are afraid of."

He told her about the infection. He told her about his skills with animals. And he told her what he had done to himself.

"And I'm alive," he said. "And I'm going to learn to walk with sticks. I'm already learning that," he said.

And then she told him what she was afraid of. She told him about her studies with Number Two. She told him about Crawler's claim, and about Archer. And about Archer's death. And about Crawler's death.

And then she told him she had to go. That she couldn't return to the village.

"Go home," he told her.

"I can't," she said.

"You can go home, Tree," he said. "Go home. Tell these things to no one. Go home. That is where you belong. That is where your son belongs."

"And what," she asked, "if I am carrying the child of Archer or Crawler? What if their mixing with me has made a new little human start to come down?"

He stared at her.

"The People would think me a whore. I have no husband. No one will know that I married Archer. No one will know that I was attacked by Crawler. And I won't know who the child's father is, unless it is a very small child," she said angrily.

"There will be no child," the medicine man told her.

"And how can we know?" She wanted to cry. Wanted to run from the old man. Wanted to leave him and leave the people. She wanted to find a place to bury herself within the earth. I am a tree, she told herself. But I have no other trees to grow beside me.

"Take your son home," he told her. "There will be no child." And then he told her about other things he had learned from animals, and about what he had done to her, and that he was almost certain there would never be another child for her. When she heard that she wanted to cry again, because though she didn't want to be carrying a little human then, she knew that someday she might want to, would want to, and that now she never would. And all the need to escape was suddenly replaced by a sense of bareness and the realization that she was a tree that would never have more fruit. A man's tale may end with the death of a son, or if no son is ever born, she told herself. But a tree can only live to bring forth fruit, to nurture that fruit and make it the finest that has ever grown. And in thinking that she knew she would return, and she knew that Stone would now become everything to her, and that she would never again seek the closeness of another tree, of another Bear Man, of another Archer.

Stone, she thought. And she wished suddenly that she were with her friend, Number Two. Because Number Two was also a tree. And Tree knew that she couldn't bear to be altogether alone, always, and that Stone, her fruit, could not provide for her what she needed from another tree. But neither can a woman, she thought. And yet she couldn't bring herself to think of ever again accepting the closeness of a man.

And then she looked hard at Broken Back. He is so very old, she thought. And so very alone, and yet he has learned so many magical things about nature and humans. And suddenly she knew that she loved him, loved him deeply, and after that she just as suddenly knew that she loved all men, even, she thought, wicked men. Even Crawler. We are all so alone, she thought. We have only each other. Like all the trees making together a forest. That is what we are, a great unshakable, immovable, green forest, struggling to bring forth our fruit. And she went to the old man and held him quietly and thanked him for her life and for telling her to go home. "We will go home together," she said. "You will learn to walk again, and so will I. And soon Stone will be walking." And someday, she told herself, I will be able to hold a man. I must.

Then she went to the pool to bring them water to have with the food Broken Back had. While she was at the water she listened to the old man talking to her son. Telling the child stories about the woods, about the small animals that live in holes. Stone was laughing. Tree turned to look at them. Broken Back was tickling the infant. She turned back to the pool and dipped a water bag into the dark water. The old man was still talking, laughing a little. A good man, she thought. We are all good, in some way, she told herself. She tried not to think of Crawler. Tried not to try and understand what must be good about him. But she couldn't help it. She kept seeing him coming toward her. Again she felt his arms encircling her, claiming her, pushing her down. Again she felt him on her, and then within her. No, she told herself. I mustn't think of these things. Not now. And then she noticed that the old man's laughter had stopped. There was only the small cooing of her son. She took the bag from the pool. It was full, bulging. She stood and turned back to them. The old man was lying back against the grass, staring into the sky.

A good man, she thought, and tired. He has done so much, for so many summers, and now in his old age he has done such a hard thing for himself. Who could have such strength? She thought of Bear Man. She thought of Archer. Her chest ached and she wanted so desperately for one of them to be there, to hold her, that she clutched the water bag to her chest, closed her eyes, and for a moment allowed herself to believe that one of them, both of them, both of them somehow merged into one man, mixed into one human body, that they were tightly against her, loving her, and that they were never going to leave her. And they never shall, she thought. Somehow, in my thoughts, inside my body and mind they will ever remain. It was true, she knew. And it comforted her to know it.

Then she opened her eyes, relaxed the hold on the bag, and moved toward the old one and her son. She put the water beside the food. Then sat down next to Stone.

"Here is the water, Broken Back," she said.

The old one kept staring into the sky.

"It's good water here. You picked a good place for your retreat, even if you say it was only because you couldn't walk further."

She held Stone and allowed him to nurse her pap.

"I'll prepare some of the food for us in a moment," she told the medicine man. He didn't object, didn't agree. Just stared into the sky, his eyes and face unmoving. Tree looked at him. His face was in the shadow of a tree, but she could see him clearly. Could see his deeply lined skin encasing the deep set, dark, dark eyes that kept staring upward. And then she realized that they were unblinking. And she moved toward him and waved her hand over his face. His eyes were still unblinking. And then she saw the blood on the ground beside him, and then the arrow beneath him.

24

She picked up Stone and started running.

"I'm here," she heard the voice calling. It was Crawler's voice, and in her mind's eye she saw his grin, wide and crooked and leering. "I'm here, Tree. Don't run from me, Tree. You can't run from Crawler." But she ran. Trees were everywhere and seemed to be moving past her, rushing toward the enemy. *Kill him! Kill him! Kill him!* She heard her heart sing the words. *Kill him! Kill him! Kill him!* She felt the rhythm of the song in the motion of her feet pounding against the ground.

And then her feet were tangled in vines. She was struggling to move. Struggling against the song of the vine. *Come down. Come down*, it whispered. *Kill him! Kill him!* sang her heart. *Run! Run! Run!* came another song within her. *Come down*, sang the vine. And she fell, and fell, tumbling, twisting, rolling, doing her best not to fall against her son, not to harm him. And then she was kicking and crawling, pushing herself against a tree. And then she felt her legs, still entangled in the growth of vines, sinking. She felt all the strength going from them, draining into the earth. And she held still, and only listened to all the songs. The windsong. The songs of trees. The song of her child, crying loudly, crying fear-pain, fear-pain. The songs within her. *Run! Be still. Run! Kill! I am a tree*, she sang. *I am a tree*, and she didn't move further. She only listened to the songs.

And then she saw him, moving easily, gliding like a small deer between the trees. Moving toward her like a bit of shadowed wind. Silent except for a whisper. And she saw his face. And she saw his smile. And everything began to be gathering darkness, except his smile.

"I'm here now," she heard him say.

"Don't leave me again," he told her.

"I claim you forever," he was whispering as he walked, glided, floated toward her. A spirit, she thought. It isn't him. It's only a spirit. He's already dead. He's at the cliff. This is only a spirit. A spirit cannot kill.

"I've come," he said, standing above her. And she knew he hadn't died. She knew he was real. She knew that he now would claim her again, and again forever. She could never escape. But I am a tree, she thought. I cannot be taken away. I can be cut down, but I can never be taken away. Not alive. And then she knew he would kill her, as he had killed the *ani soi*, as he had killed Archer, as he had killed the old one. And that then he would kill her fruit. *I am a tree*, she sang, and would not move. And then she saw the great shadow rise up behind him. The shadow of a bear, towering over him, preparing to strike him down. *Yes*, she sang, *kill him. Kill him!* She watched the great arm of the black giant reach around him. She watched the paw strike against him. Strike and strike again. She watched the great head bite into his neck. *Kill him! Kill him!* she sang within. And then she heard her voice, singing aloud the song. And then she saw him still, standing above her. Looking tall, though he was so short, so tiny she had thought. And what had seemed a bear was nothing but shadow. Crawler stood there in the shadow of branches. Nothing killing him. Nothing harming him. Smiling. Laughing at her words. Pulling away his clouts. "You're mine forever," he said. *I am a tree*, she sang, but still her voice cried for his death.

And then she felt him against her once more, smothering her, crippling her, claiming her. And once more she felt his hardness moving against her, trying to force himself within her. And her hand felt another hardness. A hardness at his side. She grasped it. Clutched it. Moved it away from his side, felt the coldness of the stone blade. Moved it between them, and pushed.

He stiffened. She pushed again, deeper. He tried to pull away. She held him with one hand, pushed with the other. Pushed and pushed and then pulled up with the blade, ripping through him, slicing him open, carving him. And all the while her voice cried to kill him, kill him.

25

The song of the child was hunger.

Hunger is the song of all things, she thought.

The song of the child was hunger.

My child is singing his hunger, she told herself. All things are hungry.

The song of the child was hunger. Hunger. Hunger.

I cannot move. I am a tree. I can never move.

The child was crying, hungry. The woman sat leaning against a tree. The evening sky was nearly dark. The child was crying. The woman didn't move. The man, cut open from his groin to his chest lay limp, dead, not hungry ever again, atop her. She didn't move. The child cried.

I am a tree, she told herself. My fruit though is hungry. And from somewhere she found a part of herself and then went searching for more. She slowly began to gather all the songs she heard from within and without. She slowly began to open her eyes once more. She listened to the songs. She listened to their clarity. Hunger. Pain. Ugliness. Fear. And among those sad songs she heard first, safety, then peace, then love, then home. And when her eyes were open she saw where she was. She smelled the blood of the man. She heard her son crying. She saw the darkness gathering in the sky. And through the heavy smell of blood, she caught the thick, heavy scent of the wolves. A pack of them, she thought, and she pushed away the dead man easily and went to her son.

After she fed him and cleaned both him and herself in the pool, she made a fire. She wasn't afraid of the wolves. She knew they would be drawn first to the dead warrior, and that if they were still hungry after that that it wouldn't make any difference, for she would have a strong fire, and they would be afraid of the flames. And so by the light of the fire she began to make a grave for the old one.

It was morning before she was finished. And in the light of the new day she put him into the earth, along with his possessions. And she said all the prayers she knew for the dead. And then she took her son, and started home, as the old one had told her to do. I loved you, she thought to him, and to Bear Man, and to Archer. I loved you. And she wondered if in the spirit world they heard her. And then she looked over her shoulder at her son, riding happily upon her back. "And I love you, little human being," she said. "And I always will."

After a while she started running. Running happily and without fear. Loving the motion. Loving the feel of the wind against her face. Loving the perspiration against her face, down her neck and chest. "I love us all," she said in time to her steps. "I love us all." And she said it again and again until it became a song. *I love everyone. I love everyone.* And she forgave Crawler for his crimes. And she forgave herself. And she forgave Bear Man for dying. And Archer for dying. She hadn't even known that she was angry with them for it, until suddenly the realization came to her.

I've hated them for dying. And just as suddenly she forgave them. *I am a tree*, she sang. *I love my fruit, and I love all things*. And she knew it was true. And she also knew that she didn't understand why. She looked at things and saw only cause for pain and anger and hatred, but instead she forgave, and she loved. *Everyone*, she sang.

By evening she was back at the village. And as she walked the streets, looking at the huts, she realized why she loved them. And something new about who she was. I love them because we are all fruit to each other, she thought. And I love them because I am the woman who loves everyone. And as she passed the hut of the chief she knew what that distinction within herself meant.

26

"He's dead," she told him.

Light Fire stared at his daughter-in-law. Dead? he wondered. The old medicine man dead? And then she told him the story. When she finished, there were tears rolling from his eyes, though he made no sound of crying. The tears simply fell silently, slowly across his face.

More than forty summers I have been in this world, he thought. Will there ever be such sorrows? And thinking once more of his dreams, he knew there would be. He knew that sorrow was only a part of living. That so long as anyone lived in this world, they would find a way to pain, find a path to sorrow. It was the inevitable destiny of human beings that they discover a cause for weeping.

And then he saw that Tree, too, was allowing tears to find their way down her face. And he put aside his concerns and thought for the time about all that she had seen, all that had happened, all her own cause for weeping. Perhaps, he thought, she is more human than any of us. Certainly she has found more reason for sorrow.

And he reached for her and drew her to his chest and held her gently, as a father will hold a daughter, a child. And her tears and crying went on, quietly but surely.

It was late into the night before she stopped. And then she stopped suddenly, as though all the pain had finally left her and there was no longer need for release.

And then she kissed him, not as a daughter, but as a woman. And after that she left.

27

Number One spoke to Number Two.

"She has been with Light Fire."

"Everything proceeds then according to the plan," said Number Two.

"Could it ever have been otherwise?"

"You know as well as I." Number Two smiled at her sister. "There was always the chance that Archer could have lived, or that she would even have accepted the claims of the little man."

"No. You taught her too well."

"That, and your spell on the little man was strong, very strong. She could never have accepted him as we made him become, and if he had failed to kill the other, then we would have found a different way to bring her from him to Light Fire."

"And what now of Light Fire?" asked Number One.

"With Light Fire, no spell will be needed at all."

The One Self is with us and we are with him, they spoke together mind to mind. *The ancient way will be preserved. The seeds of life will once more be pure.*

28

On the seventh night after her return from the woods, after the deaths of Crawler, Archer, and Broken Back, he came to her hut.

"Daughter-in-law," said Light Fire.

"Yes, father?"

He came near her and held her again. A moment later she kissed him again. In his eyes she saw the memory of a long ago woman. "Have you returned then?" he asked, speaking to a memory.

Tree answered. "Yes, dear man," she told him. "I have returned. I'll not leave you again."

Within her there was only a small resistance to the words she spoke. She knew there would be many who would look down on Light Fire for marrying his son's wife. But it would be accepted. There was no blood to keep them apart.

Two days later they were married. All through the ceremony Tree sang in her heart the song of her love for her new husband, for her village, for the People, and most of all for her son. *Stone*, my only child. *Stone*, she sang. *You are the heart of all my joy.*

On her wedding night, after Light Fire was sleeping, she rose and walked to the woods, and then to the river. There she thought of Bear Man and all that had happened since that long ago night with him. She thought of her friend, Number Two. *You have brought me through all of this*, she thought to the woman, wishing that her thoughts could be heard, wishing that she had all the power of the witch to cast her thoughts where she wanted them to fall. You have taught me well. But now I must begin to learn things apart from you. And I must begin to teach them to Stone. We cannot become you. We have our own way to go.

In her hut the sleeping witch heard Tree's voice singing in her dreams. She sang a song that told her that her plan would come to pass, but not as she expected, and that there would only be sorrow in it for her. She woke from the dream and stared into the darkness of the hut. The dream-song had been strong, but already it was fading from her memory. By the time she slept again she had forgotten it entirely.

Tree returned to her sleeping husband and sleeping son. There she watched the two unmoving forms. "I will love you both," she whispered to them. "And I will be good to you." She laid between them and held them each in her arms.

"Nothing can take you from me," she told them.

NEW HUMAN

1

Uweyv. *The River. The Long Human Being.*

River water was used in the preparation of medicines and would heal those who honored and respected it. But it would bring disease to those who treated it poorly, throwing trash into it or urinating in it.

To one who would befriend it the river would grant the gift of a long life.

2

He swam far out into the stream, his small hands moving easily against the current. The sun glistening off the water around him. A breeze shifting first one way and then another across the water's surface. The sound of his swimming small against the day and the world. And then he stopped. And then he vanished.

His mother sat on the shore, watching. She came here with him daily. Teaching him to swim. Teaching him to breathe. Teaching him about his fathers. Teaching him about himself. Teaching him about his brothers and sisters who could only be found at the bottom of the river.

She saw him vanish. In her mind she could see him pulling himself down into the river's depths. Deeper. Deeper until he reached the bottom. Her eyes were shut then, imagining his presence on the river's floor. She felt his hands traveling in search of his brothers and sisters, sifting for them, hoping to find them. And then when it seemed he had been there forever and would never return, she imagined his rise toward the surface. She opened her eyes. A moment later she saw him break the water. His face turned to hers and smiled his gladness. He raised the bag of stones above his head and then started swimming for shore.

Tree laughed with joy for her son. He's growing strong and healthy, she told herself. He will become a great warrior, and someday a great chief.

He came to the shore, stepping out with the water falling freely from his dark, naked body. He's only twelve summers old, she thought, and already his body is gaining the strength and form of a man. He may or may not be the giant his father was, but he will be taller still than any other.

"Mother," said the boy, handing the bag of stones to her. She took them and opened the bag. The boy sat beside her, eager to examine his find. Hoping that there would be the special stones among them. Tree spread the stones out carefully on the ground.

"Tell me the story, Stone," she told him. He

looked up at her. His eyes were clear, dark gems.

"Among the stones of the river," he said, reciting what she had told him again and again, "are special stones. They are my brothers and sisters. They were placed there by my father. It is my duty now to find them and save them, for they are sacred and will bring me and our people great fortune. The black stones are my brothers, the black stones that are smooth and shine like water even when they are dry. The white stones are my sisters, the white stones that are smooth and almost clear, and shine almost like the sun itself." And then he turned his gaze to the spread stones and ran his fingers gently over them. In only a moment his smile was gone. None among those he had brought up were the sacred stones. But he kept his disappointment silent. He gathered the stones carefully in his hands, stood and walked to the edge of earth and water. One at a time he returned the stones to the river, throwing them far away, scattering them far from one another. And as he threw each stone he whispered, "Go home to Unknown. It is your home and it is my friend, this great river."

"There will be other days," Tree told her son. "You will gather other stones."

"Yes, mother," he said. She extended her hand and he took it in his, helping her to stand. She didn't need any help, but his grandfather had taught him to respect his mother, to cherish her. *She is a special woman*, the chief had told the boy. *She is not like other women. Even the warriors revere her*. Stone thought about the words as they

201

returned to the village. How is she special? he wondered. He looked up at her. She was staring ahead. Her lips were moving silently, and Stone knew she was singing to herself one of her many songs. Special? he wondered again.

That night before she put out the small fire in their hut, Stone took the sacred stones from their wooden box. There were two of the black ones and one white one. He caressed them with his fingers, held them to the firelight. Then put them back into the box.

"Take care of them," Tree told him. "They will bless you in your time of need." And then she put out the fire and the two of them climbed beneath blankets, closed their eyes and slept.

Stone didn't know when he was wakened. There were strong arms lifting him. He tried to push them away but his hands were bound. He tried to cry out but something was tied around his face so that he couldn't see or speak. *Mother!* his thoughts cried. *Mother!* And then he could tell that whoever carried him was moving swiftly. But he had no idea where he was being taken or who was his captor. And all his thoughts were for the woman, wondering if she too had been captured, or worse, if she were dead. And though his eyes were covered, the cover couldn't stop the tears that forced themselves out until he realized that he was crying. Then he made the tears stop. Made himself think. I must escape, he thought. And then I must find my mother. And then I must kill whoever has done this to us.

He had lost all sense of time. He had no idea if it was still night, if it was day, or if the night had come again. He could only feel himself clenched in strong arms, jostled, tossed. After what had seemed forever the captor had stopped and put him on the ground. Then after what had seemed only a moment Stone realized he was being carried again. He had fallen to sleep while lying on the ground and so he had no idea how long he had lain there. Another forever later the captor stopped again and again put the boy on the earth. This time Stone forced himself to stay awake. He listened. Speak, he thought. Reveal something of yourself. But there came no voice.

The rest may have been minutes or it may have been hours. Blinded and weary, Stone had lost his judgment about time. But he hadn't lost his need for water and food. He wasn't terribly hungry. But water, he told himself. I need to drink. He thought of the great river Unknown. How I wish I were there, he thought. And then his thoughts went again to the woman who would wait for him while he searched for the sacred stones of his brothers and sisters. And he wanted to call to her. He wanted to go to her but there was only the forsaken, complete and unbreakable darkness of his eyes and silence of his mouth, and stillness of his arms and hands. If only I could see, he shouted inside. If only I could speak! If only I could put my hands around the neck of the one who has done this! And there was a tightness in his chest that he didn't understand. A tightness greater than the one that came when he had stayed a long while at the bottom of the river. And it made him want to breathe, but he was already breathing, so there was nothing he could do to ease the hard tightness he felt.

He thought of himself in the river at night, flowing down, down to the black depths. This is somewhat like that, he thought. This is somewhat like the pressure of the deepest waters. The deepest waters? he asked himself. Neither he nor his mother had ever ventured to the deepest waters. *They are too deep*, she had assured him. *No one can go there. Monsters may live on those bottoms. Giant black fish that would eat men.* She had always laughed when she told him these things, but when he would start to laugh with her she would always cover her face with a sudden sadness and look far upstream at a tall cliff that rose above the river. And so he would stop his laughter and wonder what the river's depths and monsters could have to do with the high cliff.

His thoughts returned to himself and the darkness that now surrounded him. It is like the dark waters, he thought. And so he slowly drew in his breath and held it, and imagined that the jostling of his captor was the turbulence of river current. Imagined himself sinking down into the familiar, cool, welcoming nest of water, stone, and mud. Home, he thought. Home with my brothers and sisters. And my mother, Tree, is waiting for me safely on the shore.

When he could stay down, as he imagined, no longer, he thought himself up toward the surface. Thought himself rising easily, gladly, a gathering of stones in his bag, a gathering of pride in his heart. He rose and watched the water grow lighter, watched it seem to thin as he came nearer the surface, and then watched it break away from before his eyes and he was staring at the sun, splashing water, sucking air.

And then he was back again, bound and blinded. And so he drew his breath once more and repeated the imagined ritual.

After ten times he still knew the reality of his situation, but what he imagined had become just as vivid if not more so than his bonds. This will keep me calm, he said. This will keep me rested. This will keep me in control, so when I am released I will be strong and able to fight them. And then he submerged himself once more in the illusion of water and downward motion, and after another ten times *it* seemed the reality, and that he was bound and blinded and being carried to some unseeable destination by an unseeable captor seemed the imagining. And he drank freely the river's water and was never thirsty. And though he couldn't see it and had no way of knowing, the sun ascended over the horizon for the second time since he was taken.

4

Oni Saquu. Last One.

Her father, Happened, and her mother, White
Box, had named their last child, a daughter, The
Last One, *Oni Saquu.* She was a child out of
season, when White Box was already an old
woman with her hair turning white as the box of
her name. And the pain of the birth and the in-
convenience of raising another infant and child
during the years that should have left her free to
work lightly and to gossip with her friends had
made her bitter, bitter toward herself, and toward
her husband, and toward Last One, the innocent
intruder.

Happened saw the bitterness and tried to make
up for it by cradling his daughter with extra
boughs of love. But his eyes were old and his arms
were tired, and he knew that he was failing, and
that there was nothing for him to do.

Happened was a chief of the *Ani Wayah*, the
Wolf Clan. *Nulistanv*, Happened. His full name
was The Man Who Made It Happen, or The Man
It Happened To. When he was a boy he had alone
saved his village from destruction at the weapons
of northern enemies, the *Ani Tsunoyeni*, the Hand
People. He had hidden well in the woods and one
by one had killed an entire war party of thirty warriors. All in a single night's cunning. Now, an old
man, he was chief of that village. A small, in-
consequential gathering of the People, he thought,
nested quietly away in the north of our lands. For

too many seasons to recall the north clans had kept at war with their enemies. But Happened's village was too small for serious fighting, and since a mere boy had so easily killed so many of its enemies the Hand People and others had thought it best to leave the town alone. So, mostly, the town lived in peace. And perhaps that is a part of our sadness, he thought. The young men of the village grew to become warriors, but always necessarily went elsewhere to practice those arts.

These were the concerns of Happened, who was husband of White Box, who was chief, who was an old friend to another chief, Light Fire, and who was father of Last One. These were his concerns on the day that his daughter left him and her People, and began the journey that would lead her first to another youth named Stone, and then to herself, and then to a land and place and time beyond the walking and hunting of the Principal People.

Far away Stone was carried in darkness.

Last One was kneeling in the sun, washing clothes, and lamenting the work of women. She hated such work and wanted to scream at it and to scream at the one who made her do it, her mother.

"Where is your smile?" her mother asked, laughing. The old woman always laughed while coaxing her daughter to labor.

"My smile is floating downstream," Last One told her. "I let it fall into the water while I was washing these," and she began to hand her father's clothes to the old woman.

Washing clothes was easy enough work. There was little of it to do, except when her mother would make her do it for others, for friends-in-need. It was the farming, the making of clothes, the preparing of food, the assisting of women, friends-in-need, who were over-ripe with children about to jump down, the doing this, that and everything else that women must do that angered, frustrated, and overpowered her. It overpowered her because there was nothing she could do about it.

She was a woman. She was nearly eleven winters old. Any day now, she told herself, I will start bleeding. And then they will start looking for a man to be my husband, and within a winter or two *I'll* be the over-ripe one, and I'll be caught forever. Caught forever and never a way to escape. Never a way to be free, to be myself, to discover who or what I am.

No, she thought, *it won't happen that way*. She had thought again and again about what she would do. Perhaps, she thought, perhaps today.

White Box helped her hang the clothing to dry. Fine clothing, thought Last One. Her father's clothing. As fine as any warrior ever wore. Now he was an old man, a warrior no more. It was hard for her to imagine that once this dark and gray warrior had been lean and strong and able to slip through the night and the woods with more grace than a shadow. But he had, she told herself. Staring past the wet garments to the hut where the old man waited, she thought again, he once was that, and so I shall become.

Women do not become warriors, something within her whispered. Women become women, laborers, mothers, wives. That is all. And they die fat, never knowing what more they might find in this world before returning to the spirit land.

She watched a group of young hunters walking from the village, off to stalk game, she thought. Off to be men. Off to discover who and what they are and what this world is about. What this world is. They will find what they search for, she thought, because they search. She wanted to run after them, to call out to them that she would join them. But such an absurdity would only gain her laughter and jeers. No, she thought. I cannot do that. But she knew what she could do.

White Box left her to visit with a needy friend, and Last One went to their hut. There she found her old father, sleeping. You sleep a slumber of discontent, she thought of him, listening to his snoring. Like the wind, old man, she thought, but wondered if it wasn't only her own discontent that she heard.

She closed her eyes and imagined wind, trees, wilderness, a breathing of animals, trees and earth. She imagined herself days away from the village and any other village. She thought herself in the heart of the Principal People's country, searching for all the meanings and truths that eluded her while she wasted away entrapped in the life of the village. I will find those truths, she promised herself, when I search for them.

She opened her eyes. Her father was still sleeping. Her mother was still gone. There was only the sound of windy snoring. Through that came the quiet of perfect silence. It was silence unlike natural silence that one often hears, or doesn't hear. It was the silence of all the great unknown things that she knew were awaiting discovery.

She let her eyes trace the walls of the hut. I can't stay here, she knew. This isn't true. This isn't right. I can't be this way.

She walked across the hut. She gathered together bow, arrows, quiver, axe and knife. All her father's. Thank you, old one, she thought to him kindly. She gathered dried food. She put all of these things neatly in a bundle. Last she added breech clouts.

She walked to the doorway of her home. There she turned, lingering a moment. "Thank you, father," she said to the sleeping man, her lips making the words without a trace of audible sound. And then she was gone.

When she was gone Happened opened his eyes. He slowly turned and looked about the hut, noting all that she had taken. Good-bye, daughter, he thought. Then he again closed his eyes.

When White Box returned she went to her husband and shook him roughly. "Where is she?" she asked. "I've work for her. Where is our daughter?"

Happened again opened his eyes. He didn't move. He felt all his age gathered in his stomach and weighing him down, not wanting him ever to move again. I'm dying, he realized. So much to happen in one day, he thought. He stared at the woman. He had seen her face for more seasons than he could now remember. He knew her face better than he knew his own hands. Then he turned to the empty place where his bow had been, his bow and his other weapons. Should I have stopped her? he wondered. He thought about it only a moment, then easily gave up the question for other thoughts. He recalled the songs of his youth. He looked again at his wife.

"Our young men go elsewhere to learn the art of war," he told her quietly.

"Where is our daughter?" she asked again.

Happened closed his eyes and refused to listen to the woman's questions. He was listening instead to the breathing of his enemies as he crept to them, one by one, and sent them to the land of spirits. He wondered if they would be glad to meet the young one who had so cleverly ended their tales.

5

"Where is she, Light Fire?" asked Number Two. "Where have she and the boy gone to?"

"They are gone," he said, staring past the woman, wanting to ignore her questions, wanting to not hear them. But he couldn't. They were his own questions. Where are they? Where have they gone?

"We must find them!" she said.

"Tree has often gone away for days," said the chief. "She has often done it without telling me. I never know where she goes. She isn't like other women."

"But I always know where she goes. I always know," the witch said.

"And how do you know?" he asked, looking at her for the first time.

The witch turned away, gazed across the village to the nearby hills. She waved her hand against the sky. "I know," she said. She wouldn't say more.

"Go away, witch," said Light Fire.

"We should search for her," she said. "She may come to harm, otherwise I would know where she has gone."

The chief said nothing.

"We have enemies yet," she told him. "Enemies to the south. Have they forgotten their young warriors who perished here twelve summers ago? And we have enemies sometimes here," she said, half smiling and sweeping her gaze across the village.

"Yes," he said, staring straight into her eyes. "I know we sometimes have enemies here. Sometimes right before us. Sometimes." He smiled as she ground her teeth at him. "But we never know when," he said.

He turned and walked away from her. Then he stopped and faced her again. "Work none of your magic on me, Number Two. I know others that I trust who can turn your magic to dust."

"I have no evil for you," she said. "And you

are a fool if you trust anyone." Then she spat at the sky. Her spittle was ugly and dark, but watching it Light Fire saw that it seemed to vanish in the air. When he lowered his gaze again to the witch she had already walked away and was out of sight.

Witches! he thought, and started away to his hut. And wives! he told himself. He thought it strongly but sadly, remembering the seasons. Either they leave you in their youth to return to the spirit land. Or they leave you in their youth to take your son again and again to the woods. Teaching him as boys must be taught, but teaching him herself instead of having him learn alongside other warriors. And why have I allowed it? He thought about that, seeking an answer to a question he had asked himself again and again. I have allowed it because I do not own her. Because I do not own the boy. I allow it because I know she has taught him far more than any other young one could know. I allow it because I would allow her anything. I allow it because I love her, and there is no one like her. There never has been. And now there is no one like her son. There has never been that either. They are something apart from the rest of us.

And then he stopped and turned to face the village. He half closed his eyes, and dimly could see the flames. They weren't the flames of twelve summers ago. They were the flames of tomorrow, of some tomorrow that he could not foretell. And in the midst of them, and yet far from them he saw the strange pale Others, and he saw Stone standing naked before them.

What is it about? he wondered. And where are you? he asked Tree. Where are you? and he ached to have her near.

6

They had planned for years. Their formula had been carefully prepared. Day by day, season by season they had laid precisely each element in place. They had taught Tree all the things she needed to know so that she would raise a son ripe for their harvesting, a son who would take Number Two's daughter as his wife against all the taboos of his people. They had offered her their knowledge, and their friendship, and their love. But behind it all was their constant purpose. Their conjured formula for power was the intent and root of all their deeds. And now she was gone, and the boy, Stone, was gone.

We must find her, thought the one, the eldest.

Yes, came the thought of the other, a whisper thought heard only by her sister.

She has been captured by an enemy who seeks to destroy our plan, said the first, her mind speaking to her twin as only twins who are witches can speak to one another.

The second witch thought about that. She thought about Tree and Stone and all the days and nights she had spent with them. She knew the woman well. And she knew how complete her learning had become. There were many things of witchcraft Tree had learned, and inevitably, thought the witch, she has brought herself to her learning and so has learned things that weren't taught by us. *No*, she replied to her sister. *She has discovered us. She knows our purpose, and she has rebelled against it. She has taken the boy from us.*

The voices of mind stopped. The women were women who were not in sight of each other, but were moving together, through woods, along paths that only they had traveled. They were moving to a small clearing that had often been their place of meeting, the place where they combined their powers and invoked their wills. Then, *I am here*, said the first.

Ah, you are indeed, said the second. They each stepped into the clearing, smiling, comforted by the other's presence. They moved to each other and held still in a silent embrace. Each of them could feel the other's fear at the danger to their work. It seemed all their lives had been spent in preparation for a magic that was threatened with being dispelled.

"We shall find her, and we shall have the boy," said Number Two.

"And what of Tear Maker?" asked Number One.

"She is cared for. Nothing can take Tear Maker from us. She is the best prepared of all. If Tree has turned against us, so be it, but Tear Maker and Stone are ours."

"Then we must go after her now. She has been gone too long already."

The sisters kept their embrace, held each other more tightly. They pressed their heads and bodies together as tightly as they could, closing their eyes to the world and reaching out from their minds. They began their search.

They stood still in the strange embrace while clouds first covered the sun, and then revealed it, again and again. They stood in the statue pose while the wind carried its music through the trees; while birds flew and landed and flew again. They saw none of that. They were seeking a trace of the woman and the boy, a recent trace of them, an echo of her having passed.

It was dark when they found what they wanted and released each other. But what they found wasn't a trace of the woman. It was the boy.

"She has not only discovered us," said Number One, "she has discovered how to disguise herself against us."

"That can't be done," said Number Two. "There is only One Self." She paused. "She can't hide from the Center Being. We have sought through the One Self to hear her. She can't hide from that."

"Perhaps she has learned more than we know to teach."

"It isn't possible, I say. It can't be done. There is only One Spirit."

"Perhaps the Spirit hides her," said Number One.

"But not the boy?"

"The boy is ours."

"Yes," said Number Two. Then, "Now we must run. We must find him and claim him."

One after the other they ran, moving like night beasts through the trees, following the echo of Stone's thinking.

He is afraid, thought Number One.

That is because she has stolen him. He is ours and she has made him her enemy.

7

On the fourth morning he was again put down. A few moments later he felt water flowing over his face, soaking through his blindfold, seeping into his mouth. At first he thought he was drowning. He thought he was in the river and that he had opened his mouth and breathed in the water while in the depths. And then understanding came and he sucked at the water, trying eagerly to drain as much as possible into his throat.

He could hear his captor walking toward him. Then he felt more water and sucked again. He wasn't sure if it was the first water he had been given or not. He couldn't remember when he might have actually had drink and when it might have only been the incantation of his imagined ritual in the river.

All his body ached, but nothing more than his

hands and wrists. They were swollen and throbbing.

Then he felt the hands grasping him again. He tried to kick and roll away. It was useless. In a moment he was in the arms. And then he was bent over a shoulder. And the captor was off again, running.

Running, thought Stone. How could he run so far, so long? He knew that running was more than just an exertion of strength and endurance. It was a sacred ritual, if done properly. His mother had taught it to him. It was a mystery few understood. Yet he understood. But to run and carry someone his size? he thought. How could a human being have such power? A human being couldn't, he concluded.

That was the first time he considered that his captor might be something more than human. Might be a great bear, he thought. But the scent, he told himself. This isn't the scent of a bear. And then he realized something he hadn't realized before. There was no scent, or at least he couldn't smell one. And so it occurred to him that it might be a spirit. And then he became afraid. How can one fight a spirit? he wondered.

8

The light of day fell through the leaves in silver-haze pillars that seemed to hold up the forest. The girl walked between trees, through the pillars of light, across long fallen and broken leaves. Her old world was behind her. There was a newness in everything around her that made her feel neither old nor young nor inbetween, but simply ageless and apart from all earthly concern. Almost she thought she was in the land of spirits, her peace was so complete.

When she had left the village Last One had been half afraid, half eager. But the further she traveled away, the more the fear went, was left behind with all the constraints that caused it. But interestingly, she thought, the eagerness had gone too. It had been replaced with a calm, a calm that told her she was coming home. That all was well within her.

Everywhere around her were the songs of life and magic that always accompany and orchestrate nature, that are nature, the natural world, the world that already her people, and all people, had departed from, become separate from. Certainly they sought to regain it, to regain themselves within it. They always failed. Only a few ever drew near their home, the earth, near enough to once more be one with its other children, their kindred the animals and plants that were everywhere.

And though her training wasn't that of a warrior, she had been trained much in the ways of plants and animals. She knew the trees and knew the flowers—the white ones, the red-white ones, the purple, the blue, all of them—and she knew what she could eat and what was good medicine. No child of the People grew without learning all these things. No child, not even a girl-child, grew without learning to use a bow, a knife, an axe. The difference came when they grew near the age of womanhood. Then they were taken away from the things of men. They were never allowed to hunt. And they were confined to village and fields, while men only were allowed to roam their land. Men only were allowed to sleep with it, to dream with it. Men only and witches, she thought. But she wasn't a witch, and was glad for it, because no witch she had ever known had been a happy human being, no matter how wildly they had laughed to feign happiness. No witch had been serene. No witch she knew played games with children.

But now I am home, she told herself. Now I am where I have always wanted to be. And in her heart there wasn't even the barest missing of that place she had been taught so long to call home, that place of smoke and voices and rituals that emulate the form of the natural world but deny the power thereof.

Home, she thought, smiling as she walked but unaware of the smile on her lips. Unaware of the lightness in her step. Unaware of her own peace because everything else was so consuming, so captivating, and she wasn't able to distinguish any of it from herself.

When she came to a stream, she stopped. There

she found a still pool. She stared into it, catching her reflection. And while staring at herself she slowly began to put aside the bundle she carried. And then, slowly, slowly, she removed her skirt of deerskin. And then her drape. She then took the breech-clout from the bundle and put it on. It was a little large, but she was able to make it snug around her waist. Her breasts were still small enough not to be cumbersome for her. She donned the weapons. The quiver and arrows and bow across her shoulders and against her back. The knife and axe at her hips. The pouch of food beside the knife.

She took the knife and cut a strip from her skirt. This she tied as a band around her brow to keep her hair from her face. Then she tied another strip around the length of her hair behind her neck. Then she looked again into the pool.

Last One was gone. A young warrior stood in her place.

"I name you *Itse Yvwi*," she said to the image in the water. New Human.

Then she tied her old clothes into a bundle, wasting nothing, bid farewell to the stream, and headed again to the southwest, where she knew there to be a few settlements of the Principal People.

As she walked away she was unaware of the eyes watching her.

9

Tear Maker watched the morning sun.

Where is my mother gone? she wondered.

The sun moved and no longer touched the horizon.

Where is my aunt gone? Where are my friends Tree and Stone?

Her mother, the witch, had sent her to stay with the old woman Wood Chip. And then she was gone, almost as mysteriously as Tree and Stone had vanished. And her mother's sister, Number One, had vanished with her.

She thought of the women, alone in the wilderness. She wasn't afraid for them. She knew the witches could take care of themselves. She could take care of herself. She hadn't been raised as a witch—they had taught her of other purposes for her life—but she knew how to take care of herself. She understood the ways of medicine, magic, and nature. She was already twelve summers. Only one moon ago she had started to bleed. In another moon she would go through the ritual of becoming a woman. But it will be a while yet, she realized, before I marry. Not until my warrior is ready. Not until he is a warrior. Not until he is a man.

She thought of the boy, tall, lean and strong. Only twelve summers old himself. And yet her mother had promised her that there would never be another like him. And that he had been prepared for her. Stone, she thought. And she knew he was special, and it took no urging for her to desire him. She had grown up with him, had played with him, had gotten into troubles with him, had bathed with him—though not for two summers—and had loved him since she could remember. But she had never spoken of their marrying. Her mother had forbidden her to do so. No one else knows, she had been told. No one must yet know, or it will be spoiled.

It seemed an impossible thing. Clans do not marry within each other. But her mother had promised it, so she believed. And now she wondered where he was, what need had taken him and his mother, and her mother and aunt away. And she watched for them, hoping they would return. It was the fifth morning since Tree and Stone had vanished.

10

Her burden was heavy. She had slept little in four days. She had walked often. Mostly she had run, always carrying her burden. The boy. Her son.

The burden wasn't only his weight. It wasn't even mostly his weight. Mostly it was the knowledge of his extreme discomfort. No doubt he suffered more even than she. Yet she felt it had to be done. So she did it.

She had never run so far or so long in her life. And she had certainly never carried such a load, and not merely a heavy one, but one that often wrestled for its freedom. And yet she had done it. And she felt proud of herself for it. And happy for her son. It was the only way she could give him what she knew he needed.

She had prepared herself well for the tasks. For weeks she had made her body ready. But what had been more important than that had been the preparation of her mind and spirit. For it all to work right she had to become something more than herself, and something different. Part of her had to turn against the boy, part of her had to hate him and want to injure him. And so she had learned to alter the pattern of her thoughts, and had learned to inwardly become someone else. It was someone who suited her needs for this purpose, but it was someone she hated and never wanted to meet, and wanted to never be again.

And then she had prepared the lotion that took away her scent and left her with no scent at all. Everything to confuse the child—the almost man. When he returns, she knew, he will be a man. Twelve summers old, the youngest warrior, and the greatest.

She stopped and gazed at the eastern horizon. The sun was low in the sky. The fifth morning since their departure. A chill came to her through the air and she began to shake. I'm getting tired, she thought, more tired now than I can bear. It is time.

She walked a few more steps. Then put her

burden down for the last time. Carrying him so far had depleted her. She would only have enough strength to get away if she rested. So once more she took the water bag mixed with the potion that had subdued the boy, and she poured it over his face, knowing it would put him again to sleep. Then she walked away from him, laid down on the ground, and slept. Not a comfortable, relaxed sleep. That would come later. She slept only enough to give her body the rest she had to have before she started home.

Before sleep came to her she heard for the thousandth time the muffled cries of her son. Tears came to her eyes as she listened, but she didn't move to comfort him. Eventually the cries stopped, and he was still. In her dreams she dreamt of the river and its enveloping depths. The peace. The sureness. And yet the control of danger. She knew that the river had been her son's constant companion the past days. It was why she had taught him to swim there in its depths, not for sacred stones, but for the sacred companionship of a power that would always stay with him and would bring him through any trial. That was what she hoped for and believed in. When he returns, if he returns, she started to think sadly—no, when he returns, I will see that what I have taught him was good. And then her dream took her to a cliff and she could see a tall young warrior with bow in hand flying away and then falling down and down. And then behind her she felt the presence of a dark, waiting monster. And then the dream ended.

11

Light Fire walked to his second hut. It was his wife's hut. She told him when they married that she had to have a place of privacy for herself. He had never heard of such a thing, but he gave it to her. The village had been outraged and had told him he was making a mistake to give a woman such a thing. He had forbidden them then to speak of it again.

He came to the hut, pulled aside the deerskin and walked in. Of course it was empty. He knew it would be. She had been gone for five days with the boy. There was no way to know when she would return. He didn't fear for her, or for the boy. They can well care for themselves, he thought. But he did fear for himself. He feared because as the years had passed he had come to love the woman more and more, and everything else had become second to her for him. And yet as the years passed she had moved further and further from him and nearer and nearer to her son, his grandson that he had wanted to raise as his own son. She hadn't allowed that, though. She had taught him all the things that he might have taught Stone. She had taken him where he might have taken the boy, as she had done now. He knew that she was already taking him through the rites of manhood, the passage between being a child to becoming a warrior. He wondered if this journey she had taken him on now was like the others. Is she teaching him to hunt? Is she teaching him the songs of the forest? He couldn't know.

He sat down in her hut. About him were her belongings. They all reminded him of her. The hut smelled of her, felt of her. And suddenly more than any other thing he wanted merely to talk with her, to again hear her voice. To listen to the words of wisdom he knew she would speak. He wanted to scream from not hearing her. But he held still and didn't scream, didn't speak, didn't whisper. He only breathed quietly. And after a while he put his head down upon her bed, closed his eyes and pretended she was there beside him.

It was late into the night when he rose and left the hut. The pretending had only made things worse, he told himself. "Come back," he whispered to the night, and his voice had a thin edge sharp as a knife.

12

The two witches stood before the midnight fire, staring into its maze of light and shadow.

"It's her, I say," said Number Two. "I know her. I know her better than you, better than she knows herself. I don't know how she's done it but she has disguised her scent, and altered her spirit. That's why our minds can't find her. But she is with the boy. It's her."

"And why has she done all this, if she has done it?" asked Number One. "So that she could escape us? Because she discovered our purpose and decided to rebel against us instead of coming to us with her discovery as we would have thought she would? It doesn't seem likely. Why not then disguise the boy? She knew we would follow him. She knew, that is, if she is running from us."

"She must be!"

"Perhaps," said Number One, "you don't know her as well as you believe. Certainly if she has done these things, then neither of us has known her so well, and she has exceeded, at least in part, her teachers."

"That worries me more than anything."

"And I think it should. If this is her, and I think you're right about that part—though we could be wrong—then it doesn't really matter why she has done these things. If she opposes us that makes matters more urgent. Nevertheless, we can't have her above us. Either she serves us, or she serves no one, not even herself."

The firelight was fading. Number Two knelt before the flames and put her hands over them. "Then we must find her and do that which must be done," said the witch.

"Yes," said her sister, "that which must be done."

For a moment Number Two thought of the years and all the moments she had spent with Tree, and what the woman had meant to her, their closeness, their sharing. And then with a single controlled thought she removed it all from her mind and faced the dark reality of what must be done. The boy must be theirs. He must be in their control. Nothing else would do. And Tree would have to die.

13

When he woke his eyes opened onto darkness. He was on the ground. His bonds were removed. And the only sounds were the songs of forest night.

He didn't move, only stared into the black. His body was numb. His mind was numb. For a moment he remembered nothing of what had been happening to him. He tried to move and couldn't. Why can't I move, he wondered. And then he remembered that he was tied. He tried to move again and through the numbness he felt his hands touching each other. There was no cord binding his wrists together. I am free, he thought. And the numbness began to ebb away and in its place came aching. He stared up into the black sky, and with each new pain his eyes also grew accustomed to their new freedom and gradually the light of stars was visible.

He thought about the time he had spent being carried. He thought back to his mother. He recalled his thoughts of the river, and he knew it was

the river that had kept him alive. It was his thinking about it, burying himself in it, allowing
himself to be swallowed by it rather than by the
defeat his captor sought to impose. He then recalled all his plans of what he would do once free.
He thought of how he had planned to kill those
who had done this to him. But now he lay still,
weak, hungry, hardly able to move. Shall I die? he
wondered. Now that I am free again, shall I die?

From the night he listened to the song of an
owl, an echo song that sounded far away but was
near, he knew. It was one of the first songs his
mother had taught him many seasons ago. Hearing it heartened him. I will not die, he told
himself. I will survive. I will find my mother. I will
return to our people. I will stay alive and nothing
will stop me. And I'll find those who have done
this, and I will destroy them. With the owl still
singing, he forced himself to stand. His legs
trembled and were uncertain. Be still! he commanded them, and he held his thighs with his
hands, giving them support.

On the breeze came the scent of water. A
stream, he thought, and slowly began to move
toward it.

The stream was near, and the closer he came the
louder came the song of the owl. And as Stone
knelt to cup water to his mouth, he silently gave
thanks to the bird for the song of hope it had sung
him. And then the song ceased. He heard the brief
folding of great wings against the night air. And
then he returned to the water, cold, dark and
delightful. The essence, *ulisgediv*, he thought, of

life. That is what the water is.

14

Tree watched her son as he came to the stream. She watched him kneel there. Watched him cup the water to his lips. And then she stopped her song of the night bird. She made the sounds of its wings taking it to flight. And then she turned, knowing that all was set, and she started home. Join me soon, she thought to her son. Learn what there is here for you to learn, and then return to me.

15

New Human lay unmoving and read the night sky, stories from the stars. They told her of the first things, the first animals, the first trees, the first rivers, and the first people. Those stars which told of the first people were the youngest stars because human beings were the last of all things that the Great One had made.

The stars held knowledge of all things beneath them, for they were the record of all things, and all things had come from them. This is what they taught me, she thought. This is what they taught and so it must be true. Would they have taught it if it were a lie? She no longer wanted to live among them, but it wasn't because they were liars, she thought. They never lied. Especially her parents never lied. Most especially her mother. Perhaps that is why I have left them even, because they never lie, because all things are so certain and true and irrefutable to them. But what if the tales are untrue only they don't know it? Then they wouldn't be lying. But they would be wrong, and isn't that just as good as a lie? But if they are wrong, then what is the truth? Does anyone know? Can anyone know?

She sat up and brought her knees to her chest. Around her were the sounds of the woods, the night, the earth. She heard them as she had never heard them before. Each one came distinct and clear from the others. The insects scratching. Birds calling, whistling, cooing. Wind whispering to trees. Trees whispering to wind. In the center of it all, her own breath and heart-beat whispering to her ears, churning within her, beating constantly, evenly, without a voice calling the rhythm, but in a rhythm just as steady as the motion of the stars. And so she watched the stars, watched those that fell and wondered at the various tales told of the meaning of a star that falls. Which of them is true? she wondered, knowing that they couldn't all be true, that two couldn't be true, that only one could be true. But which? Any? She considered that. Perhaps none of the tales were true.

And then she thought that perhaps somehow all the tales were true even though they contradicted each other. Who knows? she asked herself again and again. But the only answer that came was the sound and motion of the night. She listened to that then, thinking that perhaps it held the answers to her questions. Whether I ever find the answers, she told herself, at least I am free to search for them. And she knew she would never be returning to the world of human beings. I am New Human, she thought. And I am old human. I am New because there are no others like me. I am old because I will learn all the old ways. The ways of humans before they forgot where they came from, before the tales got mixed and multiplied, before they learned to differ from the earth. And then she heard the sounds of night alter. She heard among them a sudden silence, and with the silence the small quick sound of a footstep. Then it was gone. Its owner had been careless, but not for long. Long enough though to warn New Human. She didn't need to hear the sound again to know that she had been found. Who has come after me? she wondered. She gathered her belongings and moved quietly away. Come follow me if you will, she thought, and she tightened her grip on the handle of her knife.

The trees were thick, and thick brush made it difficult for New Human to move. Her pursuer had retreated into silence. Her own flight, a breath of quiet on the night, carried her, she thought, away from the intruder. Who could it be, she wondered. But it didn't matter. If it was friend or family, she had renounced them, she told herself. If it was an enemy, then all the worse and all the more reason to make away. Nevertheless, making away might prove more difficult, she realized, than merely gathering her possessions and moving into the night. It didn't occur to her that the footstep she had heard had been anything other than what she recognized it for. There are the sounds of nature and of animals, and there are the sounds of human beings. What she heard had been unmistakable. And now I flee, she thought.

Her knife was small security. She had never fought with one, or with anything else. Women and girls were taught little of fighting. That was a man's province. She knew how to use it for butchering, though. And that familiarity with the weapon consoled her. Had it been day, she would have felt safer. An enemy seen seems less dangerous than one which is hidden in shadow. And she knew well how to use her bow and arrow. But she didn't know what skills and weapons her pursuer had. And just as the shadows hide him, she thought, so they hide me.

She began a slight ascent. At the crest of a hill before her she could see the night sky, pale against the tree tops. She kept walking. When the brush and trees thinned she hurried her step, knowing that whoever was behind her would undoubtedly be following. He has probably followed me from the village, she thought, and isn't about to stop. She wondered how she could get away, and what she could do to defend herself if she encountered him. She thought of the pursuer as *him*, but realized it could be a woman. Or, she supposed, it could be a personage of spirit. That thought chilled her. She had never met a spirit, but had heard many stories from people who had. Not all spirits are men or women, she had been told in one tale after another. Some are neither man nor woman. Some are both. Some are not human, some are part human and part animal. But she didn't place a lot of belief in spirits, having never seen one. And she doubted that any woman would be after her. So she considered the follower a man and thought of him as such. And that seemed more frightening, though less chilling, than the thought of a spirit.

The skyline above the hill grew nearer and darker. It was important to move quietly, but also important to move quickly. Nevertheless, she knew that no speed would save her if she made sounds that would give away her position. So when it came to a choice between speed and silence, she chose silence.

She was tired and that made everything harder. She had already been traveling long hours before she had made her bed for the night. When she had stopped at sunset her load of belongings had gotten so heavy that it wearied her to carry them. The weapons and goods no longer seemed like a part of her, no longer seemed natural and in place. Now they seemed like great weights and alien things that slowed her escape and endangered her. She thought of dropping them and moving along without their encumbrance. No, she told herself. I mustn't do that. If I do that then *he* has already won. She tried to quieten her breathing and kept moving. A moment later she was standing in the middle of an open glade at the top of a hill.

She stopped suddenly and turned round and round, staring into the darkness of the surrounding forest. He's out there, she realized, watching me. She wondered how she could have let herself walk into the open. She had no idea how tired she was.

Why doesn't he come after me? Why doesn't he speak? Her chin started to shudder. She wanted to put down her burden and rest on the ground. Still she stood, staring into the unknown. No sound came except the sounds of wind and trees. Not even birds or insects sang. There was a breeze against her back carrying only the natural scents of the woods. Nothing of man. But the silence itself was a scent, she knew, a voice telling her that he was there, waiting, watching. Waiting for what? Why doesn't he do what he has come to do? She held the knife more tightly, wondering what it was he had come for, why he had followed her. And suddenly the vision and thought of home seemed something warm and good. It seemed a place she wanted to be, but she knew more than ever that whatever happened, she would never return to that place. It was a place behind her. The people there were no more than ghosts. She would never return. And with that thought she spat angrily at the black trees and the unseen waiting figure. She turned and continued across the glade. A moment later she was again in the trees, and then was descending. Come at me, she thought, feeling brave but not knowing why. Her grip on the knife seemed certain in her hand and mind. Come, she thought. I wait for you.

By the time she reached the bottom of the hill, she was frightened again. The closeness of the trees, wondering if he was waiting behind each next one, and the now and then sound of her own footsteps in leaves or twigs. And each time she made a sound, no matter how small, thinking she had heard him also, but not being certain of it. It all conspired against her, twisted her, turned her against herself. What am I doing here? she wondered, but the answer to her question was dark and hidden and couldn't be heard, like the pursuer.

She was starting up another hill when she came to the cave, small and darker than any other part of the night. She had to get onto her hands and knees and crawl to get into it. She didn't go far before she decided that it was too deep for her to explore. So she stopped, slowly managed to turn about, and then leaned against the rock wall. It was cool and moist against her back. She still held the knife, pointing it toward the gray patch of darkness that was the mouth of the cave. She wanted to call out to him, to scream at him that she was waiting. To command him to come now and confront her. But instead she remained silent, and unmoving. After a while the gray patch became a pale shadow, distinct against the interior of her hiding place. Is he coming? she asked silently. No answer came. The only sound was her own quiet breathing. Come, she thought. Let's end this. No one came. No sound. Nothing. Perhaps I imagined it all, she thought. But the memory of the foot fall was clear and real. Nothing had been imagined, she knew. Come, she thought again, tightening her clasp on the handle of the knife. Still nothing, and still nothing later when her eyes shut and her head leaned against the cold, damp stone, and the knife fell to the floor of the cave.

She knelt at the creek that flowed through her village. Her mother stood over her, instructing her in the manners of all women. This is what you must learn, the woman told her, it is the way of the Principal People. It always has been and always will be. She didn't want to listen. In her hands were the clothes of their family. She saw then that she was a very young girl. I was here long ago, she thought; now I am here again. The mother talked on and on, but the child could no longer hear her. For only a moment she saw the woman's voice moving in silent gesture. And then she saw the boys running. They ran through the village, between huts, around them, in and out of them, and then across the shallows of stream, splashing, running, jumping. They are running to be men, she told herself. I am kneeling to become a woman. This is the way of the Principal People.

She saw the boys leaping at trees, grabbing for low swinging branches, challenging each other to see who could leap the highest. They leapt and fell, leapt and fell, trying to reach the farthest branches. None could bound so high. And then the girl felt herself moving, running as the boys had run, running in long strides that took her gracefully and high through the air. And then she was approaching the trees, and above and before her was the highest of branches. She discovered that her arms were spread wide as though they were wings and she felt the air rushing past her and then beneath her. Her arms were waving, carrying her upward and the ground was moving away beneath her. And then there was the branch and she was standing on it and looking down at the boys, the village, and the creek. And there was her mother, her mouth moving violently, but no sound coming out of it. And then the girl leapt for the sky, again moving her arms, letting them carry her toward the sun. And then the sun was gone.

She was ascending through shadow, cold and wet. She looked up and saw a great black bird flying toward her, after her. Her arms froze in their motion. And for the briefest moment she hung still in the darkening sky. The bird flew nearer. And then she began to fall. She clawed at the sky, but still she fell. And all the while the giant dark bird flew toward her, its talons stretching to grasp her. And then she started screaming, and everything turned to stark blackness.

New Human woke shaking. A scream was formed on her lips, but she had made no sound, and made none. The dream was still with her, but she knew instantly that it was only a dream, and she knew where she was and remembered the necessity of keeping quiet. She did so.

She could see the first light of day outside the

mouth of the cave. It was a blue-gray light that only barely made its way inside. Where she waited all was still dark, still night.

Something seemed strange to her but she wasn't sure what it was. She started rubbing her hands together to warm them, and then she knew. Her knife was gone. I must have dropped it, she thought, scorning herself. She searched the dark floor with her hands, found the blade instantly. Already the feeling of strangeness left her. Already she felt warmer.

Is he out there, waiting for me? she wondered. Should I go out? She knew the answer before she asked it. She had to go out. Whoever it was could have killed her at any time, she decided. Whatever his purpose, it wasn't her death, or else it was more than that. But she couldn't wait in the cave forever. Either he was waiting for her, or he wasn't. Either way, she had to go out. She gathered her bundle of possessions, preparing to drag them out as she had dragged them in.

She was nearly to the mouth of the cave when she felt the cold hand against her bare back.

16

The morning woke the world, and with it Stone. His muscles were already healing from their ordeal. His mind was already calming. He opened first one eye, scantly, and surveyed the day. He was still alone, it appeared. And the day seemed clean and fresh to him, cleaner and fresher than he remembered a morning ever being. Ah, he thought, now I am alive again. Now I can go in search of my mother.

He opened the other eye and took in everything around him. Sunlight glistened off the stream where he had drunk the night before. Bird-song filled the morning air. He recalled the song of the owl. The thought of it reminded him of his mother, and that made him feel both glad and sorrowful. Where is she? he wondered. She was his life and world. Everything focused on her. Everything. But now she was gone from him, or rather he was gone from her. Where am I? he thought. Discover that and I'll discover a beginning for my search. But he didn't know where he was. As far as he could see, none of the terrain was familiar. I am far from home, he thought. No doubt about that. How long have I been gone? He had no idea. A day? Doubtful. A hundred days? Possible, though he doubted it. I'd be dead, gone to the land of spirits if it had been a hundred days, even if it had been ten. Fewer than ten then. Probably fewer than five.

Again he scanned his surroundings. Where to start? he asked himself, and knew the answer.

He began by searching all the ground around the place he had found himself. Whoever brought him here would have left some trace of their activities. So he thought. It was noon when he decided that his captor or captors had cleverly removed any hint th̲ ̲ they had ever been there. It was as though he had simply appeared on that spot. He doubted that to the extent that he didn't consider it again. What he did consider was the possibility that a spirit or spirits had brought him there. And what can I do against spirits? he wondered. Nothing. But I can find my way home, and I can find my mother. And I will.

Do I follow the rising sun or the setting sun? he thought. Or to the left of either? The rising sun, he decided. That will eventually bring me to the sea, if nothing else. I've always wanted to visit the sea. And surely along the way I will sometime encounter human beings who can help me to learn where I am. Once I know where I am, then I will know where home is. Then I will find her.

But what if she isn't there? he thought. What if the spirits or whatever took her away as well? Then I will find where they have taken her, he told himself, and he started walking in the direction of the rising sun.

It was near nightfall when it occurred to him that if spirits had carried him, that though it might not have been a hundred days, the distance traveled might be as much as a man could have gone in that amount of time, or even further. And so before the sun set he began to make for himself the tools he would need to keep himself alive, safe and fed.

That night he made himself a fire, small but warming. And before he fell asleep he heard his squirrel trap fall. He ran to it through the dark. There he found the wounded and struggling animal, trapped beneath a fallen rock. Instantly, without a moment's thought or hesitation, he crushed the creature's skull with a large stone. I end your agony, he told it, and feed my own.

It was little food, but with roots he had gathered it was ample for the day, and was in fact all that he could hold. The days without eating had shrunk his stomach so that it held little. I'll cure that, he promised himself.

Curled near the small flames, the tension in his body eased. The aches were going away. And except for his worry about his mother, he felt a peace. His thoughts wandered back to the dark riverbottom. There is home, he thought. There is the place of content. There is what saved me. Before he slept he realized that despite the seeming danger to himself and to Tree, his mother, he was glad for what had happened to him. Glad to be alone in the world. Glad for the adventure of it. It was as though his place on the bottom of the river Unknown had suddenly enlarged to encompass other places on the earth. That the entire earth was like the riverbottom, and that wherever he slept was like being there, searching for stones, searching for his brothers and sisters, and finding smooth, shining stones. He knew that he was on the verge of learning something important, but he was asleep before it came to him.

Tree dreamt. *Asgitisdi*. Dream.

The Monster stood before her, ready to rape her and then kill her. She knew the thing was only Crawler in disguise, but still it frightened her. He had already killed everyone in the village. He had already raped all the women. Now he was going to have his way with her. *You owe yourself to me*, the man-creature growled.

Everything was dark around her and around Crawler. His body was shrouded in shaggy hair, except for his penis, hard and erect and naked, jutting out of the darkness. It was huge and wet. She knew he would first rape her with it, tearing into her; and then he would kill her with it, crushing her head with it as though it were a club. *Now*, growled the thing. Tree tried to crawl away, but there was nowhere to go. Behind her was a high cliff. Far below was a raging river. The river was filled with the corpses of all her people. *Stone*, she called out, but she couldn't hear her own voice. *Stone, come home! Come and save me!* And then she felt the monster moving inside her, rupturing her. She started screaming. And then the pain was gone. Stone was there, beside her, holding her gently, touching her, comforting her. She turned to him and kissed him. And then she touched him between his legs, and what had been terror with Crawler became joy with Stone. But it confused her and made her afraid. The Principal People do not bed with their children, she knew. This couldn't be. But then she realized that it had to be because all the others were gone to the land of spirits. She and Stone were the only ones remaining. From them must come the rebirth of the People.

Then Stone was standing. He was as tall as his father had been, and stronger. On the ground near them was the dead figure of the monster. Easily Stone picked it up and threw it into the river. Then he turned and was running. Tree watched him run. I taught him to run, she thought. And she ran after him. And then Light Fire was running beside her. And then all the People. They were alive again.

"How is it that you are alive?" she asked him.

He smiled and pointed at Stone ahead of them. "He saved us all," said Light Fire. "He swam to the bottom of the river and brought us all up. We had turned into stones and had sunk to the bottom. But he found us and brought us back to life."

"Oh," said Tree, realizing that of course it must have happened that way. Then she felt something inside her, but before she could look and see what it was, she saw that Stone had stopped running, and so had she and all the others, all except Light Fire. He was running to talk to his grandson. "Don't go," he was telling the warrior. "We must not go! If we do we will die again. They will kill us!" Who are they? she wondered.

And then it was night and all the village was walking and crying, and carrying all they owned that they could carry. Behind them was fire. And again there was something in her stomach. And she looked down and saw that it was the monster.

She opened her eyes and lay shivering in the night. Her fire had died and cold had come upon the earth. The dream had left her even colder, more frightened, though, than cold. She knew dreams were many things. That more than anything they were a distortion, a mutilation of memories. But they were more than that. And this dream had seemed more. But what it was she couldn't tell. Something of the future? she wondered. Perhaps, but she hoped not because there had been little joy in it, and a great deal of sorrow.

"Come home, son," she heard herself say quietly to the night. But she knew he was far away and that it would be many days before she saw him again. She had no fear of his surviving and returning. Any direction he went would lead him eventually to communities of the Principal People. From there he would easily find his way home. Find his way to her.

For a moment she recalled the dream, his touching her. She started to shiver again. She put the thought out of her mind and got up to gather some more sticks for her fire.

She was blowing embers to flame when she heard the voices behind her.

"Where is the boy?" they said, and the words were like ice in her ears.

18

Where are they? he wondered. He had an uneasy feeling about it. Tree had taken the boy away before and had been gone longer. But this seemed different.

He got up from his bed. Slipped on his clouts and moccasins. Then gathered some dried meat and fruit into a food pouch, and then his weapons. The bow felt like an old friend in his hand, and it was, he thought.

The night air was cool but he knew he would be warm soon enough, the heat of his body rising as he moved. His stride was sure and swift.

He thought about the words of the witch. She had known this was different. And then she and her sister had vanished from the village. And then he thought about his dreams. They came more regularly. One had come tonight. It was no different than the others before it, but he woke from it worried. Where are they? Where are they? he kept asking himself until he got up, dressed, gathered his weapons and supplies and walked into the night.

Again and again he had tried to discover any trail Tree might have left. He found none. Her leave-taking had been perfectly concealed. He had no way of following her. But the witches, he thought, they may have had a way to follow her, and perhaps they have not so carefully hidden their tracks. They had been gone for days, but still he might follow them, he told himself.

He began to circle the village, discarding different signs of travel, reasoning what would possibly be them, and what must necessarily be someone or something else. It was difficult going in the dark, and there were many trails that needed to be proven wrong before they could be proven right. Finally he gave up, walked to the creek and then followed it to the river.

This is where she brought him so many times, he knew. This is where she taught him her mysteries. He sat on a stone slab. He didn't know it was the same place his son had long ago taken her to when they had first married. He didn't know it was the place where the old one had been killed. There he sat and stared into the silent waters. Have you taken them? his thoughts asked the river. Are they with you now?

He tried to peer into the dark, shining deep but all he could find there was the reflection of the night. He was still sitting there, wondering, when the day began to come. And the sun was ascending when he started the short trek back to his village. He was near the mouth of the creek when he saw the tracks.

It was where two women had gathered, had stood together, and then had departed together. He followed them. The tracks were a few days old. Two perhaps, he thought. That would be right for the witches, he told himself. This could have been them.

The tracks led away from the village. North. Toward the unsettled land at the center of the People's territory. Now and then the tracks faded and Light Fire scouted until he found them again. It wasn't difficult. They kept their direction, and usually took the clearest path.

It was half way through the morning when the other tracks appeared. They, too, were a woman's. But a heavier woman, it appeared. And there were no tracks with them that could have been Stone's. This can't be them, then he thought. But then who could it be? He kept following.

Whoever it is, he told himself, I'll find them, just for the finding. Anything is better than waiting for the woman and the boy to return.

By noon the sun was hot against his skin. It felt, he thought, as though it was reaching down and touching him, drawing against him, marking itself on his back and neck. He glanced at it, a yellow ball of heat riding the sky.

You make us thirsty, he told it. And you make us hot. His step never slowed as he spoke-thought to the sun. You are the giver of heat, and so you bless us and curse us. And so you are our friend and our enemy. His right foot fell to the earth, then lifted. His left foot stepped down, quickly, hardly leaving a print, then lifted. One after the other, eternally. Be my friend today, he told the sun.

He was still glancing at the sun, whispering thoughts to it; his feet in their rhythmed motion, when the snake reached for him, sought him, opened its mouth to kiss him.

19

Cold, cold voices. Ice, *unesdala*, she thought.

Cold voices running across her neck to hide in and freeze her ears, and then her heart.

She turned from the flames and faced the winter voices. There stood her friends, the witches, Number One and Number Two. The voices, though, had spoken no friendship. They had only spoken the demand and desolation of a frozen river.

"Where is the boy?" they said again, no warmer, still no friendship.

Are these spirits guised as my friends? Tree wondered.

The two women walked toward her, separating as they came. Then one stood before her and one walked around behind her. She had never had difficulty telling Number One from Number Two. Now the task seemed impossible. When they spoke, they did so with one voice, a frost-bitten, irredeemable voice. Their motions were in unison. And with one before her and one behind her she couldn't see them together.

"*Flames!*" they cried. They cast forth their hands and the one behind Tree dropped something over the small flames Tree had blown. Instantly there was a flash and flames billowed into the night, sparks went racing to the stars and then vanished to ash darkness.

"*Where is he!*" they screamed at her. Tree held still, awed and frightened by it all. What do they want with Stone? she wondered. What has happened to *them?* Why are they like this?

One of the witches moved toward Tree, reached her arms toward her, then with a sudden motion grabbed Tree's breasts. At the same instant the other witch grabbed her breasts from behind her. They pinched her and wouldn't stop, their voice going on and on into the night. Their face like a mask, but not a mask, not needing one. "We've come for Stone. We know you've taken him from us, he who once sucked at these," and they pinched her breasts again. "We know you've stolen him from us, that you discovered our plan and took him away from us! *Where is he!*" They let go of her and began circling her, pushing at her, spitting on her, kicking her. "You can't keep him from us! What have you done with him? Where have you hidden him!"

Tree turned her head from one to the other. She wanted to cry. These were her friends. Why are they doing this to me? she wondered. What plan are they talking of? What do they want with Stone?

Then they were holding her by her arms and dragging her toward a tree. Then they were tying her to the tree so her back was to it and her arms were stretched backwards around the trunk of it. They kept spitting on her and poking at her. And Tree was only wondering through it all what it was about and why they were doing it; not thinking to resist, not thinking to resist until she felt the rope being drawn around her wrists. *No!* her mind cried. You can't do this to me! She didn't understand what they were doing and didn't know what they planned. But all the feeling of the long ago night when Crawler had come toward her and had taken her and wounded her and left her forever in pain from it, all that and all the fear of loneliness and isolation since Bear Man had died, and all the years seeing in dreams her second love falling and falling and falling from that high cliff. All the fears and terrors and hatreds of it came to her in one single, unconquerable moment and suddenly she was jerking away, pulling away from the ropes and the tree and the women. She was like the fire, swollen with sudden flame and fury and she would not accept assault any longer. With her hands doubled she whirled and faced the witch on her right. The woman stood momentarily stunned at Tree's sudden action. Tree swung her fist across the face of the witch. It struck with a smack that Tree thought sounded like something breaking. The woman twisted and fell away to the ground. And then the other woman was beating at Tree's back. Tree ducked and turned, then rammed her head into the woman's stomach. Kept ramming, running, pushing her back, toward the flames that had again grown small. The witch stumbled and fell backward onto the flames, putting out the fire, and screaming at the same instant.

Tree straightened and turned to face the other witch again. The woman was slowly staggering up. She was holding her face in her hands and moaning.

The witch that had fallen on the fire was up again. She ran toward Tree, screaming at her.

Tree ducked and pushed at the woman as she ran by, causing the witch to trip and fall again. Then Tree was running, running, running.

20

Tear Maker had seen the chief, Light Fire, leave during the night. She slept little since her mother and aunt had gone in search of Tree and Stone. The old woman she lived with, Wood Chip, required little from her and never complained about her being awake late at night. So she sat often at the door of the hut and looked across the village, listening to the songs and sounds of her people. There was much about them she didn't understand, yet she probably understood more than most, she thought. Her mother and Number One had taught her much. It had been an education devoid of a father. He had died in combat with *ani soi* before she was born. He had gone to the north to help the Principal People there. He never returned. His mother never remarried.

It seemed strange to her that her mother should raise her for the single purpose of a special marriage when she herself had never remarried.

Stone, she thought. Stone, and she loved the thought-sound of the name. She associated with it all the images of the young boy she had grown up with. She thought visions of him when he was four summers old, tagging along beside his mother as Tree and Number Two took their children again and again to the woods, to teach them at that already ripening age the mysteries of the earth. She thought visions of him only a week earlier when she had followed him to the river and there watched him strip naked and cast himself into the water. She remembered her amazement which never ceased at his ability to stay so long beneath the surface of the great Unknown. If anybody *knows* it, she thought, he does.

At the fringe of her vision of him naked and wet, walking happily and laughing from the water, his skin dark and shining, was the memory of the warmth she felt deep within herself that seemed to rove her body and then gather strangely below her stomach, and nest there, and burn there.

Then she had watched him lie on the great stone slab and had watched fascinated at the ritual he had gone through, touching himself everywhere, and then at last touching his penis, hardening it, moving it. She had never seen him do that before, and watching him then and thinking about it now, she wanted him safely beside her. She wanted to touch him and have him touch her, and she was more glad than she could express at the promise her mother had made her that one day Stone would be her husband.

Nothing can stop that, her mother had told her. He has always been for you and none other. He always shall be. All the formulas have been made and cast. He is yours. You have only to prepare yourself for him.

21

New Human stopped and didn't move. The hand, cold and hard against her back, ran up her spine and stopped at the nape of her neck.

"So the little one has run away," came a voice from behind her. She recognized the voice. She knew it instantly, and just as instantly all the fear and anxiety left her. It was the voice of *Squaduli*, Hornet, a friend.

"What are you doing here?" she asked, relaxing and turning to face him. "And why have you been following me this way, scaring me?" There was a laugh half formed in her throat. But when she saw him all the laughter vanished, all the ease disappeared. The fear and anxiety returned. The face she saw was Hornet's, but it was something more. The boy she had lived near and grown with all her life had changed, and all the change could be seen in his face, and confirmed by his body.

New Human gasped. The creature she saw before her little resembled her friend. His mouth was open strangely, she thought, the way an animal's mouth is open when it is panting. And his teeth were black with dirt; his entire body was filthy, and now—though the breeze blew into the cave—she could smell him too well. But the greatest change was in his eyes. They were stark, black-red eyes that spoke of having not slept in days. They called out to her to give them rest. You alone can do this for us, they whispered. You alone can satisfy him and give us the peace and rest we seek. And then through shadow she saw down his body and knew how she alone could satisfy him. She saw his other hand trailing down to his belly, there to fondle and urge himself into desire, desire that had led him after her and had kindled and warmed itself all the while he had trailed her until it could no longer be denied, held back, abated, until it must be satisfied before the eyes went mad with their own dread and need for rest.

This is the way of men, she told herself, and suddenly her fear was gone. It was gone because she knew she had left behind her the ways of the people, that she was no longer one of them, and that nothing this pathetic beast could do could harm her, for she had more power than he could now dream of. All his power had spent itself maintaining his passion.

"Hello, Hornet," she said, smiling confidently.

Hornet said nothing. He just stared at her and fondled himself. His hand now on her shoulder moved down and cupped her breast. New Human firmly set it aside. It returned.

"Don't," she said and put it aside again. The eyes kept staring, hungry for peace, the hand kept moving. Spill yourself that way, she thought to him. Then his hand came back to her breast again. This time she pulled away and moved to leave the cave. His hand caught at her clouts and pulled at them. She slapped him and moved away.

She crawled out of the hole in the side of the hill; then waited for Hornet. He didn't appear.

"Going to stay in there?" she laughed.

Nothing. "Finishing yourself?" she called. Nothing, then the face again, and the eyes, still the same. Then came the shoulders, black and gray with filth. Then the arm reaching down, moving, not stopping.

It all fascinated her, to watch it, to watch one of the People so caught up in his own weakness, and to stand apart from and above it, in control of herself and confident of her control of him.

He stood easily coming out of the cave, more easily than she imagined he had strength to. Still he is weak, she assured herself. Too weak to harm anyone but himself.

"Go home, Hornet," she told him. He only stood, watching her. Both his hands were at his side now, completely revealing his nakedness, and the hardness of his penis.

The penis amused her. This is what they control us with, she thought. This is their pride. This is what makes them run faster and jump higher. She started to walk toward him. "Better get home," she said, "little one."

"You ran away," he said, disbelief in his voice and yet the familiarity that had allowed New Human to recognize it immediately. There was no trace of his wildness in his voice; no trace of his despair and passion. His voice was calm, and unlike his eyes, rested. He's not used his voice these past days, she thought. But his eyes have never closed. It didn't occur to her that he wasn't so weak and far gone as he appeared. She stepped nearer. How often have we played together? she wondered. How often as children did we bathe

257

together? You need to bathe now, my friend. He didn't move. His penis stayed erect. He waited while she came closer.

"Why did you follow me?" she asked, only three steps away. "Why?"

He lifted a hand toward her, reaching again for her breast. She took another step and let his hand come to rest on her. Then another step, and then another until she stood against him. Then her own hand reached down to where he had fondled himself. She held him gently and moved her hand as he had moved his. She stared into his eyes. They didn't alter; nothing could change them, she thought. And then she moved her hand lower, still holding, cupping the sacks beneath the penis. And then she clenched her fist.

With her other hand she thrust fingers into the staring eyes and pushed the face away from her. With relief she hadn't imagined possible she felt the heavy hand fall away from her breast. And with joy she heard him scream and scream again, doubled over, nursing his wound with one hand, his eyes with the other. She watched him only a moment, then she turned and went to her pile of belongings. She gathered them and started away.

When she got to the top of the hill she could still hear him crying, could still see him crouched in front of the dark mouth of the cave.

You disturb the earth, she thought to him. Your wailing is a mockery of the songs of nature. You are a human, she told him silently. She took an arrow from her quiver, set it to the string of her bow and drew a careful aim. I am not one of you, she

258

thought, and she let go the arrow. A moment later the woods were quiet.

After that she walked. She walked with a certainty and pervasive strength. She knew she had done the thing which would separate her from them forever. She knew she could never return to them, and that never would she be one of them again.

The sun was setting and she was staring at her face in the still reflection of a spring pond when the question came to her. If I am no longer a human being, she thought, then what am I?

Before she could answer the question she saw the reflection of the other face across the pond.

Who has followed me now? she wondered and at the same moment reached for an arrow. In the same time it took her to string and draw the arrow she took in her adversary. Another boy. Naked as the first. Filthy as the first. Weaponless. She aimed the arrow's tip between his eyes Killing *them* already seemed an easy, *natural* thing for her. Whatever I am, she thought, I am an enemy to them.

For a moment she gazed into his eyes. Whoever he was, she thought, his eyes were nothing like Hornet's had been. They were rested. They had not only found peace, they were the essence of it. Should this die? she wondered. All the while the boy held still, not moving. Then New Human answered her question about his death. She let go the arrow.

22

When he woke in the morning Stone felt at peace with himself. He was naked, dirty, alone, and lost. This, he thought, ought to seem bad, but he couldn't feel that way. He stared into the blue-gray morning sky and softly sang a short song to the morning world, the world of birds, yellow sun, cool breezes and stirring woods. It was a song his mother had taught him. All things were, he realized. All things except what he had learned in the river. But even she had led him there.

Now I am learning on my own, he thought. For a brief moment a feeling of understanding started to come to him. Then it was gone.

It's time to be away, he told himself. He got up, stretched skyward, challenging the now invisible stars. I'm going home, he told them. I'll find her. Nothing will stop me. Then he faced the east horizon and started walking.

The world opened to him and became his friend, he thought. All the fear and anxiety of the days in the darkness when he had been carried were gone, though sometimes he would close his eyes for a moment and instantly he would find himself at the bottom of the river, resting, waiting, slowing his being to match the slowness of the river at that depth.

His nakedness seemed appropriate to him. He felt himself joined with his environment, at one and at peace with the trees, birds, animals, air and earth. I *am* home he thought. He recalled then his meditation before sleeping the night before, and he realized that all the world was his home. All the villages. All people. Not merely the Principal People, he thought, but *Ani Nigadv*, All People. And all creatures and beings, spirits and temporal. And suddenly he wondered if it hadn't been a friend rather than an enemy who had taken him from home and left him stranded in the unknown. A friend who had brought him there to learn great lessons. Perhaps, he told himself. Regardless, I shall learn what there is here for me to learn, here and wherever my travels and life take me.

He came to the crest of a hill and surveyed the small valley below. Beyond the valley was another hill, and hills beyond that for as far as he could see until the world ended in a purple haze. All this, he thought and gestured at the earth and sky, is mine, is all of ours. We have only to learn to live with it, and with each other. He felt a rush flowing through him, warm and subtle, becoming instantly a calm. And when it had covered him and filled him he held still in the power and pureness of it.

It was nearing sunset when he again moved. He had stood there, unmoving, for most of the day. When he started down the hill his step was quiet and slow. He was no longer in any hurry. Eternity stretched before him with all its sureness and combined complexity and simplicity, and he saw it and was unafraid of it. He knew that his life had just begun. The twelve previous summers of living had only been a form of preparation, of waiting to come out. Now he was born. Now his life was real, he thought, and at the same moment realized that most creatures, most human beings especially, never live in preparation and so are never born.

He looked at his arms and legs. The good earth smeared them with dried mud. It didn't offend him, but he wanted to wash. He wanted to feel the cleanness of water.

In the distance he saw a glistening on the floor of the valley. A stream or pond, he thought. He turned toward it. By the time he reached it the valley was filled with shadow.

He saw her standing there, gazing into the water. She's only a girl, he thought, no older than myself. She looked odd to him, standing with her chest naked, her small breasts divided by the strap of the quiver, wearing a man's clouts, carrying a warrior's weapons. Her clothes and weapons, though, were those of the *Ani Yunwiya*. She was a friend, stranger though she seemed.

Quietly he walked to the pond and stood across from her, gazed himself into the dark water, saw his reflection and saw hers across from him. And then he saw her move. He saw her hand go to her back and draw an arrow. He watched the liquid motion that put the arrow to the string of the bow. He watched the arrow's tip rise until it was trained steadily at his face.

It all happened in an instant. It so surprised him that he didn't move against any of it. And he didn't bother to consider what he would do if she *didn't* loose the arrow. His automatic reaction was that she would, otherwise she would never have aimed it. He knew his life depended on knowing what she would do before she knew.

He stood calm, still cast in the perfect peace he had gained while standing immovable through the day. He waited for her to kill him.

23

Diatsagli. The Witches.

She saw them coming.

She saw them moving toward her through trees, brush, and early morning light. The one witch, whom she now recognized as Number Two, was still bleeding at the mouth. She moved with anger, danced through brush with hate, vanished and appeared between trees with a hunger to do violence.

She saw them coming. She felt them coming.

She saw Number One. She saw her smoulder and blaze in gray patches of early day. She's on fire, Tree thought, remembering the witch rolling across the flames of her camp fire. But the witch's blaze was her own, Tree knew, and was born of an inner heat. She could feel that heat. She could feel the anger. She could feel the hate. She could feel it all coming at her. She could feel it rushing toward her like a thousand arrows, ready to pierce her, ready to catch her and nail her to some tree and keep her there, bleeding and lost, never to leave.

They want me, she thought, and she felt them come. She felt it because they cast their thoughts and feelings out at her, assaulting her with them, wounding her with them. All the friendship. All the years of caring and teaching. All of it melted, burned to ash, evaporated in mist. All of it was gone. Only the impressions they now sent her in order to take her down came from them. That and one other quiet, almost lost but unmistakable message came to her. Feeling it, she knew she might have a chance against them. They had taught her well and she had grown strong, stronger in ways than they and their magic. What she felt, the message they tried to hide behind the onslaught of hate, anger, violence, death was their own fear, their unconquerable fear of her and what might become of them if she lived. That I can use against them, thought Tree, and she began to think through her own attack. And as her fear eased away, it became easier to avoid the attack of their thoughts.

She could still see them coming. She turned and ran, not escaping from them but leading them. Follow me now, she thought. And she ran, easily now, gladly, freely. She knew where she was going and why. There would be danger there for her, but the greater danger would be for them. She didn't understand the purpose or the reason behind all that was happening. It didn't matter. They had disclosed their true natures. They would surely destroy her, she knew. Her only hope was to lead them first to their destruction.

Between where they were and the village was a finger of swamp land extending from the east. To a careful traveler it was little danger. To one running blindly it offered many opportunities for dying. Tree had come to its southern border when carrying Stone away and had then gone around it, rather than slow her journey and endanger her son. Now she would go through it. It seemed the only weapon she had to use against them. *If* she could make it there before they caught her. If they caught her again they wouldn't be so careless with her. She realized she would only have one chance at her plan, if that. She quit thinking and concentrated on the motion of her body.

Running had become the essence of purity to her, just as lying still at the bottom of the river Unknown had led Stone to his purity. This had been a purposeful event in her teaching him. Of course she had taught him to run, and she had learned to be still and silent and watchful, waiting. But he had been prepared to master the one, while she had mastered the other, the clarity of pure motion. That is how she thought of it. And running now she drew from that, and everything else left her. The forest became a part of her, and a part of her movement. Her arms and legs sang to her their own private song of ascent and descent and ascent, again and again, out, out, reaching out and coming back, and reaching out, forever.

It was late in the day when she entered the swamp. She didn't stop to see if the witches were behind her. She could feel them. She knew they couldn't be far away. Sometimes the feelings were stronger and she knew they must be nearer. Then they would trail away. But through the day they had gradually come nearer and nearer.

The swamp was a shadow land. It was unlike

the forest in every way. The forest was clean and clear. The swamp was a place of obscurity, of dimness, of dark waiting marsh and water. Not the sweet moving water of the river, but quiet, dead water. Water that seemed to have waited there since the world began, she thought.

Her running was slowed now. An uncareful step could send her falling into mud or sand that would swallow her up. The witches wouldn't have her, she thought, but then she would never see Stone again, or Light Fire.

The past days little of her thinking had been of the man. He was a good man. She loved him. She was devoted to him, though not with the intensity of her devotion to her son. But she did love him. She knew that. And she was grateful for the freedom he had given her through the years. The freedom with her own life and with that of his grandson. She knew he was often afraid and uncertain at the things she taught the boy. She knew he wanted the boy to be his successor one day. He will, she thought, and he will be the greatest chief the People have ever known.

She sidestepped a patch of the swallowing earth, dodged a tree that rose up through the misty floor, gray and damp, and continued her run.

Her intent was to find a way to force the witches into one of the patches of earth that would trap them and suck them under. The most difficult part would be to find her way safely around them herself. She was thinking about that when her foot caught on a tree root growing above ground.

Everything slowed.

The fall seemed in slow, visible motion to her. The wet, misty earth coming toward her face. Her arms spreading widely before her. The earth touching her hands, her knees and then her lips. It was soft earth and it all seemed like a tender embrace. And then everything was dark.

24

The snake is merely an asgili, *a ghost that has come down. It is a ghost of ever-living bones. It is a ghost of ever-living teeth. It has advanced toward the man. It has lain itself upon the trail. There it waits for the man. There it waits to bite him. It is the ever-living ghost whose tracks cannot be seen. Soon the man will falter. He will have nightmares. Only the snake fern can save him, they say. Otherwise he will go to the land of spirits when the ghost has bitten him.*

25

Light Fire felt the pain streak through his leg. He looked down from the sun and saw the *inadv*, snake, clinging to him with its fangs. With a single, swift motion, he carried his knife from its sheath and cut across the head of the creature. Its body fell away with half the head still dangling from his leg.

Light Fire stopped walking and looked at the sun. I asked for friendship, he thought, and this is what I am returned. He spat at the sky. Then he sat on the ground and pulled the head away. Drops of venom fell from the fangs. At least your poison isn't all inside of me, he thought to the dead creature's head. Then he tossed it away.

He made deep cuts in his leg where the fangs had pierced. Then he lifted his leg to his mouth and started sucking. It was an old remedy, and perhaps the best, he thought, for such wounds. No snake fern grows here, he thought, so what else is there to do?

When he finished sucking he packed the wound with mud made from dirt and spit. Then he wrapped it with a strip of hide cut from his clouts. Then he started off again. He knew he should rest. He knew walking would only assist the poison that was still inside him. Still he walked. He felt old and walking seemed to be the best remedy for that ailment, which seemed worse to him than the snake bite. Weakness being worse than death.

I am old, he thought. Older than most anyway. How old now? He didn't care to count the seasons.

By night he had reached the southern edge of a swamp land. He remembered as a boy coming there with his own father. The swamp is a secret place, the man had told him. It appears to be different from the rest of the earth, but it is the same, except that where the rest of the earth sheds her secrets, the swamp makes a mystery of them. Light Fire remembered that and it made him feel not so old to do so.

He saw that the trail skirted the swamp. No doubt to take up the same direction afterward, he thought. I shall go through it, he decided, and shall find the trail again on the other side.

Half way into the night the poison struck him. When it came, he smiled, and sat down on the damp ground, not resisting the serpent's venom. It shall pass or I shall, he knew.

The dark of the swamp night turned black. He left the world of men and entered the world of dreams. A nightmare world.

It was a familiar dream, but it was made worse by the ghost that had bitten him. In it he saw flames everywhere. They were the burning of the village. In it he heard the sorrow of his people. Again and again he saw his grandson standing before the men with white faces. Come away, he called to him. Come away, he called to his people. The dream recurred again and again, always ending with screams from the women of the village as they watched their homes flying into the sky on wings of fire.

The screaming was louder, it seemed. And then he realized he was awake, and that the screams were real. For a moment he wondered if they were his own, but then knew they couldn't be. His tongue was swollen in his mouth and he couldn't have screamed if he had wanted to. It was all he could do to breathe. Still the screaming came. He started to get up but his body felt tied down. The poison, he thought.

26

Her arrow was aimed at his head.

Stone stared calmly past the arrow's tip, past its shaft, past its feathers, to her fingers. He knew that when the fingers moved he too must move. He must move that torn part of a moment. Any hesitation at all would mean his end. There could be no thought, the response had to be immediate. And so he let calm flow through him, tension would only slow him by requiring its own attention. Relax. Don't think. When the moment comes, move. Until then, wait.

The fingers moved.

The-fingers-moved-the-arrow-moved-the-head-moved—all a fluid motion.

Stone felt the edge of a flint tip lightly slicing his brow. Then he heard the thump of the arrow into a tree behind him. Then he was running through the shallow pond. The water leaping against his legs. And then while she was still reaching for a second arrow his hands were tearing her bow from her grip, tossing it aside, then stealing her knife from its scabbard. Then he had her on the ground and the blade of her knife against the softness of her throat. And through it all his eyes were the perfection of peace.

"What are you?" he asked her, and she spat in his face.

"Are you so delighted to leave this world for the world of spirits?" he asked, ignoring the spittle that ran down his cheek. She squirmed beneath him, trying to move away from him. It was useless. She realized that and gave up. Surrendered.

"Kill me then," she said, and when she said it he saw a hope and light fade in her eyes.

"If I kill you," he said, "how will you apologize for your rude behavior?" And then he started laughing which, he could tell, made her angry. He took the knife from her throat and got off her, letting her stand, but still he laughed.

"And what's funny?" she asked, blushing and trying to display the fierceness of her wrath by gritting her teeth and glaring at him.

"Does anything have to be funny for laughter?" he wanted to know.

She stared at him bewildered.

"Of course it doesn't," he said. But of course it *is*. *You* are. You are very funny. Trying to be a warrior, though you are a woman. That is funny! A woman wanting to be a man! But why do you make war against your own people?"

"I'm not woman!" she said. "Nor am I trying to be man! Nor am I of your people or of any people!" She started walking toward her bow.

Stone's laughter stopped, but still the calm remained. "Leave the bow," he said. She stopped and turned back to him. "Are you a spirit then?" he asked her.

She hesitated.

She is part of what I'm learning here, he told himself. Perhaps she is a spirit. Perhaps she was sent here to teach me. Perhaps even her attack—

"I am something new," she said. "I am something the earth has not seen before."

27

She could feel them pushing her down. Burying her. Crushing her face into the earth. I hate you! they screamed at her. Where is he! they insisted. Die! they commanded. And then the dark became pale gray and she rolled to her side. The impressions from their minds still clung to her, still hammered within her. But the reality of their bodies were still not with her, though they were close, she could tell. It was in fact the force of their thoughts that had woken her. Had they become quiet she would have slept on in the unconsciousness caused by her fall.

Weary, she stood. Already the sky was darkening. But she could see them. If trees weren't in the way and if she'd had a stone she could have tossed it and hit one of them. They were that close. But long leaved trees with vine covered branches that dropped and fell nearly to the ground obscured all but glimpses of their approach. Tree turned and started out again, this time more careful about her footing. With every moment, though, that became more difficult. The sun was setting and blackness was swiftly filling the swamp. Soon it would be complete. She could almost feel it curling around her, between her legs and about her waist, over her eyes, turning everything into nothing more than the illusion of reality.

When the blackness came she was forced to a slow walk. My plans have gone awry, she thought. But at least the witches could do no better, except that they had her mind to follow. She had only her instincts, and also was forced to try to block out the damning impressions they sent her.

When she fell the sixth time she considered not getting up. What can they do? she wondered. Whatever they want Stone for, they can't make me help them with that. Or can they? She wasn't sure. They had strange powers. Powers of formulas and spirits. Their craft was ancient. They had taught her some of it, but they knew much more than she might imagine. She had learned things on her own, but they weren't the principles of witchcraft, they were the murmurings of nature and the natural mind. Witches played with nature, and against it. They could alter the affairs of the natural world, or at least so it seemed. One thing though that was obvious to her, these witches couldn't see in the dark, and they couldn't walk on the wet sand without sinking into it. If they could they would have had her long ago. Get up, she told herself. Painfully she did so. Her legs ached. The days of running and deprivation had taken their toll.

It was midnight when the screaming began. She wondered which one of them it was. It was impossible to tell. The screaming wasn't a voice. It was a cry of agony. The agony of an animal dying that wants to live and knows there is no way to do so. Tree stopped, using the witch's death as an opportunity to rest. All the impressions from the women were gone. All that remained was the hideous wail of the dying woman, and beyond that the fainter crying of the sister.

Tree realized that one of them had at last stumbled into the sand. In this dark, she thought, it could have been any of us. It may yet be all of us. What is the point in going on? I must, she told herself. She started to rise. But first I must rest. Rest but not sleep. Do not sleep. She kept saying it to herself, trying to force herself to the wakefulness that would be necessary soon to get up and continue her journey. All the while the screaming persisted. Stay awake, thought Tree. The screaming, a hymn to sleep, forever sleeping. Awake. Awake. Stay awake. Screaming like a fierce lullabye. Sleep. Sleep. Come lovely and soothing rest. Peace. Sleep.

She woke to the starkness of silence. The screaming was ended. One of them was gone, she knew.

More than ever she wanted to allow herself to return to slumber. She couldn't do it. There was only one of them out there now, but that one would still be after her, with a greater rage.

She stood. Her body was heavy. She could see nothing but the imagined lights from within her mind. She continued her walk, slowly, carefully. The liquid earth is too easy to step into, she thought. So she seldom lifted her feet from the earth, rather she quietly dragged them along, hoping that would keep her safe.

She didn't know how long or how far she had traveled when she fell again and this time couldn't get up. She had stepped into a hole and stumbled. There was a snap. She was certain her ankle was broken.

Resigned then to her fate, she waited. From the distance she could feel the witch moving nearer. Feel her thoughts. It was a weaker feeling than the two of them had generated together. But it was still there, and coming nearer, though it moved slowly. The woman must have know I've fallen, she thought. She must sense my dilemma. She'll be in no hurry now. She's all the time she needs to find me. She'll not endanger herself by coming any more quickly than she needs.

It was daylight before the witch appeared. Tree knew immediately it was Number Two.

She looked up at the woman, once her friend, or so she had thought.

"Now there is only half of you," she told the woman. She wanted to laugh at her when she saw the blood still dripping from her mouth. I must have hurt you well, she thought, hoping so, hoping the wound would never heal.

"Soon there will be none of you," said the

witch. She held in her hand a spear freshly carved. It was how she had busied herself in the night, waiting for the dawn, waiting to complete her pursuit.

"And what plan is it of yours that I have spoiled that you do this?" Tree asked, wanting at least to know why she must die.

"Don't mock me," cried the witch, and tears came to her eyes, and suddenly Tree was full of all the agony the woman felt at the loss of her sister. Indeed she had lost half of herself. "I will find the boy," the woman said. "But you shall never see him again, not until he joins you in the land of spirits." She raised the spear with both hands, pointing it at Tree's chest. "Never! Never! Never!" she yelled until her yell became a scream. And then death had its way.

28

She had killed a man, and the power derived from it hadn't yet left her. Now another man stood before her, challenging her, questioning her. The strength gained from having killed Hornet was all that she had to support herself in front of this newcomer and his questions.

Inside she was afraid. He had moved too fast. He spoke too calmly. He was only a boy and yet his eyes held a serenity and wisdom she hadn't seen in even the very old. And though he was naked, he seemed clothed.

"What are you then?" he asked her again.

"I am New Human. That is who I am, and that is what I am." She watched him. His expression didn't change. Nothing to indicate he had heard her or that he was considering what she had said.

Who is he? she wondered. *What is* he?

"New Human?" He smiled. "And it is the way of New Human to kill her brothers?"

"You are not my brother. I am not one of you. I kill my enemies," she said defending herself and her new ideas.

"And how am I your enemy?" he wanted to know.

"The People, all people, have become enemies to the earth. It can be seen in the natural way of life."

"What do you know of the natural way of life?" he asked, challenging her. "Have you lived with nature so long? Are you above others? Have you learned what they haven't, and so saved yourself so that now you are appointed by the Great Spirit to destroy them?"

The questions came too fast for her and started her thinking about matters she hadn't considered. Suddenly she saw all the boys running and leaping. She wanted to run with them but her mother wouldn't let her. You've women's work to learn, she was told. And when she tried to sneak away and was caught by the woman, she was beaten. Every time, again and again. And again and again she tried to get away, but always someone sent her back to her mother. And always the beatings. And then she saw the arrow speeding through morning air, journeying with a whisper to its certain target, finding that target and burying itself there in Hornet's back. She saw him falling, falling and rolling, too wounded to ever stand again. Don't take me back to her, she thought. I'm not part of that anymore. I don't want that anymore. I'm new now. I belong here, alone.

She was on her knees, crying, when he came to her and touched her hair.

"Don't take me back," she said. "Please leave me here. I belong here now."

"Don't kill them," he told her. "They will do well enough not to kill themselves."

And then she was leaning against his legs, making the dirt on them muddy with her tears. And he was stroking her hair and saying nothing. And she wasn't afraid at all when she found herself kissing first his knees, and then his thighs, and then ascending. She knew that he had escaped the ways of human beings, that he was the New Human, and that she could only learn from him what she needed to know to become herself. And the realization both gave her joy and frightened her. Still she kissed him, until he stepped gently away. And then she lay back, opened herself and beckoned to him. And he didn't resist.

Stay with me here, she thought. Never leave me, she prayed. And then he was inside her and her tears stopped, and where their bodies met was the only place of life in the earth. Of that she was certain. But when they were finished the vision of the arrow and Hornet came to her again, and so did her weeping.

They slept together that night, curled first about each other and then about a fire. "Who are you?" she asked him. "I am New Human," he told her. "And I am Stone." "Who am I then?" she asked. "You are New Human also. But you aren't fully yourself yet. Nor am I. Not fully. But I am at the beginning. You are not yet at the beginning."

"But—" and he stopped her with a kiss and wouldn't speak of it anymore. Instead he touched her and allowed her to touch him.

In the morning he talked to her about villages. He learned where he was. And then he told her he was going home. "Don't return to your village," he told her. "Come with me."

They walked through half the day together. Then at noon, beside a stream where they had drunk water, she told him she could go no further.

His ever calm eyes stared at her. "Why?" he asked.

"I can't go back to the People," she said.

"Why? You can come with me. I'll teach you what you want to learn."

"I can't," she said. She lowered her head, then leaned to him and kissed his mouth. "You are New Human," she told him. "And I will be. I was afraid when I first met you. You've taken that fear from me. Your eyes and your touch have already taught me. But there are things I must learn alone. I can see that in your eyes." He tried to argue with her. She wouldn't. He tried again. She wouldn't. Finally he gave up. "Walk a little further with me," he said.

"No," she told him.

"Then touch me once more," he asked.

"No," she said. "If I touch you again now, I will go with you. I have to leave you here."

29

Tear Maker, who was named such because she caused her mother to shed many tears when she came down from her, sat beside Life, the small stream that flowed through her village.

When she looked into the water she saw the reflection of the sun many times, glistening, shimmering. There is beauty, she thought.

When she closed her eyes and looked at nothing, she saw an inner reflection, the image of the young Stone, whom she loved. He is mine, she told herself. My mother has promised him to me. It is against all the taboos of our people that he and I should marry, but I know he is mine. And so she allowed herself to love him. She had always done so. In her mind she gazed at his face. There also is beauty, she thought.

She knew that Stone cherished songs. The songs of their People. The songs his mother taught him. And the songs of nature. And so she cherished them also, and made songs for him that one day she would sing to him, one day when they were married.

Sitting beside the stream, the sun reflecting off the water, his image reflecting within her mind, she began to hum, and in her thoughts she sang to him a song she had made.

> There are many human beings in this
>   world,
> this often gray world where we have
>   chosen to live;
> this too seldom green world where we
>   have chosen to live.
> I have seen many human beings.
> I have heard them sing.
> I have seen them dance.
> I have listened to their tales.
> I have watched tears roll down their
>   cheeks.
> I have seen them in their joys,
> and have felt with them their sorrows.
> I have never seen one of them
> with a face like your face.
> Never has one of them sung songs
> that are so alive as your songs.
> Never has one of them danced like leaves
>   in the wind,
> which is the way you dance,
> and which is the way my heart becomes
>   when I watch you.
> Never has one of them stood so near me
>   always,
> which is where you always stand, though
>   you have never
> touched me, and are often so very far
>   away.

Never will there be another who does
touch me.
Of all human beings, you are the one
I'm waiting for.

She knew it wasn't the most beautiful of songs. But it was her true song to him and of him. She sang it often, and always the words changed, altered, grew.

Where is he? she asked Life. The stream didn't answer. She asked it every day. Every day it refused to tell her. Perhaps it speaks but I can't hear, she thought. Stone would say that, or something like it.

On hands and knees she bent and touched her lips to the water. There she took drink, and then whispered to the water that if it saw him to bring him her love.

Later, still sitting by the stream, she realized that Stone knew nothing of her love. Her mother had told her that must wait. How much longer? she wondered. Not long, she had been told. And though she knew well the art of waiting, the craft of giving time its need, waiting still held none of the joy that she looked for. The joy of being with Stone, of being beside him, and of feeling him not only near her but touching her.

Wood Chip, the old woman she was living with, came finally to get her, to have her cook supper. But before she left the stream she drank once more. Tell him, she reminded the water. Tell him if you encounter him. Then she followed the old woman to their hut.

Death had its way.

Tree heard the woman's voice become a scream. Then she watched the spear fall to the ground. Then saw the woman twist and fall away. She watched her writhe and moan for only a moment. Then there was only stillness and silence. Then she saw the arrow that grew out of the woman's side. It was a deep wound and had killed her quickly. She was lucky for that, thought Tree. And now what of me?

She could hear Number Two's assailant approaching. Whoever it was was making little effort now to conceal himself. She turned and tried to see who it was, but her ankle hurt badly and moving made it worse, so she gave up and waited.

A few moments later and a man she both knew and had never seen before was standing above her. She knew it was Light Fire. But he was distorted, twisted with swelling. She could tell he was in great agony, that each movement meant severe pain to him. She wished she could help him as gradually he lowered himself to the ground. His bow was still in his hand. How he had been able to shoot it was something she couldn't imagine. But thinking of the difficulty it must have been and the expertise he had still managed, expertise that had saved her life, overwhelmed her. So after all the running, after all the terror, safe now she started to cry. With the tears flowing down her face, and with sharp pains streaking through her leg, she crawled near the man who was her third husband, reached out and took his hand.

Light Fire tried to speak but couldn't because of his swollen tongue.

"Stone?" she asked.

He nodded.

"Stone is safe. Much safer than you and I." Then she put the hand to her face, and when it was wet from her tears she dried it with her lips. It was a long time before she stopped crying and began to think of how she could get them home.

31

"Where will you go?" Stone asked her. She looked around. She shrugged, then faced the west.

"There," she nodded. "I'll follow the sun." She shrugged again, then started walking away. Stone stared at her, watching her vanish.

When she was almost out of sight between trees, he called out. "I'll come back for you, New Human," he said. "One day I'll find you!"

"Follow the sun then," she answered. Then she turned and a moment later was gone.

Then he started south. Home.

Stone was in no hurry, so it was five days later when he walked into the village. His friend Tear Maker danced with joy to see him. They both danced with joy when at sunset that day Light Fire and Tree returned. Light Fire pulling Tree on a litter. The sorrow when Tree told Tear Maker of her mother and her mother's sister, of how they had sadly and accidentally fallen to their deaths in the swamp. No one ever knew otherwise, and Tree took Tear Maker as her daughter.

33

Tree watched them walking together beside the stream. She knew they loved each other. She knew as certainly that nothing could ever come from it. The People would never allow it. Sad, she thought, that those who love cannot always enjoy that gift.

She turned away and limped back toward her hut. The limp had been with her ever since her recovery. During the days that she had nursed Light Fire before he was able to build a litter to bring her home, the broken bone had begun to heal wrongly. The limp would always be there. She knew she would never run again. She had found something else, though. She knew she would never go away from Light Fire again, not even for a little while.

34

It was night. Stone went to the river.

I know you, he thought. You and I are alike.

He drank from its water. You taste of love, he told it. But that is your nature, to love, to nourish. Only those who hate and are afraid have cause to fear you.

LIGHT FIRE

1

A dream could mean many things. It could mean the dreamer was conversing with the spirit land. It could mean the dreamer was conversing with the spirits of animals or plants. It could mean the dreamer had poisoned himself or that a witch or someone else had poisoned him.

A dream that was repeated many times had principally two possible meanings. The first was that an old wound was unhealed within the dreamer. The second was that the dream was a premonition of events yet to come. Such dreams were common. Their only cure was to discover and heal the inner wound, or to wait for the event to transpire.

2

The strange, white-faced ones came from the sea.

He could see that clearly, even though a shroud of gray seemed to hang everywhere. They came and they carried fire in their arms. And then he saw his village burning. And then he heard the weeping of the women.

Running through the flames, beyond the tears of the women, tears falling now like rain from the sky, running toward the sea. He could see him running. A warrior. His son. No, his grandson. Then he heard his voice calling to Stone. *Stop!* he called. *Stop!* And he made the warrior cease running, and he forbade him to challenge the stranger-men.

And then all that could be seen was the red, burning flames of the village, and after that the red, burning flames of the setting sun.

Then he awoke.

The dream held in his mind the way smoke from a pipe holds in the air, dispersing gradually, falling away silently but not quickly, as though it wanted to stay and be a part of reality a little longer.

It was seven summers since the death of the witches. Each summer the dreams came more often. Now summer was gone. It was late in the autumn of the seasons and the dreams came each time Light Fire slept. So he tried to sleep little. It was an easy thing for him to do. He was getting older, getting weaker. Sleep held little comfort for him. When life grows short one isn't anxious to sleep it away, he told himself, especially when sleep offers only confusion and despair.

There was no understanding the dreams. He had long since decided they were no part of something within himself, some haunting of a past wound or deed. They were a warning, he knew, but of what he couldn't be sure. But because of their frequency and intensity he was sure that their meaning was not far from revealing itself. It can't be long now, he thought. And when he would watch his hands shaking as he lit his pipe, he wondered if it wasn't simply a message to himself that he would soon be gone from his people, and that his grandson would be all that remained of him. But what of the faces? he wondered. There were no answers. There was only waiting. So he waited.

Certainly, he thought, Stone had become like the image of the grandson of the dreams, a tall, strong warrior; perhaps the strongest and most able the People had ever seen. When he thought of the lad he did so with gladness. It was good to leave such a warrior as a guardian of the People. It was a fair contribution to make as he left one world to journey to another. Whenever he thought such things he surprised himself that he so casually pondered his death. But it cannot be far away, he knew. Not only did his hands shake, but there was a tightness in his chest that had never been there before.

Stone, he thought. The boy had become a man. He looks much like Bear Man, I think, the old chief told himself. Bear Man, gone, lost so long ago, only a little older then than Stone is now. Now he lifted his head to the sky, raised his palms, quivering, and silently asked the Great Spirit to give a long life to Stone. He needs a long life, he told the Spirit. And not only that, but he is the only one to carry forward my tale, and the tale of his father and all our fathers. Then he put down his hands; and besides, he told himself, his mother would perish if anything ill came to Stone. He is her life. She shares that life with me, but her son is that life.

Then his thoughts began to leave the dreams. They were away, vanishing in his mind, until suddenly his only thought was that of Tree. And thinking of her he could actually feel her nearness. She didn't have to be there. They had become too close for that to be necessary. He needed only to close his eyes and conjure her name, and she was with him. That was often. And it was made easier, too, by the fact that in actuality she was usually with him. Since the incident with the witches she had never again gone for days, or even a single long night into the woods. She had stayed instead always with Light Fire. He had never asked her to stay so near, but he was glad that she had lost all desire to do any differently. It comforted him to be with her. And now that his hands shook, and his lips trembled, and his chest ached it comforted him more than ever. It seemed to him they had grown as trees next to one another grow, with their branches so intertwined that it was no longer possible to discern where one tree ended and the other began. When their bodies were not that way, their hearts and minds were, always.

When I look into a stream, he thought, I see my face, old and creasing. When I look at my body I see it the same. I am an old man. I'll be gone soon. It saddened him, because he knew he would be leaving her. Tree, he thought, still young, still lovely. The limp in her walk does nothing to make her undesirable. Other men might turn away from such an infirmity. It is nothing. Such men know nothing of beauty. That is what she has taught me. She has taught me something of beauty. Beauty she is.

He was used to rising before the sun. It was a habit learned during a lifetime. And so he had awakened from the dream while the morning was still dark. Now, though, a gentle light was coming into the hut. He looked down beside him. He could see her there, bundled against the late autumn chill. He breathed softly on her shoulder and watched his breath curl about her bare skin. But he didn't move, not wanting to wake her until her own dreams were complete. My bride, he thought, and watched her in the pale morning light, waiting for her to awaken.

Finally she stirred. He watched her eyes open onto the day. Watched them blink, and then watched her gently rub the bits of grit from them with long, slender, graceful fingers. Then watched her stretch forth her arms and quietly yawn. It was the same each morning. It was her ritual. He always woke before her and never tired of watching the ceremony of her waking.

After she had stretched she turned to him, as she always did. She opened her arms to him and drew him near. Then began their touching. It, too, was ritual, but it never held the monotony of ritual. It was always tender. It was always eager. And it was always complete and filling for each of them. Her hands pressed gently at his back, then urgently. Old though I am, he thought, she still seems pleased with me. And she was. Truly he had no doubts of that. He understood her, and she understood him. So he likewise had no doubts that she knew how pleased he was with her, not merely in their bed, but in all things.

"You and I," he whispered when they were still again, "are the same." It was something he often told her. It was the best way he knew to express his feelings.

"You and I are everything," she answered.

They put their lips together once more before rising to begin the new day.

3

They told the tale of an ancient one. This is the tale they told. There was a great one. He was great and ancient. Some said that he was a deer, a magnificent buck. Some said that he was a warrior of the People. Some said he was a Spirit. But they all agreed he was the father of the clan. And so they named themselves the Deer People, the Deer Clan; and they called him Father of Us. He was their Father. That is what they called him.

The earth was young, they said. The earth was young and there were few men and few animals. There, though, were creatures and people who no longer live on the earth. One of them was Father. He was the sire of many. That is why he has been named Father. He had special powers. He had special powers and so did his children. Some of his children were people, and some were animals, and some were other things. Some of them could alter their appearance and be first one thing and then another, so no one could know for certain what they were. No one did know.

One day at a dance of people, people who were stomp dancing around the fire, a young man saw two of Father's daughters. They were beautiful young women. He talked to them, and then he danced with them. Who are you? he asked them. They told him they were daughters of a great wizard. That scared the young man. But already he was very much in love with the young women because of their great beauty. They were more beautiful than any women he had previously seen. There are no women like this anywhere, he thought. Take me to your father, he told them. The two young women looked at each other, and then at the young man. He is a good one, they agreed. Then they told him to meet them at the edge of his village after the dancing was done.

When they met they took him through the woods. They came with him to a river where they washed their faces and hands and had him do the same. Then they walked across a shallow part of the stream. After that they continued to walk through the night. They didn't stop and they didn't sleep. It was morning when they finally stopped. They had come to their father's home. It was in the center of a great valley.

This is our home, they told the young man. Our

father lives here. The young man stared at the hut. It was large and made from trees and was like nothing the young man had ever seen before. He started to cower at the thought of what the wizard might do to him. Then a man appeared at the door of the hut. He was smiling and was obviously very happy. His daughters ran to him and he picked each of them up and hugged them a long time. He was obviously a very strong and big man, this wizard who became the Father.

Then the young women took their father to meet the young man. The wizard looked at him. He looks good, he told his daughters. Then he spoke to the young man. There will be a contest, he told him. If you win you may have both these daughters as a reward. Go with them, he told him, through the valley. Fight whoever you encounter. When you come to the end of the valley, return with them and then they will be yours. But if anyone defeats you, then you will know you have lost.

The young man wanted the young women so he agreed. Then the wizard gave him special garments to wear for the contest. Some of them went on his arms and some on his legs. Some went on his feet; some on his hands, and some on his head. They were wonderful garments, he thought. When he had them on he felt faster, stronger. He looked at his arms and legs. They were clothed like a deer. He looked at his hands and at his feet. They, too, were clothed like a deer. They were hooved. And his head wore a crown of antlers. They were antlers of many points. It made the young man feel stronger than he had ever felt. Then he looked at the two young women. They, too, wore the garments of deer.

The young women came to him and the three of them started through the valley. They hadn't gone far when they came to the first adversary. A large buck came from the woods and challenged the young man. The young man ran fast at the challenger and the two of them butted heads and antlers. They fought only a little while and the buck lost. Then the young man and the women continued on. Soon there came a second challenger. Again the young man fought. Again he won. It wasn't long before a third buck appeared, strong and larger than the second or the first. The young man fought once more. The buck once more was defeated. This then happened a fourth time, and a fifth time, and a sixth time. Each time the buck was larger. Each time it was more difficult for the young man to defeat the buck. At last the largest buck of all appeared. As had the six others, he challenged the young man. They ran at each other. They butted heads and antlers. They each fought very powerfully. The fight continued into the night. Then just at dawn the young man grew too tired to fight any longer. He fell to the ground. The great buck stood over him. The young man thought the buck would kill him, but instead it turned and ran away. The two young women followed after it, their white tails bouncing against the green valley grass as they leapt away.

When he was stronger the young man returned to the village of the wizard. There the wizard and his daughters waited for him.

I lost, he told the wizard. I wish you had won, said the wizard. Then for a moment the wizard appeared as a great buck and the two daughters were again deer. Then they were people again but the young man knew it had been the wizard he had fought and lost to.

After that the young man spent several days at the village. At night he slept with the two young women, but he was promised that he could not marry them. Then one morning he woke to find the village, it huts, and all its people gone.

After that he went in search of his own village. He walked for many days before he finally found his way home. After he got there he told no one where he had been or what had happened to him. He knew they wouldn't believe him and he only partly believed himself.

One day, after many days, one of the young women appeared at his hut. She had two young boys with her. This is your father, she told the boys. Then she moved into his hut.

One day while she was getting water from the creek the man told his sons about their mothers and their grandfather. He looked up and watched her walking toward the hut. Then she looked at him and knew immediately that he was telling her secrets to his sons. Then she was gone, and running swiftly away was a doe with a white tail.

The young man never saw either of the young women again. But his sons grew strong and became fast, clever warriors. The Deer Clan came from them, the old ones said.

4

Whenever anyone talked of the young warrior, Stone, they talked about his eyes. He had eyes, they said, that held both all the power and all the tranquility of the earth. It is because he is like the earth, they said. That is why they named him Stone, they said, for all the earth is a great stone. So conversations went when he was the subject. All this at nineteen summers old.

Stone never thought about his eyes. When someone would mention them to him, someone like Tear Maker, he could only wonder what they saw. They are only eyes, he would say. I am merely a man. Never merely anything, not you, he would be told.

Is that right? he would wonder. Am I not merely a man? Then, no, he would tell himself, but he never spoke of such things with others, and would disclaim them when others would speak of them. And he would try to disclaim them to himself, but that wasn't possible. And it made it more difficult when others would insist. Don't say such things, he asked them. Still they persisted.

His knowledge of himself, though, didn't come from what others told him. They could tell him nothing he didn't already know, except for the nature of his eyes. There they knew what he did not know. And no matter how often he had stared into the stillness of the great river stream, or even the quiet of a pond, he could never see what others assured him was there.

But otherwise, he thought, I know myself. And Deep, the River, has been my teacher; and All, the Earth, too. *The river knows all deep things, and the earth is all things*, he sometimes sang. *The river is Deep; the earth is All.* And he wanted to learn all things, and he wanted to know how deep the river ran. But that was unknown, and remained so, even to him. So the river kept its name. *Unknown*. But someday, he thought.

We are all of the earth. The earth is all. And life is a stream of unknown depths. And swimming through it, we live. That was his song. And so when he spoke of the earth he spoke of all things, all creatures, plants, and objects, even the clouds and stars of the day and evening skies. When he spoke of rivers, he spoke of life. When he spoke of swimming, he spoke of living, breathing, walking, breeding, hunting, and even of death, the greatest mystery of life.

His arrow moved sleek and silver-gray through autumn air. The buck lifted its head, cropping leaves from a low branch. The leaves were like honey on its tongue, sweet, moist, green-rich. And then, without warning, it ended. The leaves were gone. The sunny clean autumn air was gone. All that remained was a sudden and new aching, piercing pain. Then nothing. The arrow broke the skull and sunk like a fast light into a dark expanse. It sliced the brain. The creature fell, dead while falling. Stone watched it all. The best kind of kill, he thought. Then with ease and casual, careless concern he moved from his hiding to claim his prey.

300

Hunting, fishing, harvesting, he thought, the balance of the earth. Here I sustain myself. Here I am a part of nature, not an enemy to it.

He was a half day's journey from the village. It was a big buck. No matter, he thought, and straining only a little he hefted the cleaned carcass onto his shoulders and started walking. While he walked he sang and whistled. When birds sang he sang with them. When the wind sang, he sang its song.

Under the weight of the big buck he let his thoughts wander to other deer he'd taken from the forest, and to his father, Bear Man. Bear Man the Great. Greatest Warrior. Greatest Hunter. So went the legends already forming. He thought of his father, whom he had never known, hunting these same hills and hollows. Likely that he did so, he thought. He imagined the dead man alive, imagined him stalking a great buck like the one he now carried. He imagined Bear Man sitting beneath a tree, singing the songs of nature. Was he really Father Buck's greatest grandson? he wondered, and for a moment his thoughts took him walking back to that ancient myth of the mysterious father of the Deer Clan. Could such creatures as he have ever really lived? he wondered. Could they still? No, he answered, not still, but perhaps once. Perhaps when the world was a very young place.

Life is good, he thought. All things come to those who wait for them. Waiting is the cleverest kind of hunting, and again he saw his father waiting beneath a summer tree. It was as he had waited that morning in the fall of the year, knowing game would come his way. Finally the buck had come. The earth had provided. Now he carried it homeward, heavy on his shoulders, but not more than he could manage.

He stopped now and then to rest. While resting he rubbed his arms and shoulders with care, keeping away the stiffness and soreness that carrying the carcass wanted to cause. When he came to water he drank his fill. The water was always good to him. Wash me, water me, cool me, he thought to it as he drank. It was a small song, a song of incantation.

When he came to the village he was tired. He'd already gutted the beast, so he hung it and spread its ribs with a stick. Then he skinned it. The hide was for Tear Maker, his adopted sister. He'd promised her his next kill's hide. It was an easy gift to give, because he knew she would use some of it, if not most, in making something for him. New moccasins, perhaps. Perhaps clouts or a new quiver. He could use a new quiver, and probably she'd noticed.

His hut was next to Tear Maker's. Her's was beside Light Fire's and Tree's. Stone put away his weapons and tools, and then started for Tear Maker's hut. But no, he thought, first Light Fire. He draped the hide over his hut and went to his father's hut.

The old man was there. His health had been weaker with each season. He seldom left the warmth of the hut now that the season was getting cold.

"Come smoke with me," the father-grandfather said.

"I've had a good hunt," Stone reported, folding his legs beneath himself as he sat.

"Then smoke and tell me about your hunt," said Light Fire. "I want to hear about your hunt. I want you to tell me everything since I can't hunt much anymore. Tell me what it was like."

Light Fire relit his pipe and passed it to Stone. Stone drew the gray warmth into his lungs, held it there calmly as he passed the pipe of wood and feathers back to his parent-chief-friend.

"I waited," he began, "for I found waiting to be the finest way to capture the greatest beasts." The tale went on. He included songs he'd sung while waiting. He spoke of the silent hours, the thinking he had done. And then he spoke of the smaller deer that had come his way, the ones he'd allowed to pass. And then of the buck he'd killed. He spoke of his bow and of his arrow. He told of drawing the string. He told of letting it go and of the swift tickling of the feathers against his cheek. He told of the whispering motion of arrow through cold air. He told of the instant dying of the beast. The sudden jerk it made when the arrow arrived and shattered its living. He told of the sound of the creature against the brush and the earth while it fell. He told of the blood, of the gutting. He recounted his journey home, his thoughts of hunting, of his father and of the Father Buck. Last he told of the hide he'd gotten for Tear Maker, and of his hope for a new quiver. A good hunt, he ended. Yes, agreed Light Fire. A good hunt.

Then they smoked again, burning dry leaf in the pipe.

He took the fresh hide from the hut. It was already getting dry, hard. Then he headed for Tear Maker's hut. With water and urine and lots of work, he knew, she'd make the raw skin into tanned cloth, softer than a child's face.

"Tear Maker," he said outside the door, and then pulled aside the cover and stepped in. And there she was, not expecting him or anyone else, naked in the center of the small, low ceilinged room. For a moment she didn't move. She only stared at Stone, now an intruder. And he returned the stare, too surprised to say or do anything. Then with a quick, unhesitant bow she picked up a blanket from her bed and covered herself.

It wasn't the same as when they were children. As a woman he had never seen her naked. And suddenly feelings he had hidden for many seasons were no longer willing to wait buried within him. They wanted expression. That's impossible, he thought. That's impossible, he knew. So he forced them back, buried them again, yet still stood there, not speaking, not moving, and from far away in his past there came the memory of a long ago season where as a boy he had met or had imagined a strange girl in woods. He felt again what she had done to his body, and his being. And he felt the pain of leaving her. Not imagined, he knew. She had been real, just as Tear Maker is real, he told himself. And all he had long ago felt, he felt again, and more. He felt more because his feelings for Tear Maker had been growing for a long time. *Feel yourself, feel your mind, your body, your needs*, came a voice from within him. No, he commanded it. They cannot be. They must not be.

"This is for you," he said, remembering the deer hide, and he held it out to her. She didn't take it. She only continued to stare at his eyes, and he could only wonder what she saw there. Then, without warning, just as his feelings were becoming secure in their hiding, she let the blanket fall away.

5

Udaniyadv was his name. Orphan.

His father had died nineteen summers earlier when his people had raided Light Fire's village. That winter his mother had starved because she was old and had no man. She could have lived but she obeyed instead a stronger impulse to preserve her children. Even at that his brother and sister had perished.

He looked out across the next valley. Hills and valleys. They had been crossing them for days. We will be outcasts no more, he thought, though he knew that their band of two hundred couldn't regain the long lost territories. What they could do was to atone the loss. This they would do by destroying the village of Light Fire, and after that others would join them. Their numbers would grow. Soon they would be thousands. Then the *Tslagi* would be driven out. Soon the old lands would be returned to their rightful heirs.

He started down the hill into the valley, following his brothers. Ahead of them all walked their chief, *Aqueluga*, I Shout. *He* can lead us to our certain victory, thought the young warrior named Orphan. *Aqueluga*, I Shout. He will stand one day at the council house of the *Tslagi's* seven clans and shout his song of victory. He walked on, dreaming sweet dreams of fighting and revenge. It was the only song he knew.

6

The messengers arrived at sunset. They stood panting and sweaty outside Light Fire's hut. One of them a boy, the other a warrior, the boy's father.

Light Fire stooped to step through the doorway, then stepped out into the evening air. He twitched his nose at the smell of the man and the boy. Then he smiled; raised his hand to hail them.

"You have the fragrance of hard work," he said and laughed a little.

"It's been a good, long run here, Light Fire,"

said the man. "But we've hurried to bring you the news of this new thing that is happening." Light Fire motioned that they should sit and he sent Tree after his pipe. "Go get my other chiefs," he whispered to her.

"A wondrous thing has happened," began the messenger, but before he spoke further Light Fire's smile vanished. A hard, cold expression set in his face. The man stopped speaking.

Light Fire stared at them. They were still breathing hard. The sweat was still wet on them. The boy looked confused, wondering why his father had stopped speaking. Then the boy looked at Light Fire and his own face grew quiet.

"I know what you have come to tell me," said the chief. He stood slowly, walked away from them. Stopped. Raised his hands and stretched them out to their greatest breadth. He would hold all the village in them if he could. He knew the time of the dream had come. He knew it was with them and that nothing could stop it. Still he wished he could do so.

"*Dla! Dla! Dla!*" he cried, *no, no, not this!*

Then he turned and returned to the messenger. "When the others are here," he said, "then tell us your story. Tell them. I know what you have come to tell."

"But it is not a terrible thing. Light Fire. It—"

"I have seen things others have not seen," the chief answered. "I know what is terror. I know what is happening. You have no message for me. It is *I* who has a message, a message for the Principal People, for the Council and all our chiefs there. You bring us news. I will return with you and take them the fullness of the news you carry. Then they all will know the horror of it." Then he spoke no more until his own chiefs came and sat with them. Then the messenger told the story of the white, hairy faced men who came from the sea. He told of their meetings with the villages in the east. He told of the wondrous gifts they had brought, and of the great friendship they offered the Principal People. And then he told of the strange spears they carried that sent forth fire and thunder and magically brought down any game the strange ones chose.

When the telling was done, all sat silent and amazed. All but Light Fire. He had seen most of it many times. But he had never seen the aspect of friendship that the messenger spoke of. That confused him. Everything in the dreams had foretold of terrors. Terrors only. Now this message of the strangers' friendship.

They want a Trust, he thought. And then they will deceive us. And then he told his dream to the others.

"We must go to the Council," he told them when he had finished the tale of the dream. "We must warn them."

He took the pipe from Tree. A small fire had been made within the circle. He lit the pipe. Gray smoke billowed from it. Then, after holding it long in his lungs he allowed the gray-white smoke to curl from his lips. Then he passed the pipe to *Tsula*, Fox Man, his war chief. Then it went to *Gohiyudi*, He That Proves, the peace chief. Then to Has No Hair, the priest, and to *Kayvsilugi*, Pugnose, the medicine man, and then it went to the warrior who had delivered the message.

"Find my son," said Light Fire, taking back the pipe. "He must smoke with us. He must hear the message, and then he must hear my dream." He drew smoke again from the pipe. "Then we must all travel to the council," he said, smoke warming him inside. He turned to Tree. "Find him," he said.

7

She stood before him naked. For a long, long while neither moved.

Outside the sun was setting. The cover had fallen across her doorway. There was a small fire though in the hut, and the light of its flames played games of light and shadow across the gentle land, her body. Shadow rolling, then soaring—up her thighs, into the dark places, across her stomach. Light cupping and caressing her breasts, her arms, her shoulders. Light and shadow dancing on her face, hiding in her hair, black, complete and ultimate black-night hair.

Stone moved toward her. Nothing mattered so much as to touch that world which was her body. But he moved slowly, not wanting any of the moment to be hurried. Everything he was thinking was forbidden them. It didn't matter. What mattered was being with her, near her. His hands wanted to hurry. He held them back. His lips wanted to hurry to her lips. His breasts wanted to hurry to her breasts. He held everything back, and moved slowly, letting the desire grow. And she waited, waited. She waited as she had waited all her life. But now she turned her body to him, opened her hands and extended her palms to greet his. Slowly his hands moved from his side, reaching for her, extending toward her, to first touch her fingers, then her palms, and then all parts of her. His hands drew near, nothing ever moving so slowly and yet still moving, nearer, nearer. And then their fingers touched, and at the same moment Stone felt the beating of her heart inside his own. And then the door cover was pulled aside and Tree stepped into the hut.

8

"Go to Light Fire," she told him. She was staring past him, glaring at Tear Maker. "Go," she said, still not looking at him.

Stone turned to Tear Maker. She had gathered a blanket about herself and was cowering on her bed, facing the floor, afraid to look at either of them.

His mother came to him and put her hand on his shoulder. "I don't know what this is," she said to him, "but if it is what it appears, then surely you know you both must die. There is no other remedy for this transgression." She was looking at him then. "My son, my son." He faced her. Turned his eyes to her.

"There is nothing here," he said, gazing at her forever with the eyes that everyone spoke of, "that should not be. And there is nothing here that any others need ever know." His eyes reached into her, spoke to her, promised the truth of what he said with words.

"Your father needs you," she said. She wanted to say more. She couldn't.

Stone walked to Tear Maker. Reached out and took her face between his palms, turned her to face him. And again his eyes spoke for him, confirming his voice. "All is well," he said. Then to his mother, "Stay with her, dear woman. Comfort her." Then he crossed the hut and was gone.

The women stood silent, not looking at each other. Neither of them moved. Only their breathing and the small crackling of the fire could be heard in the room.

When the fire was low and about to go out Tree put some fresh wood on it. Then at last she went to Tear Maker's bed. She sat down beside her. Put an arm around her. Held her near.

"I wish all were well," she said, "but all is not well. Stone has no doubt discovered that by now." And then she told Tear Maker of the messengers, the strangers, and Light Fire's dream. And nothing was said of Stone and Tear Maker.

"They will leave tonight," said Tree. "I have to

go now to help make preparations."

"Will you journey with them?" asked Tear Maker.

"I may. That will be Light Fire's decision. But I must leave now to go to him." She paused, then once more embraced the younger woman. "All will be well," she whispered in her ear. Then she left. In her mind she wasn't at all certain all would be well, not with Stone and Tear Maker. Stone was everything. Stone would be chief one day. One day perhaps Chief of all the People. Nothing could interfere with that. But the way he had been looking at her when she walked into the room. The way he had spoken of Tear Maker. This is all too much, she decided, and putting thoughts of it out of her head walked resolutely to her hut where her husband and son waited.

After Tree was gone Tear Maker sat in the warmth of her fire and tried not to consider everything that had happened. But there was no way to keep the thoughts of it out of her mind. Everything she had lived for was in the balance. And how now, she wondered, could she ever hope to have the promise of her long dead mother, that she would one day marry Stone? She had given up the notion the day she learned her mother was dead. But she had never given up her love for the young warrior. And she knew she never would. They couldn't marry, she had told herself, but she could love him. Always though from a distance, until this night. And now comes the mysterious revelation of Light Fire. And now Tree knows of us, she thought. Us? she asked. Is there an us?

No. And there never can be. But Stone, Stone wants *us*. All is well, he said. All is well. She stared into the flames. They cast warm heat onto her face and eyes. She heard again the warning of Tree. All is not well.

I'm tired, she told herself. All is not well, and I am tired. Still naked beneath her blanket she lay down upon her bed. Tired, so tired, she thought. So many seasons have passed. So much is lost. Mother, where are you? What am I to do?

Her dream was a familiar one. It was her wedding night. Stone took her to their new hut. There she sang him all the songs she had made for him. No other human being has your eyes, she sang to him. And then he sang to her with his touch, and with his eternal eyes. Eternal eyes. Eternal touch. In the dream he touched her forever.

She woke to his touch, soft, gentle, the same eternal, infinite touch of the dream. For a moment she didn't realize she was awake. Then through the dark, lit only by the glow of coals in the fire, she could see him. She couldn't see him well enough to recognize his features. But she sensed it was him.

"Stone?" she whispered.

"There's no need to speak," he told her, and it was his voice, a voice with all the calm and assurance she had so many times listened to. And his hands were touching her, caressing her shoulder, her neck, her arm. And then touching her thigh. And then his lips touched her lips. And then she was opening all of her being to him and he was lying beside her, and then within her.

313

Then she woke. This time she knew she was awake. The fire was gone. There were no red coals. Stone had never been there. She shivered from the clear memory of the dream. But that was all it had been.

She got up and dressed. She was walking through the door as Stone approached her hut.

"Stone?" she asked.

"I've come to tell you we're leaving," he said. He stopped and stared at her. She could see the eyes even in the night. And she could see something new in them. It had nothing to do with her.

"What has happened?" she asked.

"My father, my grandfather," he said. "Has had a dream, a vision of things to come."

"And is it a true vision?"

Stone hesitated. Then, "Who can be certain of such things. He believes in his vision. I can't say he is wrong, and something about it touches." He paused. "Frightens me," he said. That is it, she thought. That is what is new in the eyes. Fear. I've never seen that in him.

"I—" she started to talk; then didn't know what to say.

"Come inside," he told her, and nodded toward her hut. Then he stepped in front of her and went in first. She stood there a moment, uncertain what to do. The dream was still with her. She could still feel his touch. She wanted his touch.

"Let's sit down," he said when she was inside. And in the dark, hardly able to see him, she heard him finding a place on the floor. She wanted to find a place near him but was afraid to do so. She sat across the room from him.

"Here," he said. And then instead of waiting for her to move he moved to her side. He took her hand. Tear Maker's heart began to beat rapidly. What is happening? she wondered. What is going to happen?

"You are my friend," he told her. "You are my sister." These weren't the things she wanted to hear. Love me, she thought. Touch me. Touch me forever. "And I can't put you in harm," he said. Then he took his hand from hers. There was a long silence. Outside, Tear Maker could hear the voices of those preparing to depart. He is already gone, she thought. Gone forever. The touch gone forever. And then Stone was speaking again but she had hardly heard him. What was he saying? What had he said? A way? That there must be a way? And then he was touching her face, lightly, softly, and it was just as in the dream. And then he kissed her.

"Now I must go," he said. "But I will return. And there *will* be a way." Then he kissed her again, and for the briefest moment his hand lightly brushed her drape, touching her breast. And then he was standing, and then gone.

She sat alone in the dark. I shall sing him my songs, she thought.

It was nearly dawn before she returned to sleep, and to her dreams.

9

It was midnight when they stopped to make camp.

There were twelve of them. Light Fire, the presiding chief. Fox Man, the village's war chief. He That Proves, the peace chief. Has No Hair, the priest. Pugnose, the medicine man. On Time, a warrior. Tree, Light Fire's wife. Stone, her son. Down The Mountain, the messenger, and his son, Good Boy. And Sounds Good and his younger brother, Sounds Better, warriors. Sounds Good's father named him such when he was born because he screamed so well. His younger brother sounded better, the father said.

Their fires were low, but they were curled around them against the cold. Stone sat wrapped in a blanket and watched the others. He didn't actually watch them so much as to stare into the space they occupied. His thoughts weren't with them or with the journey. He was thinking of Tear Maker and of New Human. He hadn't thought about New Human for a very long time. Tonight had brought back all the memories.

Sounds Good and Sounds Better were talking. All the others were asleep. They should sleep too, thought Stone, and so should I. But sleep wasn't in store. Only thoughts. Memories of the young warrior girl who had declared herself *agadainvda*, outcast. How terrible a thing, he thought, to be lost from the People. And yet it was what she had wanted. For many seasons he had even thought that perhaps it was what he wanted, and he had considered going after her, following the setting sun. But he hadn't, and he knew he never would. He could never leave his town, his father-grandfather, or his mother. And now he knew he could never leave Tear Maker.

How long have I loved her? he wondered. His memories traced their way back through the seasons to their early days together as children. Did I love her then? He saw them playing, swimming, bathing, laughing. He brought himself forward. He recalled the songs she had sung at the creek named Life. Something in him knew all her songs had always been for him, but he had disregarded such impressions in the past. Now he no longer could. And he realized that he had always loved her, liked her, thought her important, was happy near her. Even as a child. And he knew that when he had returned from his journey in the wilderness, his test of manhood, that long lost yesterday when he had known for too short a time New Human—when he had returned and it was Tear Maker waiting for him and not his mother, that it had been nearly as important seeing her as it had been to see his mother. That had been a good day, he mused, coming home. She ran to me, took my hands, danced with me, singing me some glad song I had never heard. What was it? Only the barest trace of its echoes came to mind. I remember, he thought, her glee. Yes I loved her then. I didn't know it then. My head was too full of thinking about Tree, my mother; and about New Human, and about all the things

I'd come through. So many things had happened I hadn't yet ordered them, placed them in their proper understanding. Now I know, though. But what to do about such knowledge? *Death to the man and woman who marry in their clan.*

And, he wondered, am I not already married to New Human? The act of coupling is the act of marriage, ceremony or no ceremony. Part of him very much wanted after all these seasons to search for her, to find her if she were alive, to bring her home. Part of him knew it was impossible. Probably impossible, he thought. And, he told himself, these feelings for her return only because of my feelings for Tear Maker. And he knew he must find a way to be with her. That I shall do, he thought, wanting to believe the thought, hoping that thinking it would make it possible. But how? How? No answers came. Sounds Good came instead.

"I see you have the gift of *utsoasedisgi*, melancholy," he said.

"I have the gift of thinking too much tonight," Stone told him. Then he laughed. "But you and Sounds Better seem to have the gift of talking too much." Sounds Better came walking to them; heard Stone and laughed with Stone and Sounds Good. Then they all sat together to enjoy the gift of chatter.

"What do you think of all this about strangers?" asked Sounds Good.

"I've given it little thought," said Stone. "My thoughts sadly are on less adventuresome considerations."

"I think it is wondrous," said Sounds Better, who was sometimes simply called Better. "I think that perhaps these are old ones returned from where they went long ago. Perhaps they have brought back the great magic that they took away."

"Light Fire sees no such wonder in it," said Sounds Good. "He sees them as spirits of fire and wrath."

"He's had dreams," said Better. "Dreams are strange combinations. No one can know with certainty what message they deliver, if any."

"Don't let my grandfather hear you say that of his dreams of these strange ones," said Stone. "He's certain and certainty, right or wrong, has no heart for wayward arrows."

Better stared at Stone a moment, then smiled. "I'm no wayward arrow, Stone. My allegiance to your father is not questionable." He said it with force, but still smiled.

Stone put out a hand and rested it on Better's shoulder. "Of course, my friend," he said, and then he too smiled, letting Better know that they were friends and that he had never doubted the warrior's loyalty to his father.

After that the two brothers returned to their fire, huddled together in blankets, and gave up their gift for talking. Soon Stone could hear their rough breathing as they slept. He was nearly asleep himself when he heard the footsteps behind him.

"Stone," he heard her voice, and half asleep it sounded for a moment like Tear Maker's voice.

Possibly because he was thinking of her. Then his mother, Tree, was sitting beside him, huddling near to keep away the cold.

"Tree?" he said, wondering why she had come to him in this cold late night. "Is Light Fire well?" he asked.

"Light Fire sleeps. But his sleeping is a hard thing for him. Always he dreams. Asleep he dreams. Awake he suffers from the memory of the dreams, and from the aging of his body." It was the first time she had ever spoken to her son about Light Fire's aging. It was the first time she had ever let herself worry about him. Always he had been strong. Always he had held the power within himself to be whatever life required him to be. Now he was weakening. Now with the news of the strange people a shadow had fallen across his spirit. She could see it there, darkening his countenance, shading his eyes.

Stone looked at the woman, his mother, still young, still lovelier than any other. Lovelier than Tear Maker, lovelier than New Human. Her beauty was remarkable to him. It reminded him of the tale of the daughters of Father Buck. *There never were such beautiful women*, he sang within. And though she seemed wise and grown, completely a woman, there was nothing of oldness about her, with the possible exception of her limp. But that was something he had stopped seeing years earlier. For him she had no blemish.

"What do you need?" he asked her, and put his arm about her to further keep her from the chill of night.

320

"I just needed to sit with you a moment," she said. She leaned heavily into him, at the same time staring into his fire. It felt good to him having her there. He was glad she was with the party, not only because Light Fire needed her there, but he needed her, he suddenly realized. I need, he thought, to tell her. I need to tell her about New Human and about Tear Maker, especially Tear Maker. I need her to help me find the way. And with that thought he knew that in this woman beside him, this woman who had led him through so much, this woman that had taught him all things, that in her was his best hope, perhaps his only hope, in finding the way for him to take Tear Maker as his bride. He was about to tell her so when he realized that she was crying. He could feel her tears wet against his arm. And then his concerns for himself were gone, and he was listening to her, and he understood that for the first time in his life she had come to him for help. Not for help, he thought, but for comfort.

". . . have all died," she said. "All of them have. And now he is going to die." and then she was quiet a moment and there were only the tears and the energy of fear. "And I'll be alone again." She talked about it some more. He wanted to cry with her, her pain was so close to him. But he could sense her greater need for him to simply sit silently and listen. So he did. Finally her tears stopped. Then she too simply sat silent, motionless except for the rising and falling of her breasts as she breathed.

Stone was about to doze when she spoke again.

This time there was no fear, no pain, just the strength of her wisdom. This time it was his mother speaking, the woman who had been his guide. She was back, ready to guide him further. "You are my son," she told him, "so I tell you truly. There can be no way for you and my adopted daughter, your adopted sister. The people will never allow you and Tear Maker to be together. I tell you what you must learn, forget her. It isn't possible." Then after a long pause she stood and went back to her husband.

Stone stared into the flames of the fire. Eventually his eyes closed on them and he was given the gift of sleep.

10

Nagoligvna. The Strangers.

"They are savages," said the Lieutenant.

"No," answered the Captain. "But we will regard them as such because we have been ordered to do so. And someone, though not I, shall make of them what was made of the Aztecas. It will be the same story for all of this new world." They were walking along the beach. They could see their ships anchored off shore. The Captain stopped and gestured inland. "Can't you see it," he asked, "all this territory, owned by these simple and beautiful people. Soon we will own them. It is too sad a thing to consider."

"Perhaps, sir, it won't happen that way."

"Are you a fool, my friend. Can't you see the hand of destiny when it is held before your face."

"No sir, I am not a fool. And if as you say this is the hand of destiny, then there is nothing to be done about it, and—"

"That is true! There is nothing to be done about it! We are stronger than they, and we come bringing gifts. And they will fall before us. But destiny or not, it remains a sad thing."

The Lieutenant said no more about the subject. He considered the preachings of the Captain to be, not eccentric, but overly sentimental. *He* was the fool. Someday it will cost him, thought the Lieutenant, but he kept his thoughts to himself.

"When we go to their city," said the Captain, "and speak with their council. Then perhaps you will see what a sad thing we do to these strangers."

"They *are* strange, sir," said the Lieutenant. The Captain pretended to ignore him and kept walking. Eventually he came to a sand shark that had died and washed to shore. Most of its body had been eaten by other creatures from the sea. Perhaps, he thought, it will be different. Perhaps we shall be like the shark, and not them, but he didn't believe it.

11

Orphan knew that something was going on, but didn't know what. Scouts had reported something unusual to the chief, I Shout. Then I Shout had given orders that a temporary camp be set up until he had more information. More information about what? Orphan wondered. Are we never going to attack the *Tslagi?* There was no way to know. Wait. Wait. That's all there had ever been it seemed. He was tired of waiting. It was time to avenge his family. But the scouts had gone back out, and I Shout had said nothing about it except to wait.

Orphan thought about home. Now his son and wife waited as once he and his mother and siblings had waited. Will they wait forever as we waited? He thought of Faraway Eyes, his wife. Already he missed her. Missed her laugh and smile. Missed her touch. Missed her body.

It was the first time in the seven seasons they had been married that he had been long away from her. He was used to joining with her. He missed it. Joining, he thought, and he felt an ache of pain and pleasure in his groin. Part of him wished very much that he was home. Another part of him wished very much that the war-group was on its way. That same part of him, though, wondered if he would ever return.

To die in service to the tribe, that is a noble and worthwhile thing, he knew. But Faraway Eyes, what of her? What would then become of her, and of Morning Sun, our child? They were unanswerable questions. Having to make camp and wait made them worse.

12

When they reached the central village of the Principal People the days had grown short and the nights long, and everything had grown cold. The paths between huts were muddy with cold, and the air was damp with drizzle. They arrived in the middle of a gray afternoon. Light Fire, coughing badly, and walking with the assistance of his grandson led the party. Children and warriors and women crowded around them to welcome them, their brothers.

Light Fire forced laughter between the coughs. Forced himself to offer salutations. Forced himself not to stumble as he walked. Will their greeting be so joyful, he wondered, when they hear the story of my dreams? Because already he could sense that the People had accepted these strange ones as friends. How would they hear another view? What would their reaction be to that? Wait and see, he told himself. He smiled at that. Of course he must wait, he reminded himself. There are things one can help with worrying about, but tomorrow isn't one of them.

The village was large, spanning an entire valley,

with a river running between it. The central lodge of the Head Council was in the center of the village beside a bend in the river.

Light Fire had to be carried on a litter the last distance to the lodge. Have I come too late? he wondered. Will I be able to tell of my dreams and warn my brothers?

"These many seasons I have seen them," Light Fire insisted. He still lay on the stretcher, the center of attention in the evening fires within the great lodge. Surrounding him were the chiefs of many towns, and all the chiefs of the clans. Presiding over the affair was *The One*, or *The One Who Is Chief Of All The People*.

"Aren't these the dreams of one growing old?" suggested a young chief named Dry Day, a chief of the Blue Stone Clan. Then he laughed. A few others laughed with him. Light Fire could see immediately that the opposition here was mainly Dry Day's bid for attention. He was ambitious. Challenging Light Fire was a step forward, or so he hoped. But most of the council room was quiet, seemingly ignoring the young chief. Light Fire continued. "I have seen them coming. I have seen them attack us with their spears of fire. I have seen them destroy *my* village."

A few started to laugh again at a comment made by Dry Day but not heard except by those near him. Then The One stood; the laughter stopped. The attention shifted from Light Fire.

"Light Fire," said The One, "I am your old friend."

326

"Then listen, my friend," said Light Fire, "before they do us harm."

"I have listened. I have listened to you, and I have listened to the reports of others. These strangers claim friendship. But I have asked myself, how can they offer friendship to those they have not met. Yet they claim to do so."

"That could be deception," said Light Fire.

"I know, old friend. And that is why I have listened to you. And that is why I want you to go and examine them, and then to report to me."

Light Fire twinged at the words. He wanted nothing to do with these strange ones. He looked at the Blue Stone chief. The young chief was smug with disdain.

"They are already invited to come here to visit our council," said The One. "You, Light Fire, and your party will go to them, and bring them here. After you have traveled with them you will be able to tell me the truth of their nature. Then when they appear before the council we will have a better knowledge of them." The One started to sit, indicating that he was finished and that the subject was adjourned until Light Fire returned, but Dry Day spoke.

"The One," he said, "perhaps it would do no harm for another, such as myself and my warriors, to accompany Light Fire's party."

"Nothing is needed from you," said Light Fire.

"But, old one, your health is obviously not best. What if you were not able to complete your task? The council needs the report of a chief. And what if as you say they are indeed our enemies?

Such a small party as yours—What is it? Ten?—would be no contest against them?"

"Your argument isn't worth answering," said Tree, suddenly standing beside her husband. "You know well you've no interest beyond embarrassing Light Fire and extolling yourself."

"And of course if I'm wrong, then I'll be the one embarrassed," said Dry Day.

The One intervened. "It may be well to send others along. Dry Day has volunteered, so he and his warriors shall go. But only a small number of them, say another ten in total. We must not send a war party in greeting strangers who claim peace. If they intend to deceive, we will have sadly sacrificed a few. But their sacrifice would not be in vain, nor should it happen will it go unavenged." He turned to the Blue Stone chief. "You, Dry Day, gather nine of your strongest and most able warriors. Go with Light Fire. When you return you also shall report to the council your observations. That is enough," he said and then quickly sat. After that various chiefs and their wives stood and moved from the lodge. The One walked to Light Fire and stood beside his friend.

"Go, Light Fire. I know you. I know you never speak but truth. But dreams, dreams are often not what they seem. You know that as well as I. Go and test your dreams. I will wait for your report, and I will consider it well."

Then Stone drew the litter carrying Light Fire from the lodge. Tree walked beside her husband. He reached for her and took her hand. "There is nothing else to do," he told her, and then he coughed roughly.

"This journey may kill you," she told him.

"Not until I prove my dreams," he said. And then they were outside, and the drizzle had stopped and the late moon was clear in the sky.

13

Orphan and Fast Man sat eating. Fast Man had returned to the war party with more news of the strange ones. After reporting to I Shout he went to his friend Orphan to share what he'd learned.

"They make preparations to travel to the council lodge of the *Tslagi*," said Fast Man.

"Yes, Big Ears," Orphan joked, "tell me more."

Fast Man shrugged, then laughed. "My big ears learned something else, that is true." He paused.

"Yes, yes?" Orphan was anxious.

Fast Man leaned to his friend and whispered in his ear, making a drama of it all. "We have prepared an embarrassment for the *Tslagi*. A terrible one." Then he pulled away, smiling, delighted with himself.

"Well? What is it?"

Fast Man grinned. "The Tslagi have been offered peace and friendship with these strange ones. The Tslagi have accepted. And so when the Tslagi attack the strange ones, making war, it will be not only an embarrassment, it will be a disgrace. It will be one they can never escape.''

"But why would the Tslagi do that?" asked Orphan, not yet understanding.

"Why, my simple friend," said Fast Man, "*we Tslagi* cannot be trusted at anything. Haven't you heard the tales of our deceit?"

Orphan stared at his friend a moment. Then the shape of the drama was clear to him. He laughed a moment and Fast Man's laughter joined him. But inside he felt uneasy about such arrangements. Is this truly the way to make war? he wondered.

"I Shout has asked for a dozen warriors to leave tomorrow," said Fast Man. "Will you join us?"

Orphan looked at him. He took a bite of the dried meat held loosely in his hand. He turned southward and stared a moment, trying to seek an answer from the past and from his family. He could dimly see his mother's fading, shriveled, shrunken body. He turned again to Fast Man. "Of course I shall come," he said, and then with his friend laughing and patting his shoulders, he continued his meal.

14

He saw the strange men as he had seen them many times before. But this time it was not a dream. Almost, he thought, it seems a dream. It was evening. There were sunset shadows reaching across the sea. In the shadows, far from shore, were the ships. Ships, he knew, were something no one could have imagined. Great canoes, is how he thought of them, then as more, as great floating lodges. That is what they are, he decided.

They were wondrous to him, and suddenly he felt small, felt dwarfed, and felt afraid for the Principal People. How can we ever expect to stand against such men as the ones who have learned to live and travel upon the sea? If my dreams are true, then what can be done about it? Could there ever be hope for us if these strangers prove to be our adversary? And then he hoped that all he had thought and dreamed was wrong. He wanted the friendship of these unknown men who moved upon the waters, arriving from unknown and far away places.

Has No Hair came to his side, knelt beside him. "Yes, priest?" said Light Fire.

"I had not believed," said Has No Hair. "Your dreams, certainly they must be true!"

"We shall see. Let us hope they are not entirely true."

The Party had stopped on a hill looking down at the small settlement of the strange ones. "Let's go to them," said Light Fire. Stone began to pull at the litter. The others began to follow, Dry Day walking beside Stone.

They were still coming down the hill when they heard the war cries of the *ani soi*. Then they could see their enemies running through the camp of the strange ones. They could see axes swinging and blood spilling. Light Fire's warriors and Dry Day's started to run toward the battle, Dry Day leading them.

"*Wait!*" cried Light Fire. The warriors turned, wondering why they were being stopped from fighting their enemies. Dry Day walked to Light Fire.

"Don't you see what's happening, old man!" He spat at Light Fire. "They've dressed as though they were The People! They do this in our name! They shame us!" He turned and signaled the warriors to follow him.

"*Wait I said!*" Light Fire climbed from the litter, coughing, stumbling, his voice cracking as he screamed. Stone came to his father and helped him to walk.

"We must help the strangers, father. They have asked for our friendship. Our enemies have attacked them, and as Dry Day has said, they have done it disguised as the Principal People. We must."

"My dream is true," said the old man. "The *ani soi*, though, may save us from it!

"Old woman!" said Dry Day, and this time he spat in Light Fire's face. Stone stared coldly at the young chief. Twice he had defiled Light Fire. Light Fire was too weak to resist. Stone was not.

But such matters would have to be settled when the matter of the *ani soi* and the strangers was settled.

"After I kill the *ani soi*, I shall make good my challenge of a coward," Dry Day told Light Fire.

Stone put forth his hand and laid it on Dry Day's shoulder. "You shall make good your challenge with me, Dry Day," he told the Blue Stone chief.

"Gladly," said Dry Day, smiling. Then he turned. "All *true* People will now follow me," he commanded. "Only women, old men, and cowards will remain behind," and he started running down the hill.

Dry Day's warriors went after him without hesitation. Light Fire's party looked to him for instruction. "Stay here," he told them. Stone glared at him, then turned and ran after Dry Day.

"*No! Stone! Come back!* I'm your father and your chief! *I command you to stay here!*" And then Light Fire fell to the ground, coughing and spitting blood.

15

The Lieutenant dodged the swing of an axe and dove for cover. The first sweep had been such a surprise that the musketeers had all been taken without firing a shot. The Lieutenant had been talking with Valenzuela, a navigator, when an arrow unexpectedly grew out of Valenzuela's throat.

On his belly, crawling to stay covered, the Lieutenant headed for a fallen soldier, seeking the dead man's musket. The savage's screams were still echoing in his mind. Sand was in his face and his eyes. Then he was up, open, running for the musket, diving for it. It was in his hands, he was rolling, then coming to rest against a log. No, he realized, not a log, one of his men.

He tried to ignore the bloodied face beside his own. Instead, he looked at the musket. It had been primed but never fired. Its owner hadn't had time enough. The Lieutenant surveyed the situation quickly. The first attack was past. But he could see the second descending from a nearby hill. In a moment they would be on him. He raised his weapon and aimed. From behind him he heard more screams. He turned; the first attackers had already returned. The Captain and three musketeers were lined against them, aiming muskets. The weapons exploded. Four of the savages rolled forward as they ran, blood spilling from the wounds in their chests. Good, thought the Lieutenant. Then he saw the Captain fall forward, clutching an axe buried in his own chest. He turned back to the savages coming from the hill. There was little time. Quickly he raised his musket and let it fire at the savage in the lead. The ball caught the dark man in the temple and took away the top of his head. Then the Lieutenant drew his sabre and charged the onrushing savages. He caught one easily with a quick thrust through the abdomen, quickly withdrew the red-wet sword and charged on. He was bringing his blade against another when something struck him from behind, all blurred and then became black. He didn't even feel the force of the blow as his face fell against sandy reef.

16

Stone stopped, watched Dry Day and his warriors run into the fighting. Everything within him and about him urged him to go with them, everything but his father-grandfather. He turned to face Light Fire and the rest of their party. Then he saw the old man on the ground, blood trickling from his lips. Immediately he was running back to Light Fire, then helping him onto the litter. "I'm all right. I'll be fine," he was whispering between coughs. He isn't though, thought Stone. Then, kneeling beside the litter, he turned again to the shore. Dry Day was still in the lead as warriors of the People went to defend these strange ones from the sea. And then he saw and felt the thunder. And then there were three of the *ani soi* falling dead. And then more fire and thunder, and this time it was Dry Day falling. And then there was more. And through it all Stone watched, wanting to go down and die with them, but not willing to disobey his chief. Nor did Light Fire's other followers. And within Stone knew that his own obedience came entirely from loyalty to Light Fire, but he also knew that part of him was glad, not because he was afraid to die, but glad because the fire and thunder did frighten him and he wasn't sure what would become of a spirit that had been killed so.

When it was done the *ani soi* were gone. Several of them had been killed. The rest had escaped. It hadn't been so fortunate for the warriors of the Blue Stone Clan. When their chief had fallen at the hands of the strange ones' fire and thunder, they had at first scattered, naturally frightened. Then realizing that their chief was dead, they were committed. They turned quickly upon the strange ones, and just as quickly they fell to long knives and fire-thunder. All of them perished. I, too, should be in the land of spirits, thought Stone.

He walked beside his father in silence. The old man was asleep on the litter, with Has No Hair pulling him. On the other side of the litter was Tree. She, too, said nothing. Through it all she had said nothing, and now in her eyes there was a distant look that Stone had never seen before, a look of being lost, and of being afraid.

This is how it will be from now on, thought Stone. Silence. Fear. Lost. We all should be dead, he thought. We all should be with the warriors of the Blue Stone Clan. They had died honorably; we have lived in dishonor. He dreaded the journey back to the council. He dreaded the inevitable report. He dreaded returning to the village. Ever after there would only be shame. We ought to be dead, he thought again. It would be better. As it is we are worse than dead. No one said the words, but he knew they would be coming. He knew he would hear them at the council. It was necessary. He wondered if his father understood it all. His sickness was worse. He might not even live to make his report, Stone thought. It will be a kinder thing from life if he doesn't.

17

When the Lieutenant woke he was aboard ship. "What—"

"The savages, sir," said an uneven voice. The room was dark. Only one small candle was burning. "The savages attacked us. We drove them off, but not until they killed eight of us." Then there was a silence broken only by the creak of the ship rocking in the waves. At last, "We might have fared better, had they not surprised us. They might have fared better had they not been so surprised themselves by the muskets and the sabres."

"The Captain?" said the Lieutenant. His head was throbbing and his face felt packed with some heavy weight. He raised his hand and touched his cheek; pulled the hand away quickly. The pain had been sharp.

"The Captain, he's dead," said the voice. For a moment the Lieutenant saw again the Captain falling forward against some savage's axe.

"Yes," he said. Then he fell back to sleep, allowed himself to be swallowed again by darkness. His last thought was that he didn't know what would come next, but that he was glad he had lived to see what it would be, and that the savages had proven him right. They held no right to this new world. They were not people, they were animals. It made his wounds hurt less to think so.

18

Tree held him within her body.

It was seven days since the battle. They were still three days away from the council. Each day she had seen him grow more withdrawn. She had seen his eyes close while he was still awake, wanting instead to sleep, to shut out the reality of the days and the nights. She had seen him grow weaker. For four days it had rained. Now the rains were gone. Light Fire had called her to him on the first dry evening.

"I need you near," he told her. He held her face close to his own. "I miss the closeness of your body," he said. "Come to me." And though he was weak, she came to him. She found a place for them to be alone, away from the others. And she drew him within her, and did everything for both of them.

"You are everything," she whispered when their bodies were still. Light Fire said nothing, but his hand again and again made its way lightly, almost like breathing, across her arms, shoulders and back.

When he was asleep Tree walked back to the others. They, too, were sleeping. She found her son, curled around a fire. Sounds Good and Better were near him. She recalled the night only days ago when she had talked with him by a similar fire. Things had seemed difficult then. Now they seemed impossible. She knelt and whispered in his ear.

"Stay with me," she said. "I need you. He is going to leave me. I need you now, as you once needed me." Then she stood and returned to her husband.

Stone listened to her leaving. Yes, he promised her. I shall stay with you, as I remained by his side I shall remain by yours. Now more than ever, all of us must stay together.

By dawn the rain had again begun to fall.

19

It was still raining when they reached the council.

There was silence while Light Fire, coughing, weak and hardly able to speak above a whisper, gave his report. The only sound was the patting of the rain upon the roof of the lodge.

When he finished, the silence continued, broken only by Light Fire's coughing. His body was tied in pain to the litter. He kept trying to stand while he was speaking but was never able to do so. After he finished, and after the long silence, The One stood.

Now cast me out, thought Light Fire. He knew it was coming. He was prepared for it. It was a terrible way to end a life of love and loyalty to the Principal People. But it must be. He knew that. For this they won't kill me; they will exile me. It would be better if they would take my life. They won't be so kind.

The One spoke. "There is no need to confer on this thing," he said to all those gathered. "We all know the law. The penalty for such is affixed. Even this old and dying one before us must know what penalty is waiting."

Then he walked to the center of the council floor. "*Ahee! Ahee!*" he screamed and began to dance wildly in a circle, at the same time tearing off his clothes. "*Ahee! Ahee!*" Then when he was naked and panting for breath he walked to Light Fire's litter. "*I wish I could kill you!*" he screamed at the sick man. "I wish I could kill you with my own hands! Then perhaps my own shame would not be so great! You *know* what you have done! This is *udehoisdi*, disgrace of the worst kind, *old woman*." He called the chief old woman so everyone would know that Light Fire was no longer a chief of the People. He raised his hands and shook them in the air. "Once I knew you! Once I knew all of the people of your family and village. Now I tell you, and I tell all your old women, those who once were chiefs of the People, and I tell all the people of your village. *I know you no more!* The Principal People know you no more! You have gone somewhere. You have gone somewhere that no one can find you. You have not gone to the land of the spirits, but you have gone from the land of the Principal People! That is certain. No one can deny that! And now that you are gone no one will remember you and no tales of you and of your village may ever be told. This I say to you, Light Fire, and to all your town, for your people followed you and helped to bring this disgrace. This is a terrible thing you have brought to us! It can only be forgotten if you and your village are no longer among us.

"*Indeed your dream has been a true dream!* But you have seen it falsely. It was not the strangers who burned your town! But it was because of your fear of them that your town burned. And you, yourselves shall burn it. *You must do so!* Go! Burn your huts! Go and never be found!

"You shall become the *unigimi*, the people who are gone. Burn your homes. Let the rains that come in the new seasons wash the ashes into the river. Let the river take the ashes to the sea. Let the grasses and shrubs and trees cover all trace of you. Let the Principal People never see you or hear from you again! And only if the Great Spirit wishes it may you ever find *udasdelvdi*, salvation, for yourselves. I think not. I hope not. Go now." Then he quickly sat. The council was adjourned.

As they left in the middle of rainy night, Light Fire was filled with coughing. For a while the bleeding came again from his mouth. Perhaps, he thought, if I cough enough I shall die and save myself from having to face my village with the terrible news. But he knew fate would not be so kind to him. He knew he deserved no such kindness. That is what he told himself. Of course The One had pronounced the correct punishment. What amazed him, and saddened him, was that he had not realized or not allowed himself to realize what the extent of that punishment would be. But as he looked at those around him, at Tree and Stone, at Has No Hair and the others, he could see that they had realized. Why had I not? he wondered. Was I afraid of that, too? Have I been a coward for so long now? he wondered. Indeed, how long have I lived a life of fear? And he knew then that it was his own fears and cowardice that had brought all of this about, or so he convinced himself, and he knew that no one could convince him differently. I have brought myself to the justice of my life. But all these others they deserve none of it. What, though, are they to do? And in the middle of his

342

coughing he began to weep, not for pain, but for realizing that there was nothing his people could do. The penalty was unalterable. He wept because he knew their lives were gone, and he loved them.

20

Orphan thought of his friend, Fast Man. He was among those who had fallen to the fire-spears of the strange ones.

It could have been I, Orphan who fell, he thought. But it wasn't. *Not yet*, something inside told him. *There is still time for you*. Orphan knew it was true. Not only would the Tslagi return an attack upon them, but I Shout was now returning them to their original purpose: The village of the old chief, Light Fire.

Then, he thought, if I must join my friend, Fast Man, so be it. He was only glad to live long enough to journey with his brethren and I Shout to destroy the people of Light Fire. And only for a moment did the memory of the woman who waited for him dim his vision of the need to find the revenge he had longed for all his life.

STONE

1

The rains fell. On the tenth day from the council they stopped and made thatched shelters. Dryness was hard to come by, but Stone gave special attention to Light Fire's and Tree's shelter. Light Fire was worse than ever, and there were still two days travel ahead before they reached the village. And then—Stone felt limp at the thought of what came then.

In the darkness, through the rain, Stone couldn't see Light Fire's shelter. But he knew the man and woman were there. Now and then, even over the sound of the rain, he could hear the man's coughing and gasping. He could imagine his mother holding him, caring for him, trying to keep pain away from him by the force of her concern. He wants to die, thought Stone, and who can tell him he shouldn't? Don't I wish for death? The *udehoisdi* is too much. He wished again he had gone to Dry Day's side, and then with him to the world of spirits. But wishing was futile. He knew that, too. Still, he wished.

He felt his tiredness moving through him, creeping over him like the winter cold moves onto the land. He had slept little since the battle. Sleep wouldn't come, didn't want to come, it seemed. If he slept too much he dreamt. And it was Light

Fire's dream. He had inherited it. But now instead of a dream of things to come it was a dream of events past. In the night, unsleeping, listening to the rain, he wondered if he would ever again regain the inner peace he had lost, the peace that came from being in harmony with the earth, the river, his people and himself. He had terribly violated that harmony, and now couldn't see a way to find it. The rain, he thought, a river from the sky. *Oh river*, he sang silently, *my friend, where are you? Where am I? All was mine! Now nothing is mine.*

He fell asleep before the rain stopped, so when he woke it was to the sound of his father's coughing. He opened his eyes onto a clean, green-blue world freckled by the rusting colors of the season. Soon, he thought, all the world will be colors, a rainbow of trees, and then will come the white and gray and black of winter. Perhaps, he thought, that will come sooner than usual. Already there had been frozen rains now and then during the past days. An early winter, he considered. That will make the *leaving* even worse, if not impossible. But it had to be possible, no matter what, because they simply couldn't stay. He knew that. And so if winter came early, then they would move through it. And if they died along the way? he wondered. Then so be it. The earth would perhaps be doing them a goodness, giving them a gift.

They broke camp, scattering the materials of the shelters, and started out. Two days, Stone thought, and then flames.

That night Tree came to him again.

"He may be dying," she said.

"Good," he told her. "I am glad for him. He wants to die." She stared at him, then without any more words she put her arms around him and held him for a long while.

"What will I do?" she finally asked.

He put his own arms around her, held her tightly. "I don't know," he told her, "but whatever happens, I'll be with you, my mother, my Tree."

The world was dry again by the next morning. A cold, stripping wind blew through the sunny day. Traveling was quicker, and for most of the day it seemed Light Fire was recovering, but by late afternoon he was worse than ever.

They came to the village shortly after sunset. Before they arrived Light Fire gathered the travelers about himself.

"Say nothing," he told them, barely able to speak. "Say nothing until morning." He coughed wildly. "Don't tell them," he said again. His voice came like the scraping of bark from a tree. Then, wearily, he waved them all away, and Stone helped him to his hut. Stone left him there in Tree's care.

He hadn't seen her as they entered the village. It surprised him. Most of the people had come dancing and singing, laughing and shouting to welcome the travelers home. She hadn't been among them. But then, he thought, there should be no surprise in that. After all, she had grown up learning independence from her mother, and from his mother. And though she had never become the wanderer that Tree had been and that Number Two had been, it still wasn't unusual for her to be away from the village. What had made him feel surprised, he realized, was that he had been anticipating seeing her there, waiting for him. He had been anxious for it, and it hadn't happened. The emotion he felt wasn't surprise, but disappointment.

He went to her hut. She wasn't there. He looked about the small, empty building. Everything was much as he remembered last seeing it, except that there was no fire, and there was no Tear Maker standing naked and beautiful before him. Thinking about her that way began to stir again feelings both in his heart and in his loins. The dual feelings created other feelings, amusement, excitement, and fear. Where are you? he wondered, not wanting to think of the fear that thinking of her evoked, the fear of knowing that he must find a way to a forbidden desire.

Wait, he thought. She'll return soon. But what if she's away? something inside insisted. If we leave the village tomorrow she'll return to find it gone, to find us gone. No, he thought. She'll return. She'll come back tonight. And if, after all, she shouldn't, then someone will wait for her. I'll wait, he told himself; and he half hoped she wouldn't come back until everyone else was gone so that they would have time to spend alone together. Then again the feelings began to stir. Go away, he told them, not willing to feel them while there was still nothing he could do about them.

From the hut he went alone to the river. It will be the true homecoming, he thought, coming back to the river. And deep within he felt yet another emotion, a deep remorse at having been gone so long from the river. That is what he told himself the feeling was, a missing of his truest friend, the river named *Unknown*. And he told himself that his fears and uncertainties, and doubts would fade once he had come back to the river, once he had dived to her bottom and rested a while within the embrace of the waters. Home, he thought. And he didn't allow himself the thought that in another day he would begin the journey that would take him away from this place forever.

At the river's edge, beside the large stone slab that his mother had so often brought him to, he stripped away his clothes and waded into the shallows, then further, toward the deeps. And then he dove. The river swallowed him, took him in. Take me home, he asked it, and went deeper. But something was different, he knew. He could feel it, the difference. He didn't know where it was or where it came from, but he had sensed it when he had first come upon the waters of the river where the smaller stream named Life poured into the large flow.

At the bottom of the river he realized that he was a stranger. It was likely the very same place that he had swum to hundreds of times, and yet there was difference.

Beyond here, he thought, while waiting for his breath to dissipate, waits the greater deeps, the unknown deeps that give the river its name. In all the times he had come to the river he had never been able to find that lost, dark depth. It had remained a challenge that he had now and then worked at, but that within he had known must remain apart from him. Something within had assured him that the time hadn't come for him to reach that place and learning. So he hadn't resisted the inner voice. Now, he wondered, will I ever find what waits there for me? Already his lungs were aching as though he had been there too long; he hadn't been there but moments, not even half the time he would ordinarily spend. What's wrong? he wondered. What's wrong with me? You're a stranger here, came his inner voice. You are no longer a part of us.

He considered the answers he had given himself only a moment. Then the pain in his chest got too strong and he pushed himself upward, toward the surface. The journey up seemed long, seemed impossible. How could I have ever come so deep? he thought, and he began to fight to regain air.

When he broke free he was burning inside and so hungry to breathe that the breathing he longed for almost seemed as impossible as a moment earlier the water and darkness had seemed.

On the shore he stared out at the water. He felt things he hadn't felt since he was a boy first learning to delve the river. Old pains had returned. Old fears had come with them. He cast his sight far out to the center of the river. There, he knew, waited the unknown bottom of the river. Perhaps, he thought, I should have stayed under. Perhaps I shouldn't have come up. But it wouldn't have been possible, he knew also. It wouldn't have been possible because it was the river that had rejected him, had sent him away. No, he thought, don't do that to me. Don't, he told it. And then he was back in the water and swimming out to that far center, that far place where the great deeps waited, knowing that only there could he prove himself again to his friend, only by at long last finding the river's deepest terrain would he be able to again acquaint himself with the river, and that then it would no longer have its name, for he would know its secrets.

And then he was going down, plunging, cutting, falling through the black waters. Everything above was only memory or illusion, he told himself. This is everything; this is home; this is where I must be. Down he went. After a while he knew that he was far deeper than he had ever been before. Still he went down.

Eventually, everything above did become a dream, and then a dream that he could no longer remember. He had no thought of above. All that existed was downward thought and motion, and the water, cold and black. But there was no end to it, no bottom, no bed where he could rest. And he never knew when the lack of air in his lungs caused him to lose his sense of balance and direction and to swim up instead of down. One moment he was covered in the wet land of water, the next he was splashing and breathing and wondering where he had come to and what had happened. It took him until he reached the shore to realize what he had been trying to do, and what he had failed at, and that he was still alone, and still outcast from both the People and the river Unknown.

He was halfway back to the village when he encountered Tear Maker walking toward him.

"I knew you would be here," she said, and she stopped a little distance from him; stared at him. "I was walking, and when I returned they told me you had returned. I knew you would come to the river."

He didn't say anything. He just looked at her. Then he went to her, not slowly, not easily, and he put his arms around her and held her tightly. He didn't kiss her. He simply held her. And for a long time he didn't want to let go, though he didn't know why. Everything has changed, he thought. Nothing anywhere is the same. Except, he thought, and then he knew why he was holding her so tightly and not letting go, Tear Maker, Tear Maker has not changed; what I feel for her has not changed.

When he finally stepped away from her, he looked at her. He gazed at her face, and she returned the gaze, stared into his eyes. Looking at her, watching her watch him, he knew he had been wrong. She, too, had changed. Nothing remains as it was, he thought. Nothing waits. In her eyes he could see a difference, something gone. What? he wondered. Then he asked her.

"What has happened?" he said. "What has changed about you?"

"Nothing," she told him. "I'm the same."

"No," he said. "I can see that you've changed. I can see it in your eyes."

She looked at him a moment before speaking. Then, "It isn't my eyes," she said. "It's yours. What you see in my eyes that seems different is the reflection of your own eyes, your own way of seeing. Your eyes have changed. There is something gone from you." Then she stepped forward and leaned against him, putting her head against his chest.

"My eyes are tired," he told her. "That is all." But he knew that she could see more than that, and he knew that what she had said was true; that it wasn't her, or the river, or the earth, or the village, or anything that had gained a difference, except himself. He was different. Because of all that's happened, he supposed, but he didn't understand why.

"Let me tell you about the strangers," he said, "and about the council. Let me tell you about Dry Day and the *soi*. I'll tell you about all of it." And all the while he spoke he kept looking for what it was in the tale that had changed him. What it was that had altered him so deeply.

When he finished talking he sat in silence. The small stream named Life flowed before them. He had said it all and still it seemed to him there was something left unsaid, for in all the telling he hadn't found what he was looking for. After a long while Tear Maker leaned gently into his shoulder and then drew her arms around him. "You're home now," she whispered. "This has given *us* a way. You shall be with me, for we of this village will have no others. You and I shall be together now. Think of all of this as a strange but necessary gift.''

It felt good having her near, and yet he thought her wrong. This couldn't be necessary, and if this was the price of their combining, then was that good? He didn't know, but it seemed wrong. But there is nothing else now, he thought. All other things are gone from us; at least we do have each other. So he turned to her and held her closer, and slowly began to let himself ease, and to let his hands ease; and on their own they began to move across her body. Soon her hands were touching him.

Their touching became the world to him, became the river, became all the things he thought he had lost. And he realized that in this nearness he was discovering a part of himself that he had lost. It was a part of himself that had been gone not recently but for many seasons. He had begun to rediscover it the last time they had been together. Now the rediscovery continued. It wasn't the part of him that was rendering him different from all things; it was displacing that lost thought, he thought. Then he realized that they were lying together; her body stretched before his. She was gently helping him to move over her. He could feel her legs, soft and warm beneath his own. His hands were touching her breasts, and then her arms, and then her sides. Then again her breasts, playing with them, discovering their soft perfection. He could feel his hardness growing, demanding, pulling him against her. Then he could feel her hands pulling him too, and pulling away his clothing and then her own. And then, against his loins and against his hardness he could feel her heat making warmer his flesh. He could feel the wetness of her. He breathed the scent of her readiness and it stirred him more. He wanted her, wanted to be with her forever, and he knew that terrible as things were that indeed events had led to the way for them to be together. After all, as she had said, if they were cast out from the People there would be no other way for them to marry other than among themselves. So we are no longer forbidden. There is no one but ourselves to tell us no, and if we desire one another, then there is no one. I can do as I choose here, he thought. I can do what I want. And he started to gently press against her, leading himself within her. And all thinking became clear, and he knew. He knew why the change. And he stopped, and softly, more softly than anything he had ever done because he didn't want her to be frightened, he moved away.

She tried to cling to him. Still he moved away. I know, he thought. I know why I have changed. He stared down at himself. He still felt his passion. He looked at Tear Maker. He saw the fluid crystals starting from her eyes and finding their path down her cheeks. He could see her nakedness, just as he had before. But now he could do nothing about it. Because he had to be certain. He had to be certain from now until his last day that he never again did to himself what he had done at the battle. All his life had been trained against it. All the hours in the river had taught him differently. And he had gone against everything. For he had *known* what he should do there. It had been true *vgatahvi*, knowledge. He had known its importance, and yet he had gone against that. When Dry Day and the others had gone forth, he knew—with *vgatahvi*—that he should go with them. And in not doing so, in going against his knowledge he had not merely betrayed the People. In a terrible, unforgiveable way, he had gone against himself, and against the earth and truth which had given themselves to him. And in so doing he had become not only an outcast from the Principal People, and the river, and the earth, and now Tear Maker, but worse than all these, he had become an outcast from himself.

So now I am lost from all things, he thought, staring at the woman's body, now seeming distant and untouchable. And as he stared all the fear and distress he had long felt when one night he was carried away by an unseen captor came back. He closed his eyes, seeking the dark of the river, but all that came was the vision of Dry Day falling, and then the others.

He felt Tear Maker's touch. He opened his eyes and looked at her. How I want you, he thought. He leaned to her and put his lips to her ear.

"Not yet," he whispered. "This cannot be the time."

2

The burning began at mid-morning. It was finished by noon. All through it the women wept and screamed. Many of the men wept and shouted with them. More than five hundred of them, standing beside what possessions they could carry or pull on a litter, watching their homes ascend into an ever blackening sky. The dance of flames against the earth gave no delight, only anguish. And none of them understood, least of all the children, who did little screaming but cried just as loudly and sincerely as their parents.

None of them understood, and yet they had obeyed. They had felt for themselves the shame of the disgrace, they understood that, but they would never be able to understand what was happening to them. The place of their fathers and their fathers' fathers was being destroyed, adn they were working the destruction of it themselves. That was something that they couldn't even imagine. Doing it terrified them. And yet they did so. The Council chief had spoken. There was no thought for reprieve.

When there was nothing remaining but ashes, they left. It was slow, almost impossible movement. There had been no intention to go far that day, so before nightfall they had begun to make their first camp beside the river Unknown.

"This will do," Light Fire had said. His voice was so weak that he could hardly be heard. Still they followed him. He was all they had.

* * *

That night Stone was sitting bedside the river, watching its silent flow, when he heard the coughing. A moment later his father-grandfather was sitting beside him.

"You should be resting," he told Light Fire, startled that he was walking about.

"I shall rest soon enough," said the old man. There was a strength in his voice that Stone hadn't expected. Light Fire looked back at the camp. "They are the saddest of people," he said. "Only my own sorrow is greater. Not only do I bear the disgrace, but I bear the blame for their suffering." Stone looked at him; he could see the old man's pain. "They are going to die, many of them," he said, "because of this. Perhaps all of them will." Then he sat silent for a long while. Sounds from the camp came to them. Their crying still continued. There was no laughter, no singing.

"But The One may have been wrong about us. I deserve this punishment. They do not. Nevertheless they are cast out. They are damned. But they may yet be saved. There may be *udasdelvdi*. But if it is to come, it will only be after much suffering. Of that I am certain." Then he was quiet again. Stone said nothing. He felt there was nothing he could say to help, nothing to comfort. He didn't believe in Light Fire's hope for salvation, especially for himself. We are all lost from ourselves, he thought. There is no return.

"I think I am going to go to the spirits soon," said Light Fire, with a sudden strength. "I think I will if they will have me. I may be outcast from there also, though. My spirit may have to roam with the wind, waiting for this people to find their salvation. That is part of why I am talking to you. The other part is that I want to say it to someone, and Tree won't let me talk. She'll be finding me here soon and making me go to bed. So I must talk fast now. You must listen. This is important. These people must find their salvation. When I go, you must lead them and help them to find it. I tell you to do that. I would tell one of the others, but they could not do it. I think only you can do this." He paused. Then, "I love you, my son. I think you have a special goodness. That is why you must become chief when I am gone." Stone started to protest. "No! That is the way it must be. There can be no argument. I will tell the others in the morning." Then he stopped talking and was taken by an attack of the coughing. Stone could see someone approaching. It was Tree. Then the old man was speaking again. "And you, son, you know that you are perhaps the most lost of all. I know that. I can see it by what is gone from your eyes, and by what is new there. I can see it in your walking. I hear it in your voice. You are most lost, though, because once you were nearer to yourself than any of the others. Once you have found your- self, and your *udasdelvdi,* then you will be able to help these others to theirs. All this you must do."

"It's too much," said Stone. Tree was almost there.

"No! Not too much. It is only barely enough, for I think it is the only way for you to regain yourself also. Your fate is in their hands as well as theirs in yours."

"Old man," said Tree, half angrily.

"I know, I know," he claimed, coughing and choking. Then he struggled up to his feet.

"Why didn't you bring him back?" she demanded from Stone, but didn't wait for an answer. Instead she started back to their beds.

Stone watched them go. The old man hobbling. The still young, still beautiful woman limping. Then he sat again and stared once more into the river. He wanted to swim. He wanted things to be as they had been. He wanted to be as he had been. We are the people who are gone, he thought. His thoughts came back to his father's words. Could it be? he wondered. Is that indeed the only way for us? Shall I find myself by leading them to themselves? A cripple leading cripples. A lost man leading the lost. It cannot be, he thought. But then who will lead us? If I could go again to the bottom of the river, he thought, I might find answers. He stared at the dark water; he was afraid of it.

While he sat she watched him. She was across the river, hiding in the dark. She had watched him many times through the seasons since they had first met. She had never let him know. She didn't now. She didn't know why they had burned their homes and left. But she had cried with them when they did so. Watching him now she wanted to be with him, as she had wanted so often. But something in her told her she must wait for him. So she waited, and watched.

3

Orphan could hardly believe what he had seen. But he had seen it; it was real. After the *Tslagi* were gone he had even gone into the valley and walked through the ashes. I Shout will be amazed, he thought, even more amazed than I.

But when his scouting party returned, I Shout was not amazed at all. He laughed at it.

"But it is true!" Orphan insisted.

"Of course it is true," said I Shout, still laughing. "Don't you see, my young friend? We have shamed them. Our attack on the strange ones caused this. Somehow Light Fire was shamed. He and his village are cast out from the People." It was a long while before his laughter faded. Later Orphan heard, as did all the warriors, that in the morning they would move out for the attack. At last, he thought. But as he fell to sleep he saw his friend Fast Man falling, and then the faces of his wife Faraway Eyes and of his son Morning Sun. And these images became his dreams.

4

He was still sitting beside the river when most of the others were long asleep. He could hear someone walking toward him. Then Tear Maker was sitting beside him. Imploring him to let her near.

He kept staring out at the river. "No," he told her, trying to be firm but not unkind. The water flowed by in a vast seemingly still darkness.

"You tell me no," she said, "but I know you want it to be otherwise. I know you have changed, but I know that your desire for me has not changed."

Beneath the darkness of the surface, he thought, lies a greater darkness, a complete, untouchable darkness. He turned toward her slightly, looked at her for only a moment. Then made himself turn back to the river, afraid of deceiving himself. In the moment he had glanced at her he had thought or felt something of his old self, and that, he thought, is what frightened him most, not himself but the illusion of himself found in another.

"Not yet," he said. "There will be time, but not yet. Too many other things are happening." Then he looked at her again and saw that she was holding back the tears of her name. No, he thought. We've enough pain. And he drew her to him and held her and allowed her to loose her tears against his chest.

When she had cried herself to sleep he picked her up gently and carried her through the cold night. He found her bed and left her there. Then he went in search of another.

The black of night was grayed by the small, irregular fall of snow. The cold of the snow, he thought, will catch us. Then what will we do? He kept walking. He wanted to talk to her. He wanted to see her. She will know what we must do, he told himself. She'll know what I must do. And from the back of his mind came for a moment the echo of a thought held earlier about finding himself in another. But she will know, he reasoned, and dismissed his own warnings.

5

He touched her shoulder lightly, wanting to wake her but not to frighten her.

"I'm already awake," she whispered. Then she was getting up from her bed, pulling aside the covers. It was dark but still he could see her. He hadn't seen her naked since he was a boy. Then it had meant nothing to him. Now he could see that indeed she was a beautiful woman, more beautiful than any other. He felt a pride in that, that his mother should be so perfectly lovely. Then quickly she was covering herself with a skirt and drape; and then she took his hand and led him away toward one of the fires.

"I knew you would come," she said. "I haven't slept." She marveled him. She knows all things, he thought. His mind was racing back to the times when again and again as a boy she had taken his hand and helped him to find what he was looking for, or helped him to discover some hidden part of himself. And for a moment he was that boy again.

When they were sitting before the small flames she took his other hand and looked directly into his eyes.

"What do you see?" he asked her.

"I see my son, my child," she said. It was true, he knew. He was again that child he had long ago been, at least part of him was. "And," she said, "I see my son, a man. And both the man and the child are confused. Both are lost."

He tried to speak, couldn't.

"And I see, hiding deep inside, the peace and calm that seems to have forsaken you. Fear not, Stone, it will return." And then she drew him near and held him as she had done for many seasons, so long ago. "I'm confused, too," she said. "He is leaving me, you know. I'm going to be alone again and I don't want to be. I don't want to again learn to love another." After a while they each closed their eyes, the eyes that told so much, and they slept, on the earth as they had often done when Stone was growing from infancy to manhood, before the small flames until the flames were gone and until the morning sun was about to cast its first light into the darkness.

6

"I saw him last night," she told the child.

"You should have taken me," Earth said.

"You've seen him often enough."

"No I haven't. I never see him enough. I like him. I like to look at him. You said he is the best of them, but you won't let me go to him."

"Someday he will come to us."

"Never." Earth pouted. "He has forgotten us."

New Human moved near the child, embraced her. "No, my dear. I'm certain he has not forgotten us. And some day he will come to us. Wait, you shall see." Then she held the little girl tightly and rocked her. Earth was strong and able enough to take care of herself alone in the wilds. That at only seven summers old. But she was still young enough to seek often her mother's embrace. And New Human didn't mind giving that. It was something she had never known as a child, and she found that part of her was still young enough to seek it often from her daughter, Earth. And part of her was both old and young enough to wish that she didn't need to wait for Stone. How many times had she nearly walked into the village and gone to him, claiming him as her husband. Certainly she had that right. No, she thought, I have no right among them, for they are not my kind, nor am I theirs. I am no longer of the People. Then she thought about the burning and she realized that perhaps now they too were not of the People.

"Soon," she whispered to Earth. "Soon I think he will come to us."

7

When Stone woke, his mother was already gone. The cold was worse, but the light snowfall had stopped. The morning was gray, the sun hidden behind a gray sky. Others were awake and preparing to break camp. Someone had rekindled the fire for him, to keep him warm against the morning chill. He squatted before it, warming his hands and legs. Suddenly he heard someone near laughing. Then laughing louder, louder because he realized that it was himself laughing. Nothing was funny, but he felt good, and he realized that like a babe in arms he had slept well last night for the first night in many, since the messengers had come with the news of the strangers.

When he was warm he got up from the fire and started working. Moving five hundred people was a lot of work. Everyone was needed. Everyone shared jobs. Warriors helped with work that ordinarily women would have done. Hunting parties were sent out. Scouts were sent ahead to find a place for the village to camp that night. Other scouts were sent out to watch for the possible approach of enemies. The war chief didn't think there would be any real worry while they were still in the lands of the People, but now, he said, was the time to begin what must become their new way of life. At those words many, including Stone, had been stunned. Our new way of life, they had thought. It was a hard thing to think about.

Because of Light Fire's illness Stone stayed near him. Several times during the day he saw Tear Maker. Each time he tried to avoid her. He didn't know why, but he wasn't ready yet to talk with her, to be close to her again. It made him wish he had gone out on a hunting or scouting party.

By noon it was raining. Cold, hard rain. Everyone was drenched before they could put up tents and shelters. Then most of the wood was wet and it was hard making fires to get warm and dry by.

The five hundred were scattered along the river valley. The river was headed to the south and to the west. Light Fire had told them to follow it until they were away from the lands of the People. From there we will decide what next we do, where next to go.

It was nearly nightfall when Stone finally climbed into his own shelter and got a fire going. It was dark when Tear Maker appeared there. She stood in the rain and looked in at him. He watched her, saying nothing. She didn't move. Finally, "Come in," he said, and then he smiled. He loved her, he knew. He just felt so confused, so not himself. He wanted to get nearer himself, not further away.

When he told her to come in, she too smiled.

Then she unrolled a wet blanket she had and draped it over the entrance to his shelter. "It will help keep out the cold," she said, and she left just enough of the entrance open for the smoke of his fire to escape.

And then she was beside him, wet and trembling from cold. And before he knew what was happening she was stripping off her clothes and hanging them on the small stick-walls of the shelter, and then she was naked. She had another blanket then, which was also wet, but not so wet as the first. She unrolled it and sat on it, making room for Stone.

He wore clouts, so didn't have much clothing to get wet. But the clouts were wet, and so were his moccasins. She helped him untie the moccasins, then slipped them from his feet; then hung them over the fire. Then with her hands and belly she warmed his feet. And when they were warm, she began to untie his clouts. He wanted to say no, but all the while he had only been able to stare at her, her breasts swaying gently as she moved, the dark place below her belly; and then when she had put his feet against her, he was lost. He knew it, and he wanted it. He knew it was what he desired. He knew that it was the kind of losing that would somehow help him to find a part of himself. And he knew that had he lain with her that first night after returning from the Council that he would have found much healing for himself. And so when she began to loose the strings of his breech clouts, he didn't object. He wanted for only a moment to say no, and then he welcomed her. He began to caress her as she did so, first her face, lightly, softly, gently, the back of his fingers tracing her chin and lips. He felt her pull away the clouts. His hand moved to her shoulder, lingered only a little while and then moved to her breasts. Meanwhile her hands were busy touching him. So that while his fingers felt the hardness begin in her nipples, he knew that her fingers were directing a hardness beginning in him.

And then she was lying before him. In the firelight he could see all her beauty and mystery as she spread her legs slowly before him; and holding his hardness gently pulled him toward her, opening herself. He touched her, soft, warm, moist. She pulled lightly, guiding, leading. He could feel himself against her, barely parting her. And then the screams began.

For a moment he thought it was her, thought he had hurt her. He pulled away quickly. The screaming continued. And then he knew it came from outside. It came through the rain, through the night, above and through all things. And he knew what it was but couldn't believe it was true. They were under attack. And he was grabbing his clouts and moccasins, and then realizing there wasn't time, so grabbed instead only his weapons.

"Run!" he told her. "Find shelter in the woods! *Run!*" And then he was pushing aside the blanket that covered the shelter. The sound of screams and rain grew suddenly louder. He ran naked into the night, ready to kill, ready to die.

They were the *ani soi* from the south. The same ones, he supposed, who had nineteen summers earlier attacked them. Now they had returned, come back to complete their destruction.

Women and children and warriors were running everywhere. He ran past a woman lying still on the ground, blood from her back was mixing with the rain.

"*Stone!*"

He looked up. It was Has No Hair. He was running toward Stone. "Behind you!" he cried. Stone turned, dove to the ground, mud caking his face and chest. A *soi* spear flew over him. Then his own axe, swung from the side, was flying. It hit its mark. The Other went down. Stone turned to thank Has No Hair. The priest was writhing on his back, his hand clasping his stomach, blood flowing from under them as they struggled to push against pain and at the same time pull away an arrow. Stone was up and running to him. Kneeling beside him. Pulling at the arrow. Then he was picking up the priest and running with the man draped across his shoulders.

"No, no," said Has No Hair.

"Don't talk now, old one," said Stone. The priest said nothing more. When Stone put him down beside a tree, the priest was motionless. His eyes were fixed open, staring at the rain, the mud, and the battle. "Farewell, my friend," said Stone, hoping Has No Hair's spirit was still near enough to hear. Then he turned and ran for his parents' shelter.

The screaming became so loud that the rain seemed like a silence within it. The fighting came in waves. The first wave was nearly through, Stone thought. He came to Light Fire's and Tree's lean-to. It was empty. Where are they? he wondered. Something hit him from behind. It had hit hard and hurt. He turned and saw an axe in the mud behind him. He reached to his back. He was soaking from the rain. He touched himself where the pain was. Pulled his hand away and looked at it. There was no blood. The axe had hit by the handle. He grinned, picked up the weapon and started after his enemies.

After the third attack there was a long silence. Stone used the time to look for Tear Maker and his parents. They couldn't be found. Then the fourth attack came. He was fighting beside Sounds Good and Better when a spear caught Better in the leg. Sounds Good picked his brother up to carry him away to the shelter of the woods. Stone started off on his own.

A little while later Sounds Good was back.

"Your brother?" said Stone.

"My brother, with many others, has gone to the land of spirits."

Stone was amazed. "From the spear?"

"No. From an arrow. I took him to a hiding place where there were women and children. I told him I would leave him there. I told him he would be safe there. Then I started back. I wasn't far

373

away when I heard the screams. I returned. All those women. All those children. One of them was Sounds Better's wife. All of those people were gone. Sounds Better was gone with them. There were arrows in most of them. Some of the women had been gutted. Some of them worse." He stopped talking a moment to stare at Stone. "These are monsters, I think, that do these things. These are not people of any kind. These are monsters in the form of men."

"Yes," said Stone, his mind imagining that Tear Maker had been among them. Yes, he thought, they are monsters. We must kill these monsters.

He saw a young one moving between trees, then hiding. He motioned to Sounds Good and then whispered to him. They moved out.

The young Other wasn't far away. Most of the fighting was close. Most of the attackers simply ran through the camping place and hiding places of the people of Light Fire. Stone moved in one direction. Sounds Better moved in another. A moment later Stone was standing before the young *soi* warrior, taunting him. Stone held no weapon, offered no defense. The *soi* raised his axe, preparing to throw it. Before he could bring his swing around, Sounds Good had come behind him and brought the blade of his knife across the *soi's* throat. Neither Stone nor Sounds Good smiled at their victory. "This is good,"said Sounds Good. "Let's do more of this." They moved away, in search of more enemies to kill.

Halfway through the night the rain turned to

ice. Still the fighting went on. Through it all Stone hadn't seen his mother or Light Fire, nor Tear Maker. He could only hope they were safe.

The cold both helped and hurt. It helped very little, only by forcing everyone to keep moving, to fight. The women and children, though, thought Stone. They will be freezing. He was freezing, so he had to move rapidly. His arrows were long spent since many of them had found their target. Mostly now he fought with axe and knife. Now and then he gathered a spent arrow or spear.

After the ice started falling the attacks came slower. There were long moments of silence, and then a few *soi* would rush from cover and attack the waiting warriors. It went that way through the night. Shortly before dawn it began to snow heavily.

This was an early snow. This kind of snow shouldn't have come before another moon. But it did. And with the snow, the attack ceased.

The sun rose on a new white land, a land of crying voices. Everywhere there were bodies half buried in the white, dark figures patching the fresh white earth with a fresh bright red.

Stone stood beneath a tree and stared at the scene. He was shivering, naked and unprotected from the frozen flakes from the sky. He wondered if they had gone, if they would return. It was too soon to know. Perhaps they think they have killed enough of us, he thought. He hoped so. He didn't want to fight them any longer. He wanted to find his mother, and of course, he told himself, he wanted to find Light Fire and Tear Maker. And he also wanted to get warm.

He started walking among the dead. There were living now coming out from their hidings, walking with him. Among the dead there were many who were wounded. These had to be gotten to warmth and shelter before they froze. Already, though, the snow was melting. Stone knew it would be rain again before noon. He wasn't sure which was worse. The snow of course, he thought, because of the cold of it. They will freeze, he told himself again, looking at those who cried and struggled from where they lay.

He went to them, began the work of carrying them to the fires that were already being prepared. There were many young among them, young warriors whose tales had ended before they had given seed to carry them on. And there were children and women among them too. Many dead. Many wounded. It was the end of all their songs, the end of the village, he thought. The smell of blood in the air was so strong that it made his stomach tighten, and he wished he could stop breathing it.

Where is she? he wondered. And he realized that he was wondering about Tree and not Tear Maker. And it felt odd to him that his concern for his mother should be greater than that of the woman he had chosen for his wife. Where, too, is Tear Maker? he asked, hoping the question would ease his confusion.

He was helping a woman who had been wounded by an arrow to her shoulder. He was carrying her to a fire and treatment. She was crying in his arms. You'll be all right, he was telling her. My children! she wailed. She was an old woman with no young children, he knew. Nevertheless he told her that her children were safe. Then he saw the *soi*.

The Other had been wounded himself, and had been left for dead. But he still had the strength to hide himself, and to draw an arrow in a bow. That's what he was doing. He was kneeling behind a tree and brush, and he was aiming his arrow at Stone. And Stone knew there was no place for him to hide, and no defense for him to take. So he waited.

9

Orphan had fought well. His ancestors would approve, he thought. He had killed three of the *Tslagi*, and had badly wounded two others. Then he had taken an arrow in his side. It hadn't killed him, but it had stopped him. He pulled himself along the ground until he found shelter in the woods, and there he let himself rest. He didn't know when he fell asleep.

When he woke, snow was covering the valley. His people had gone. His enemies were tending to their wounds. So he waited. They would find him soon, he knew, and finish what the arrow had not completed. He had managed to keep his own bow and quiver, though. And so he hoped that before he died he would have the opportunity to send one more of the *Tslagi* to the land of spirits.

The land of spirits, he thought. I shall go there soon. I will join my friend Fast Man. And my father and mother and their children. Faraway Eyes and Morning Sun, he thought. Someday you, too, shall join us.

Then he saw his opportunity. A warrior was lifting a woman from the snow. Blood was running down her arm. The warrior was helping her then to walk, but he was having to move her slowly. It gave Orphan the time he needed.

Pain flooding his body and centered in his side, he pushed himself to his knees. Then he took an arrow from his quiver and strung it. It hurt almost more than he could bear to draw the string. It was his last act, though, and he knew he must do it. The arrow drawn, the pain intense, it was difficult to focus, difficult to aim. One moment he thought he was ready to shoot, then the moment passed too quickly. He tried to concentrate. The next time the arrow leveled at the warrior he would let go. Almost, he thought, the tip wavering. Almost. And then he felt the new pain. He let go the arrow instantly, never knowing if it met its mark. Another arrow was buried deep in his back.

10

The arrow's tip lightly cut his brow, bringing out only a trickle of blood. It was only a finger's width away from a slight scar he had gained seven summers earlier when another young archer had sought to kill him. That had been New Human. Then he had saved himself due to his own quickness. This time he had been saved due to someone else's. An arrow was in the warrior's back.

Stone looked through the trees and brush to see who it was that had saved him. He caught only a glimpse. The warrior wasn't staying to be thanked. But it had been one of the youngest ones, he thought. It was a small figure dashing away between trees and shrubs.

Then he continued his walk to the fires. The woman was shivering; in much need of help. We all need help, he thought. By the time he got her to the fires where other women were already making beds to nurse the wounded, the woman was dead. He put her down and stared at her. The bleeding, he thought. The bleeding and the cold. Then there was someone touching his shoulder. He turned around. It was his mother.

He looked at her a moment, then hugged her. He wanted to laugh but was too tired and too cold. "Light Fire?" he asked.

"Light Fire is safe," she said, "safe from the *soi*, but he is growing weaker. He's asking the other chiefs to come to him. He has named you his successor. He wants them all to know and to pledge their loyalty."

"Have they done so?"

"Those who have come have done so. He is still waiting for others. He's waiting for you. He wants to see you."

Stone held her again. "Are you all right?" he asked her. "I'm fine," she whispered to him. "I'm fine." They moved away from the embrace. Then they started walking, Tree leading the way to Light Fire.

"I should continue working," he told her. Then, "Tear Maker. Have you seen Tear Maker?"

Tree stopped and turned to him, concern in her eyes. "No," she said. "You haven't seen her?" He shook his head. "We must find her," she told him. "But for a moment come to Light Fire." They started off again.

Death had reached out in an untimely manner and touched the village, he thought, just as winter had reached into autumn and touched the land.

By the end of the day it was known who had survived; and it was known that more than a hundred had perished. And there were many more who were missing. They were lost, wounded, captive, or dead. Most likely, Stone realized, they were dead. Tear Maker was among them.

Late that night another joined the dead.

11

"Did I ever tell you the tale of the deer that ate his tail?" asked Light Fire. Stone and Tree and others were gathered around their chief. He spoke in a coarse whisper. Most of those around him couldn't hear what he said. Outside the small shelter the business of pulling the people together, nursing the wounded and burning the dead went on. It seemed to those involved that it would go on forever.

A few had gathered around Light Fire because he was chief. He had been so for as long as most of them had lived. It didn't matter that it was his act that had plunged them into their current situation. What mattered was that he was about to die.

"Yes, father," said Stone, "many times." Then smiling, "But tell it again. It's a wonderful story." And so the old man told it. He told about the crazy animal that had determined to be unlike any other deer, and so it had eaten its tail, only to discover that doing so had made it less than others instead of more. And then he told the tale of the man who married a wolf. And after that he mentioned other tales but didn't have the strength to tell them. He would mention one and then close his eyes as though he were inwardly telling the story to himself. Then he would open his eyes and mention another. "These are the important things of life," he whispered at some point, the things we tell each other to make ourselves laugh. Sometime after midnight he stopped talking. Long before the next dawn he had ended his personal tale, passing it to Stone.

Later, walking with his mother, watching the work of nursing and burning continue, Stone started to laugh. It wasn't loud laughter, or easy laughter. It was quiet, sinister.

"Don't do that," Tree told him. He continued. She grabbed his hand. *"Don't!"* she ordered. He turned to her suddenly.

"Don't you see!" he said. "Don't you see at all? *That* is everything! That's what we're here for! More than learning, more than mating, more than eating and singing. We are simply here to *laugh!* To learn that all of this is a grand and funny tale and to laugh at it! That's what he was doing tonight." Then he started walking again, but didn't laugh. And Tree followed him.

Eventually they came to the river.

Stone stared at it, which was all he felt he would ever do again. "I would like to swim in there," he told her. "How much I would like to do so."

"Then do," she said, and while saying it laced her arm in his.

He watched the water, cold, dark, deeper than anyone knew. Deeper than I know, he thought, or ever will know. Unknown.

"No," he told her. Still he watched the stream flow by.

"Someday," she said, "you must."

"Must I?" he asked. "I think not. I think I shall never swim there again."

"Tomorrow," she said.

"Not tomorrow. Perhaps never. Perhaps someday, also.''

After they stood there a long while she took his hand again and started him walking back to the camp. ''You must sleep some,'' she said. ''I'll sleep beside you, to help you. You must be rested when you meet with the others in the morning. You must show them your strength. They'll need to see that in their new chief.''

He knew she was right, but he said nothing.

She took him beyond the camp, into the woods. There she made a fire. And while he sat at it, warming, she built him a shelter around it. Then, ''Wait here,'' she said, and she left.

He stared at the fire. Light Fire gone, he thought. So many gone. Chief. The river, Unknown, Unknowable. Tear Maker. Tear Maker. All of it is too much, he thought. Tear Maker. They hadn't found her among the dead, but that meant little. There were so many places for a body to be. There were others still missing. Likely some of them would never be found. But Tear Maker? He had forced himself not to think much about her. Now he let the thoughts come. He allowed himself to remember her face and her touch. Her songs wanted to come to him but they were only vague memories. Not only have I lost myself, and now my second father, he thought, but I have lost her, and have lost her without ever having her.

When Tree returned she brought blankets. She found him laughing again as he stared into the flames. He kept laughing while she wrapped the blankets around him and made him lie down. Then she lay down beside him, covering herself too within the blankets, and holding him tightly. She did so as much for herself as for her son. Light Fire has left me, she thought. Just as the others are gone. She knew she would be alone forever. And Stone kept laughing. "Don't, my son," she whispered. "Don't." She held him more tightly, pressing against his back. "Don't, don't." After what seemed like a long while his laughter faded, and his breathing eased, and he was asleep.

Tree watched the flames. Whenever they grew too low she added another small bundle of wood, and watched the flames kindle higher.

Is it all a funny tale? she wondered. Are we merely fools, here to discover how we have fooled ourselves, and to laugh at the revelation when the dark moment comes?

There seemed no answers. Certainly, she thought, life has been grim enough. Holding Stone, she could still feel herself holding Light Fire as he closed his eyes and stiffened and his spirit went out of his body. She could still see his body where it lay dead, waiting for dawn and his private burning.

It was Light Fire himself who had declared there be burnings instead of burials. We must not leave our bodies in this land, he had said. That is forbidden us. Someday the Great Spirit will have new bodies for us. Until then these must go to ashes.

It seemed to her that all things must go to ashes. Alone. Alone forever. She closed her eyes.

Tried to find sleep. Sleep couldn't be found. She thought of all the nights when with Bear Man or Archer or Light Fire he-they had loved her to sleep. Never again, she told herself. Never again. She kept staring at the flames.

It was nearly dawn when understanding came to her.

We are the people who are gone.
There are none others.
We live in a world our own.
All old laws are gone from us.
All old ways are gone.

It is true, she assured herself. And if we are to live, if we are to survive all of this, we must learn to make new laws and new ways. We must learn to be alone, and by being together *not* to be alone. Otherwise we shall perish. That was the beginning of her thinking.

What came next she hadn't realized until it happened. And yet with each movement she knew that it was part of what must be the new way. Indeed, she told herself, she could look back at the motion of events and see that it had come as a part of a strange destiny that had been shaping for a long, long time. It was all as though some unusual formula were at work and had finally completed its purpose. And what must happen, she told herself, is part of what must be the new way for us. And deep within her something sang that it was what had been prepared for her all her life. This child-man was hers. She was his.

* * *

In the gray dark before sunrise she began the gentle motions, preparing herself, and then preparing her son without waking him. It was an art she had mastered.

As she worked the new way she thought. All the seasons of their running together in woods, swimming in the river huddling in the dark before campfires, all of it, all the songs and all the silences, it all became clear and purposeful to her. This is the new law, she thought. This is the new way. And quickly then, easily, while he still slept she opened herself and brought her son's body within her own and held him there.

It is the new way, she sang to herself. Stone will understand. I will make him understand. And then she began a gentle motion with her body, bringing him awake.

He opened his eyes.

"I've something new to teach you, my son, my love," she whispered.

12

"A new way," he heard her say. And then he became aware of the strange new feeling centered in his loins, and then of her nakedness and her nearness, and that he was within her. He started to pull away, but she moved with him; and moving felt so good that it eased his fear and made him want to draw nearer instead of apart.

"Why?" he asked her, and when she started the rhythmed motion against his body he surrendered and didn't care why. He moved as she moved, danced within her, beside her, then under her, then above her. It was a dance he had never done, but one she knew so well that so long as he allowed her she led him perfectly.

It is like, running, he thought. And like swimming. And like singing all the songs of nature at one moment. He felt like she had become the river and he had immersed himself in her. This beautiful woman, unlike any other woman. This woman, my mother, he thought. And only for a moment, at his own unknown deeps, there was a small voice telling him, giving him warning that this might be a betrayal. But he forced away any recognition of such thinking. She could not betray me, he knew. And though he didn't understand why this was happening, he didn't want it to stop. Sing to me, he said to her body with his. And the rhythm moved faster. And he felt her hands pressing against his back. He felt her legs drawing around his own. He felt her belly against his belly, and her breasts against his breasts. His mouth found her mouth, or hers found his; he didn't know. But it was her tongue that opened him and plunged within him, seeking out my soul, he thought. And while he moved within her, again and again, deeper, deeper, she moved within him, filling his mouth and throat as he filled her womb. And then the song and dance and running they were making ascended. It was like breaking away from the bottom of the river and rushing to the surface. He knew the surface was coming. He knew air was waiting for him there. He knew that life was waiting for him there. He was about to be born once more from the very same place he had many seasons ago been born. It was a new birth. A new way, she had said. It is true, he thought, though only barely thinking. Still, he had begun to understand what she had meant, what the new way was, and that it wouldn't be only them. There must be a new way for all of us, he realized. A new birth for each of us. And then he felt himself, something within himself, jumping down, being born, shattering the surface of rivers and life, filling him with breath and shuddering, and returning to his place of beginning the seeds of his fathers, the same seeds from which he had begun. The birth was complete. It was done. A new way had started; now it would continue.

Gradually he moved slower, as did she. They both were warm and breathing hard. They both were tired and yet full of energy. It was an energy he had never felt before. He wanted to feel it again and again. Once more for a moment there was a deep voice of descent within him. He shut it away and pulled her close, pushing himself once more deeply within her instead of allowing that deep part of him to come close.

"Stay near," he told her.

"I shall," she answered. "I ever shall."

13

I Shout looked at her. She was naked and shivering.

"Get her a blanket," he said. Of the four women they had taken, this one was the strongest and loveliest, he thought. He already had four wives waiting for him to return. This one I will make my fifth, he said to himself. To her he said, "What is your name?"

"Tear Maker," she answered.

"No longer," he told her. "Now you are Smile Maker, because you will make me smile many times."

The woman didn't answer. Instead she stared at him. You I will make cry, she thought. And you can never keep me with you. Either I will escape or you shall have to kill me. But she said nothing because she didn't want to die. She thought of Stone, waiting for her. She thought of her long dead mother and her mother's sister and of the plan they had lived for. I will yet bring them their hopes, she thought. The true way for the seeds of life won't be lost. Wait, she thought. Escape. Return to Stone. She promised herself she would.

"Get her some clothing," said I Shout. A warrior took hold her arm and led her away. She was removing herself from all of it, seeking the voice of the Center Being. She wasn't a witch as her mother had been, but she knew much of the craft, and it was to its mysteries and the power of the Center Being, the One Self, she turned for guidance. Help me, she asked, but no voice came.

Later, after the *soi* chief had finished with her and she was still bleeding between her legs, she thought again to the One Self. Where are you? she wondered. Why have you brought me to this? And then she cursed him. *You are not!* she thought. *And there is no true way!* And she realized that Stone would not wait for her, because he would think her dead. But I will return to him. There is no One Self. There is no true way. But there is Stone and there is Tear Maker, and I will find my way back to him, and then he will welcome me. It will happen. I will make it happen. Then she tried to sleep but could not for she kept seeing in her mind the face of I Shout, and his telling her how glad she had made him and that already she had given him his first smile.

14

"But he survived?"

"Yes, I told you so."

"But are you certain?"

"Yes. I'm certain because my arrow saved him."

The child, Earth curled then into her mother's arms.

"I want us to be with him," she said.

"We will," answered New Human. "Soon. We shall follow them. When the time is right we will be with them."

UNKNOWN

A human being may be born many times in this life. That is told. It is told around fires to children. A human being may be born many times and in many ways. This is the way of the earth. There are seasons. With each season the trees are born new. With each fall of rain the rivers are born once more. The birth from the womb is only the first birth. There is a second birth. There is a third birth. There may be many births. All of this is because the birth of things is not the beginning of life. The birth of things is the renewal of life. The birth from the womb has been spoken of as the first birth. But it is also told that before that human beings and all things were elsewhere. That is so. That is so, and it teaches us that even the birth from the womb is merely a jumping down from another place, a renewal.

Darkness was everywhere. Cold was everywhere. Silence was everywhere.

Above him was the ice. Beyond the ice was the snow covered shore. Beyond the shore was the winter camp of his people. After the first snowfall it had been another moon before the snows fell again. Then the snow stayed on the ground. Then the river began its freezing. They were near the end of the lands of the People by then, but they didn't stop. Finally they came to a place unclaimed. It wasn't a good land. No one would object to their using it through the winter, if they lived through the winter. We will stay here then until spring, he had told them. They had agreed.

The darkness was complete. The cold was complete. The silence was complete. It was home for him.

Above him they waited. They had objected when he began to make the large hole in the ice, large and far out on the middle of the frozen river. He had ignored them. Tree, his wife-mother had objected most of all. He had ignored her more than any other. If he hadn't she would have dissuaded him.

After they had made camp and settled in they had made small breaks in the ice that they fished from. He had gone out often and stared into the cold, dark silent water and wondered if he would indeed never swim it again. For a long while his wife-mother, Tree had urged him to, telling him it would restore him, that it would renew his faith in himself. I have faith in myself, he had told her. She hadn't argued with that, but she had continued to encourage his return to the water. She knew he was afraid of it, and that he needed not to be. But finally she grew weary of prompting him and left him alone about it. It wasn't long after that when he began to think what she had said was true. But then the ice came.

The darkness was in him. The cold was in him. The silence was in him and part of him.

Above him there was light. There were warm fires. There were voices, songs, laughter. Their songs and laughter had been slow in coming. The sorrows of their journey were great. Their fears were greater. Still they had followed him. Even the new way hadn't shaken their loyalty. It had been a hard thing for them to hear, and harder still to practice. But they had done so. He was their chief. He was their head. The body could only go where the head led it. So when he began to make the hole in the ice and they understood that he intended to swim down to the deeps, the deepest and unknown parts of the river, they were afraid. If they lost him, they were afraid they would lose all. They told him that no other could lead them now. He told them he must go swimming, and ignored any other objections they offered.

He had walked out on the ice each day for half the winter. He had stood there and stared down into the fishing holes. I'm waiting there, he had told himself. I was born anew when Tree took me into her. My people began their renewal when they burned their homes. They continued it when they accepted the new way. But there are other things awaiting us. There are other things awaiting me. Some of them are down there, he thought. I must go to them. All good things wait, but I shall make them wait no longer.

Darkness. Cold. Silence.

Above him was the universe, waiting. Dark. Cold. Silent. Like himself. And Light, Warmth, Singing. Like himself. He looked up from the darkness. He saw it all. He saw himself. For a moment he saw what must be done. It was what he had come for. It was all he needed.

Such a long way to go, he thought, considering what waited ahead. And then to his grandfather, I will take them there. And then he moved. He pushed himself away from the river's floor. He began his ascent. The passage to the surface was a long one, he knew, but the one beyond it was longer, far, far longer.

Darkness. Cold. Silence. The river was no longer Unknown. He gave it a new name. Anigisid. *Journey.*

Above him there was a break in the ice, waiting to complete the birth.

About the Author

James Tucker was born in Oklahoma City October 2, 1948. He is a descendant of the Cherokee and Choctaw Indians. He served as a medic in Vietnam and later as an infantry officer. He is a graduate of Brigham Young University, and currently resides in Salt Lake City, Utah where he spends his time reading, writing, going for long walks, singing songs, and riding his motorcycle. He loves movies, children, books, animals, music, and Susan.

FICTION FOR TODAY'S WOMAN

EMBRACES (666, $2.50)
by Sharon Wagner
Dr. Shelby Cole was an expert in the field of medicine and a novice at love. She wasn't willing to give up her career to get married—until she grew to want and need the child she was carrying.

MIRRORS (690, $2.75)
by Barbara Krasnoff
The compelling story of a woman seeking changes in life and love, and of her desperate struggle to give those changes impact—in the midst of tragedy.

THE LAST CARESS (722, $2.50)
by Dianna Booher
Since the tragic news that her teenaged daughter might die, Erin's husband had become distant, isolated. Was this simply his way of handling his grief, or was there more to it? If she was losing her child, would she lose her husband as well?

VISIONS (695, $2.95)
by Martin A. Grove
Caught up in the prime time world of power and lust, Jason and Gillian fought desperately for the top position at Parliament Television. Jason fought to keep it—Gillian, to take it away!

LONGINGS (706, $2.50)
by Sylvia W. Greene
Andrea was adored by her husband throughout their seven years of childless marriage. Now that she was finally pregnant, a haze of suspicion shrouded what should have been the happiest time of their lives.

Available wherever paperbacks are sold, or order direct from the Publisher. Send cover price plus 50¢ per copy for mailing and handling to Zebra Books, 21 East 40th Street, New York, N.Y. 10016. DO NOT SEND CASH!